I0788180

WOLVES OF LUNARA - BOOK THREE

USA TODAY BESTSELLING AUTHOR
HEATHER RENEE

CONTENTS

Selaris
Cav
Alklo Falls
WOLVES OF
LUNARA

Portal Cave
Lunara Academy
Venaris
The Bridge
...aris

CHAPTER ONE

SLOANE

The fire crackles in the hearth, its warmth reaching my skin but doing little to thaw the icy weight that's settled in my chest. For weeks, that coldness has plagued me—a constant reminder of my failures. My kingdom is dying. My pack is suffering. Everything I've built over the last two hundred years is crumbling, slipping through my fingers like sand.

Soon, all that will remain of my reign are whispered memories.

I once called myself a warrior queen. I stood strong, unshaken, certain of my worth and the promise I'd made to my people. But now, as I lie in a bed that isn't mine, in a castle too far from the land I swore to protect, I can no longer hold on to that certainty. The woman I was feels like a distant stranger, a faded reflection of someone I can't claim to be.

Clara, my top advisor and closest friend, sweeps into my room like a whirlwind, the door banging against the wall behind her. She doesn't bother with niceties or even a glance in my direction as she strides to the midnight-purple curtains and flings them open with a flourish. "It's time to get up," she declares, her voice sharp enough to cut through my haze.

Sunlight pours into the room, golden and relentless. Its rays settle over my skin, but still, they don't offer me warmth.

I groan, burying my face deeper into the pillow. "No."

My refusal is met with a snort of exasperation. Clara yanks the comforter off with one swift motion, followed by the sheets, leaving me exposed to the morning air. When that doesn't rouse me, she grabs my ankles, her grip firm. "If I have to physically drag you out of this bed, I'll dump you straight into an ice bath," she threatens, her tone as serious as the narrowed green gaze she throws my way. "Maybe a shock like that would do you good."

"Don't you dare," I warn, my voice low and edged with irritation.

Clara doesn't flinch. Instead, a triumphant smirk spreads across her face. "There's my queen. I thought I'd lost you." Her tone is teasing, and her expression softens as she steps back and heads for the drink cart. She pours a cup of coffee, her movements brisk but unhurried, before glancing over her shoulder at me. "We've been in Venaris for a week, and every single day you've grown more...*pathetic.*"

I arch a brow at her, the force of her harsh truth pressing against my already bruised pride. "You might want to choose your words carefully, Clara."

Her green eyes sparkle with defiance. "I'm not here as your advisor right now," she says, picking up a second mug. "You need a friend more than anything, and today, we're going to get your head right so we can figure out what our next moves are."

"We have a few more weeks. What's the rush?" I mutter,

sitting up slowly, though I regret meeting Clara's gaze as I do. The glare she levels at me is harsh enough to pierce the lingering fog in my mind.

"Cut the bullshit, Sloane." She stomps forward, her heels clicking against the oak floor like a warning drumbeat. Two steaming coffees sit precariously in her hands, a friendly offering, yet her frustration doesn't wane. "I know you're hurting. I know you feel like you've failed, but the time for self-pity has passed. Your people need you. *I* need you."

Her plea stings more than I'd like, but I take the coffee she thrusts at me anyway, gripping the warm cup like it's my last tether to reality. "They won't be my people for long," I murmur, the bitterness in my voice matching the dark liquid swirling in the cup.

Clara doesn't flinch. Instead, she grabs my shoulder with her free hand, shaking me hard enough to spill hot coffee onto the bed. My long ebony hair falls forward, creating a curtain between us, but I can still hear the fire in her voice. "Enough of this, Sloane. As much as I don't like this plan, I'm here because I've read that agreement a thousand times. You will still be queen. Your pack will still be your responsibility. Just because our kingdom is all but dead doesn't mean you've failed. You're here, searching for solutions. Now it's time to accept the path you're being led down."

A blanket of emotions slam into me like a wake-up call, but she doesn't stop as I look up.

Her eyes blaze with determination as she tightens her grip on my shoulder. "I need you to believe what I'm saying and tell me what we're doing next. I can give you all the facts, but what we really need right now is your intuition. Your instincts are what make you a great leader. We can't afford for you to wallow anymore, letting your doubt overshadow your good judgment."

Her words pierce through my mind and straight into my heart. I set the drink down beside me, my gaze meeting hers. For the first time in weeks, a flicker of resolve stirs in my gut.

Coming to Venaris was supposed to provide answers, a sense of clarity amid the chaos that's consumed Alcaris. Instead, I've allowed my dark thoughts to take root, sapping my resolve and blinding me to the duty I still owe my pack. Clara's right. I need to be the queen I was once capable of being. That means leaving this bed, stepping out of this room, and truly seeing what this kingdom has to offer.

Because while bonding with King Aeson of Venaris may seem like the most logical choice, it isn't the only one.

I could walk away from it all—my crown, my land, my people. Queen Isla and Queen Estee would never turn away the shifters of Alcaris. Their mates, Asher and Theo, may be kings, but they'd listen to their queens. I could relocate everyone, give them a chance of survival in another kingdom. It's a possibility I've considered, even though it would shatter me. The thought of letting Alcaris fade into memory feels like ripping my own heart into pieces, ones so small they could never be put back together.

And yet...staying here and choosing Aeson constricts my chest in a way that feels just as unbearable.

His offer is generous, maybe even lifesaving, but it comes with stipulations I haven't decided if I'm capable of agreeing to. He doesn't just want to unite our kingdoms. He wants me as his mate. His queen, who will stand by his side *and* lie in his bed.

For him, the choice is easy. His fated mate was killed by his brother over a century ago in a jealous fit of rage. But for me? I've never met my fated mate. Settling for a chosen one feels wrong. It's a loss I don't know how to articulate, a grief that lingers like a shadow I can't escape.

My wolf stirs, her presence steady but quiet, a faint warmth in the back of my mind. Oddly enough, it's her that has made me feel any glimpse of ease within these walls. She seems to be at home here, as though this is where we were always meant to be. That sense of comfort, combined with Aeson's patience and unwavering support, has allowed me this time to wallow. But Clara is right.

That time is over.

I gave myself one moon cycle to decide if I would become Aeson's mate. That decision can't be made from a place of despair or my wolf's uncanny sense of belonging. It has to come from me being the queen I've always strived to be.

I stand then cross the room, feeling Clara's gaze burning into me the entire way. I grab clothes from the closet, and her smirk tells me everything I need to know about how she feels in this moment. Still, she can't resist a jab.

"I knew yelling at you would work," she quips, leaning casually in the doorway. "Though I'm a little disappointed I didn't get the chance to toss you into an ice bath."

I brush past her with my bundle of clothes, heading for the bathroom. But Clara isn't one to let silence linger.

"So, what's the plan?" she presses, grabbing a brush as I strip out of my pajamas. "I've been scoping out King Aeson's office. He's usually in there until lunchtime. We could sneak in, go through his desk, maybe find—"

"No." My response is harsher than I intended. I pause, meeting her eyes in the mirror. "Aeson has been nothing but kind and welcoming. We're not going to invade his privacy."

"But—"

"I said no." My icy blue eyes tighten, cutting her off. "I appreciate the pep talk, and I know you mean well, but I won't jeopardize this opportunity for our pack by pissing off the one man who's offered to save us. He's given me no reason not to trust him."

Clara raises a brow, clearly unimpressed by my logic. "Do you really believe that?" When I don't answer, she continues, her tone softening but her resolve unyielding. "He's been after you for years. He could've chosen any unmated female, one in a similar situation to his. Yet, he's become almost obsessed with having you, and we have no clue why."

I have my thoughts about that *why*. Ones I've ignored because they make no sense, but I can only assume it's the same reason for my willingness to come here.

While Aeson might not be my mate, there's always been a connection between us. A pull of sorts that's been present throughout all our meetings, though I've never understood it.

One that has me wondering now if this was always meant to be my fate.

A chosen mate. A love built out of obligation rather than passion. A partnership forged not by destiny but by necessity.

Either way, whether my decision comes from duty or my heart, I'm going to find the best path forward.

Even if not continuing to wait for my fated mate might destroy me in the process.

I've barely started picking at my breakfast in the formal dining room when we're interrupted. Clara and I exchange a glance as Dasha, Aeson's top advisor, steps into the room. She hesitates, standing across the table from us, her brown eyes downcast and her fingers fidgeting in front of her waist. Her demeanor is the complete opposite of Clara's brash confidence.

"I apologize for interrupting, Queen Sloane," Dasha says softly, her voice almost as fragile as the unease now coiling in my chest. "But an urgent call has come through from your castle." She hesitates, glancing between me and Clara, before adding, "There's an issue with your water supply. Easton is requesting to speak with you immediately."

Clara stiffens beside me, her gaze snapping to mine. We don't need to ask what that means. We already know because there's only one problem there could be at this point.

The well has officially run dry.

The last thread of hope that Alcaris might revive itself has finally snapped.

The weight of that reality settles over me like a

suffocating blanket, but I push back from my chair, refusing to let it pin me down. Clara rises with me, her comforting presence grounding. "Thank you for delivering the message, Dasha. I'll return Easton's call promptly," I manage, my voice steadier than I feel.

Before I can take a step forward, the door bursts open, and King Aeson strides into the room with his signature flair, his dark blue eyes scanning the space until they land on me.

A sliver of warmth pools in my chest, but it isn't attraction. It's something softer, something that feels like a reminder—an unspoken assurance that, no matter what, I can rely on this man to help.

"I came to find you as soon as I heard," Aeson says, closing the distance between us with purpose. He reaches for my hands, taking both in his. His touch is firm, his concern palpable. "I'm so sorry, Sloane. What do you want me to do?"

His kindness is overwhelming. Almost too eager, too generous. Unrelenting.

"I need to return the call to my pack and speak with my advisor," I say, stepping back.

But he doesn't let go.

"Tell them all to come here," he insists, his tone leaving no room for argument. "Your people can't survive long without fresh water. I know we've yet to make things official, but my kingdom is open to them regardless of what happens."

His offer sounds perfect, but doubts simmer beneath the surface. Why does he want my pack here so badly? Yet, my wolf stirs, bristling at my hesitation. She trusts him without question, her belief in his sincerity unshakable, thanks to this strange connection between us.

Still, I'm not so easily convinced.

I nod and offer a polite smile. "I'll let my other advisors know and see what they think."

"Good," he replies, his smile growing wider. There's something unsettling about it, as though I've just handed him exactly what he wanted. "I'll send carriages across the bridge to help your people begin moving," he adds as if it's already been decided. His tone is deceptively light, but the words slam into me with the force of a final blow.

My stomach churns. I want to be furious, but I also know my people need security.

I glance at Clara, using our pack connection to speak privately. *"What do I do?"*

"Let him send the carriages," she says firmly. *"The people decide for themselves. We'll make sure they know you're doing the best you can, and this option is for them to accept or not."*

Gods, is this really happening?

Is my kingdom really going to be deserted already?

I'm not ready to admit defeat—not yet. But it's impossible to ignore the truth: I'm out of options. The reserve water supply we painstakingly saved for emergencies like this will barely last the pack a week. I could go home, try to rally, to find some miracle solution. But deep down, I know it'd be a waste of time. If there were still other avenues to pursue, I wouldn't be standing in the Venaris castle, wouldn't have left Alcaris in the first place.

Clara and I exchange another look. She might've spoken with confidence, but the agony in her eyes mirrors my own.

"I'm going to have to sign the treaty."

She nods ever so subtly. *"I know."*

But knowing and accepting are two very different things. And I'm not ready to tell Aeson yet. Not until I'm absolutely certain this is the best path forward. A voice in the back of my mind, faint but persistent, keeps whispering alternatives —spreading my pack out across the other islands, seeking aid from allies like Isla and Estee. But those options come with their own sacrifices. By choosing Aeson, I can remain queen. I can still lead them. Anything else would strip me of my alpha power, and while I'll endure anything to save my people, that *just* might be worse than death.

"*It will be okay*," Clara says, though I'm not sure if it's for my sake or hers. "*We're going to figure this out. This is why we're here.*"

Definitely hers.

Aeson and Dasha quickly leave the room, presumably to go 'save the day.' Their absence gives me the moment I need to steady myself.

I step forward, holding Clara's shoulders tightly. My voice comes out firmer than I feel. "This *is* why we're here."

Clara's breath stutters. For a moment, she closes her eyes. When they open again, the strength I've always relied on shines through once more, steady and unwavering in the depths of her green gaze. "You're right. I just needed a moment to remember."

I smirk. "It's nice to see you not so composed, even if it only lasted a couple of seconds."

She rolls her eyes, but her lips twitch into the smallest of smiles. "Says you." She pulls away, shaking off the moment with a flick of her blonde hair. "What now?"

"Now we call Easton back," I say, the words bitter on my tongue. My hands fall to my sides, my fingers curling into fists. "Make sure he and the other advisors have already begun enacting the emergency plans. And…" I hesitate, hating what I'm about to say. "Make sure the pack is prepared for what's coming. They might need time to decide and everyone should know they don't need to leave today if they don't choose to."

Clara nods, her respect evident in the quiet determination that returns to her stance. "Of course."

We leave the dining room, the remains of our untouched breakfast sitting cold behind us. As we walk, the gravity of it all presses down on me. Every step feels heavier, every breath harder to draw. But there's no room for weakness now.

The moment I close the door to my room behind us, I square my shoulders and lift my chin.

It's time to be a queen again.

THE SKY IS AN ENDLESS STRETCH OF BLACK VELVET, DOTTED WITH faint stars, and a chill wraps around me like a second skin. I shiver, but it isn't from the cold. It's something deeper, something I can't name.

Aeson emerges from the darkness, his gaze locking onto mine with an intensity that burns straight through me. Those piercing azure eyes see only me, and the way they light up the shadows leaves me breathless. His light brown hair is longer than usual, falling across his forehead, and his powerful frame moves with purpose. Each step sends a ripple of anticipation coursing through my veins.

He's bare-chested, the moonlight carving shadows into the sharp angles of his muscles. His shoulders are taut, tension coiled in every fiber of his body. I can feel it—his need, his desire. It pulls at something primal inside me, something I can't resist.

"Mate." The word falls from his lips, deep and possessive, and it unravels me completely.

A moan escapes my throat before I can stop it.

Gods, I want this man.

No, I need him.

I grab his biceps, my nails digging into the firm flesh beneath my fingers. "Love me," I plead, my voice raw with desperation.

"Always," he answers, his voice like thunder, low and commanding.

He pulls me into his arms, his lips trailing a path down my neck, and when his teeth graze the sensitive curve of my throat, I melt. The connection is intoxicating, all-consuming. It's as if every nerve in my body is tuned to him, to the promise of what we could be.

How is this possible? I can feel him—every inch, every emotion —as though the mate bond has already tethered us together. Happiness swells in my chest, unlike anything I've ever known.

He starts to strip me of my clothes, and I reach for him, my movements frantic, desperate to touch more. But just as his fingers brush my skin, the dream begins to dissolve.

Aeson pulls back, his eyes darkening. "Don't leave me," he pleads with vulnerability.

"Never," I vow. But it's too late.

The scene shatters, splintering like glass, and I wake with a gasp, the sheets twisted around me. My heart pounds as my eyes dart around the room, searching for anything to root me back in the present.

I'm in my suite. Alone.

My chest heaves as I struggle to pull myself together. That wasn't real. It couldn't have been. It was just a dream.

But gods, it didn't feel like one. The connection was so vivid, so raw, it was almost tangible. Like a fated-mate bond.

I press a hand to my racing heart, trying to steady the tumultuous emotions swirling within me. Could this be what's waiting for me if I accept Aeson as my chosen mate? Could it really be better than I've allowed myself to believe?

My wolf paces in my mind, restless and alert. The fog of sleep fades, and with it comes a pull—deep, magnetic, undeniable. I feel it in my bones, in the very core of my being.

We need to find him.

The sun hasn't risen yet, but through the window, the faint glow of dawn edges across the horizon. I don't care how early it is. I throw on pants and a sweater, not bothering with my hair or even glancing in the mirror before I slip out the door.

The pull guides me, tugging at something instinctual, and I follow it eagerly. My bare feet move soundlessly across the cool floors as I race through the halls, urgency thrumming through my veins. I let my wolf help, her instincts sharper than my own, her focus unshakable.

At first, I think she's leading me to Aeson's chambers, but as our path twists and turns, doubt creeps in. We're heading downstairs now. Maybe he's in his office.

But as I turn left instead of right, something shifts. The tug doesn't waver, but a faint nervousness trickles down my spine.

Where are we going?

We circle the first floor, but each path we take leads us back to the base of the stairs.

It's okay, I tell my wolf silently, trying to soothe her discomfort. *I'll find him.*

She whimpers, her despondency tugging at the edges of my resolve. I don't understand her reaction. It feels so unlike her usual strength, but the dream lingers, a haze in my thoughts and a need in my chest I can't shake, no matter how confused she might feel.

I sigh, turning back toward the stairs, only to stop short when Aeson appears at the landing. He's already dressed for the day in black slacks and a matching shirt left unbuttoned at the collar.

"Sloane?" he says, tilting his head as he studies me.

For a brief moment, I expect strands of his hair to fall

forward like they did in the dream. But his hair is slicked back, neat and controlled. Everything about him is polished and deliberate.

Still, concern softens his sharp features as he steps toward me. "Are you okay?"

I grab his hand, the movement almost impulsive. "Let's go to your office."

His gaze flickers to my bare feet. "You're not wearing any shoes."

A dry chuckle escapes me, though the sound is far from steady. Of all the things to notice, that's what catches his attention? I don't bother responding. Instead, I reach for the handle of his office door, only to find it locked.

Keys jingle in his hand as he moves around me. "Allow me," he says smoothly, slipping a skeleton key into the lock.

The door opens effortlessly, and Aeson gestures for me to enter first. I don't hesitate, stepping inside as my gaze sweeps the room. The industrial design doesn't surprise me—the metal fixtures and sleek desk suit his personality. But what does shock me is the photograph sitting prominently on his desk.

It's me.

A candid shot from the day I arrived in Venaris. I'm not even looking at the camera, my smile soft and unguarded as I turn toward something just out of frame. The intricate crown atop my head catches the sunlight, the polished metal glinting against the dark waves of my hair. The blue dress I wore that day makes my eyes appear brighter than usual, almost luminous.

All this time, I've been building this situation up, too afraid of the unknown and what I stood to lose. Because of that, I've failed to see the moments of calm and trust that, no matter what happens, everything is going to be okay.

I've been searching for a solution, and it's been right here the whole time. I just didn't want to believe it was the right one.

Aeson.

"Sloane?" His voice pulls me back to the present. He's watching me with a mix of confusion and curiosity, his brow slightly furrowed. I must seem so strange to him, wandering the halls barefoot before dawn, my emotions written plainly across my face.

I turn to him, offering a small smile, one I hope conveys the clarity I've found. "I want to sign the treaty."

His head tilts slightly, his expression unreadable. "You don't have to rush into anything, Sloane. I'll help your people regardless. I'm not trying to—"

"This offer's been on the table for months," I interrupt gently. "I'm not rushing into anything. I know what's in my heart, and this is the best solution for all of us."

For a moment, a crease forms between his brows, but it disappears so quickly I might've imagined it. Then his lips curve into a broad grin, and he reaches for a stack of papers on his desk. "Then let's make this official."

He shuffles through the documents until he finds the treaty and slides it toward me along with a pen.

My fingers close around it without hesitation, and I begin signing, my initials marking the bottom of each page.

This is it. The questions, the doubts, they have to end here. That dream showed me what I needed to see. Being Aeson's mate doesn't have to be a death sentence just because we aren't typical mates. He's kind, eager to help, and no matter his reasons, he's capable of doing things for my people when I'm not.

Finally, I scrawl my signature across the last page. When I look up, Aeson is grinning.

"Now we can plan our mating ceremony," he says, his voice laced with satisfaction.

Before I can respond, my wolf howls within my mind. The sound is raw and sorrowful, a piercing ache that sends a chill down my spine.

My stomach twists, dread coiling low in my gut.

What have I done?

CHAPTER THREE
SLOANE

The soft chime of the castle bells marks the arrival of dawn, but I've been awake for hours. Sleep hasn't come easily since I signed the treaty two days ago. My wolf is quieter now, but her sorrowful howl from that morning still echoes in my ears. I shift beneath the covers, trying to shake the restlessness that's lingered since I placed my name on that final page.

I've done the right thing. I have to believe that. But my instincts whisper that I've missed something—a detail, a truth hiding in plain sight. I still feel the connection to Aeson, but it's…faint. Yesterday, I expected some of the emotions from the dream to return when I was with him. They didn't.

Maybe that will change after the ceremony. Even though our bond won't carry the blessing of the gods, it will still tie us together in ways I can't fully comprehend yet. Chosen mates are rare, and I've never had a reason to learn much about them before. Now, I suppose, I'll need to start researching.

But one thing I do know: if my fated mate were to

appear—if he found me after all this time—everything would change. Whatever feelings I might grow to have for Aeson would evaporate. That's just how it is. A fated mate is an unbreakable connection, one that defies logic or desire. Leaving Aeson for my true mate would be the only choice.

I stare up at the ceiling and groan. Gods, this all seemed easier when I was hyped up on sexual tension from that damn dream.

There's a soft knock on the door, but it creaks open before I can get up. Aeson steps inside, a tray of food balanced in his hands. His smile is radiant, his every movement exuding an unfaltering confidence. "Good morning, my queen-to-be," he says, his voice warm enough to melt ice.

I sit up, forcing a small smile as he sets the platter on the bedside table. The aroma of freshly brewed coffee and sweet pastries fills the room.

"You didn't have to do this," I murmur before a yawn slips out.

"I wanted to." His gaze lingers on me, heavy with something unspoken. For a moment, it feels too much, and I reach for the coffee to avoid his eyes.

I'm sure he means well. He always seems to. And yet, there's an undercurrent to his kindness—something I can't put a finger on.

"You didn't sleep well," he observes, pulling a chair closer to the bed. His concern feels genuine, but his expression flickers with something hidden, though gone before I can place it. "Is it the ceremony? I know it's happening quickly, but it feels as though we've been building toward this moment for months. Waiting any longer might make me combust with anxiousness." His grin is charming, almost roguish, as he adds, "Don't worry about anything. I'll handle it all."

Yes, that's what he said yesterday. I've barely had time to process it. Aeson insists the event will be grand, even though it won't carry the blessing of the gods. I wonder how his people feel about a bond unblessed, how they'll view me as their queen. But when I voiced my reservations to Clara last night, she reminded me that there aren't any other options. Not for me. Not for my pack.

"You're being too generous," I say lightly, trying to match his tone. "You've already done so much for me—for all of us."

Aeson reaches for my hand, his grip firm but not harsh. "You deserve it, Sloane. After everything you've endured, you deserve to feel safe. You deserve happiness."

The words should comfort me. They don't. Not entirely.

I pull my hand away gently then slide out of bed and grab my robe. Aeson protests, but I promised myself I wouldn't wallow any longer. This next conversation needs to happen from a position of strength, not while I'm lying in bed.

I grab another chair from the small mahogany table in my room and sit across from him, our knees almost touching. My posture is straight, my thoughts clear. Each breath I take reminds me of who I am, what I stand for. My confidence builds with every beat of my heart.

I've fought and won wars. I've outwitted kings and queens. I've stood before gods and refused to flinch. Just because I've suffered a blow to my pride, just because I couldn't save my kingdom on my own, doesn't mean I can forget who I am. Not when I'm needed most.

I'm still Queen Sloane of Alcaris, and it's time I started acting like it again.

"I know I signed the contract—" I begin, but Aeson cuts me off before I can finish.

"You're not reneging, are you?"

The flash of darkness in his eyes is unmistakable this time. It lingers, pointed and unyielding, long enough to send a chill down my spine.

"No. Well, not exactly," I say, my tone firm despite the desire to do so creeping into my chest. "There's something I need to be sure you understand before we continue down this path. That morning…I wasn't entirely myself, and I realize now this conversation should've happened before I put my name on those papers. For that, I apologize. But it's not too late."

"You signed the contract." His words are soft, almost measured, but the tightness around his eyes betrays him.

"Yes, and if I lose my title by not following through, so be it." I meet his gaze head-on, refusing to buckle under his scrutiny.

For several beats, neither of us speaks. The tension thickens between us, but I wait him out. Finally, his expression shifts.

His smile returns, and the spark of warmth reappears in his eyes. "Fair enough." He leans back, relaxing into his chair. "What is it you need me to understand?"

"First," I say, sitting straighter, "while I know I'm agreeing to be your mate, I fully intend to be an active queen. You need to accept that I'll have my own opinions and desires for this kingdom. I expect my voice to be heard and to act as a true partner in ruling Venaris."

His chuckle is low and smooth, but it cuts through me like a blade. My wolf bristles at the sound, her agitation mirroring my own.

Still, I keep my composure, waiting for him to respond.

"Oh, Sloane," he says, his tone bordering on patronizing. "Do you not see how much I already cherish you? I'll give you the moons and the stars to make you happy. Of course, you'll be able to do as you please."

Now that my head is clearer, and ever since that dream, I'm trying to see him in a new light. Aeson has been patient and willing to accommodate me. But as I study him, I can't ignore the nagging suspicion that creeps in. What if his patience isn't the virtue I'm trying to believe it to be, but a calculated tactic?

Knowing I need to tread carefully and be certain of my thoughts before I push too hard, I let this subject go for the moment.

I'd convinced myself that this option was the only way to keep the thing I valued most: being the leader to my people. Aeson might think he can hold that against me, but as long as I remember that being a leader is more than wearing a crown, I'll find a way to make this work—or break free if I have to.

My smile widens. "I appreciate your understanding. There's just one other thing." I pause, holding his gaze with deliberate intent. "My fated mate."

Aeson doesn't blink. He doesn't even flinch. His casual response is unnervingly smooth. "What about him?"

"I don't intend to go looking for him," I begin carefully, "but if he happens to find me in this lifetime, I'd like an amendment to the contract. One that ensures I'm free to walk away without consequence. You've been mated before. You know I won't have a choice. A true mate bond isn't something I can deny, nor should I be forced to out of obligation. I want to be certain that won't be an issue."

His reaction is almost immediate. He leans forward, gently holding both my hands. His thumbs stroke over my skin in slow, deliberate motions.

"My Sloane," he murmurs, his voice heavy with sincerity.

"My queen. I know you don't trust easily, but I hope you'll believe that I have only the best intentions. If you're blessed to meet your mate, I will not hesitate to let you go, no matter how much I love you. I only want your happiness."

I study him, not reacting to his use of "love," but also hating that he sounds so damn convincing. His authenticity makes me wonder if I might be searching for lies where there are none.

Something for me to keep in mind as things progress, but that doesn't mean I'm letting my defenses slip away again. Dreams or no dreams.

"Thank you, Aeson." I mirror his smile, keeping my expression warm and open. "You've been more than patient with me, and I appreciate that you continue to do so."

He winks, leaning back in his chair. "Except when it comes to our mating ceremony," he teases, his tone light but purposeful. "But that's only because I think it'll offer peace to the people. Bringing in all these new wolves without you officially joining the Venaris pack has some on edge."

It's a rational explanation, and I can't fault him for it. In his position, I might have done the same to keep my kingdom calm amidst changes they didn't ask for.

But something inside me remains unsettled.

I need clarity, but I suspect time will be the only way to find what I'm searching for. Time and an unshakable resolve to stay true to myself.

The crisp afternoon breeze carries the scent of pine and freshly turned soil, mingling with the faint murmur of approaching carriages. I stand at the edge of the castle's main courtyard, my crown resting lightly on my head. The perfectly manicured area sprawls before me as I wait.

The expanse of carefully laid cobblestones, worn smooth by centuries of footsteps, and manicured hedges frame the space, their emerald leaves trimmed into precise shapes. Clusters of vibrant wildflowers—deep purple, white, and crimson—spill from stone planters placed along the perimeter. In the center, an ornate marble fountain bubbles quietly, its cascading water catching the sunlight in glittering arcs.

Clara's at my side, her usual sharp gaze scanning the procession of wagons rolling through iron gates embellished with a wolf-head design. Behind me, Aeson's pack moves efficiently, preparing to guide my people to their new homes.

The first transport comes to a stop, its wheels creak as the driver pulls the horses to a halt. About a dozen people step down, their expressions a mixture of exhaustion and uncertainty. My heart clenches at the sight of them. These are wolves who've endured so much. Wolves who've been uprooted from the land they've called home for generations.

But I don't let the sorrow show. I can't. They need a queen, not a grieving woman.

Clara steps forward as the first family approaches, her presence as commanding as ever. "Queen Sloane is here to welcome you personally," she announces, her voice ringing clear and strong.

A young girl clings to her mother's skirts as they approach me. Her wide eyes meet mine, and I drop to one knee, bringing myself to her level. "What's your name?" I ask gently.

"C-Cleo," she stammers, glancing up at her mother for reassurance.

"Cleo," I repeat, letting her name linger with warmth. "It's very nice to see you. You're going to like it here. Venaris is a beautiful place, and we'll make sure you and your family have everything you need."

She nods hesitantly, her grip on her mother's hand tightening.

I rise and place a soft touch on the woman's shoulder. "I know this has been a lot," I say, my voice steady. "But I'm going to make sure you're all taken care of. If there's anything you need, anything at all, please don't hesitate to tell me."

"Thank you, Your Majesty," she says, her voice thick with emotion.

As they move toward the waiting pack members, I catch Aeson out of the corner of my eye. He's helping an elderly man off one of the carriages, his hands firm but gentle as he steadies the man's trembling frame.

"You're stronger than you look," Aeson teases lightly, earning a weak chuckle from the elder wolf.

"I've still got a decent right hook too," the man retorts, his voice rough but good-humored.

The exchange stirs something in me—relief, perhaps, that Aeson's handling this transition with such care. For now, my people are in good hands.

The carriages continue to roll in, their wheels rocking over the cobblestone courtyard as family after family steps into the unfamiliar. Each one is met with warmth and guidance, not only from me but from Aeson's pack, their belongings unloaded with care and efficiency. Some are escorted to the guest quarters within the castle—a temporary arrangement until more houses can be prepared—while others are led toward the village homes that have been readied.

The late afternoon sun casts golden light over the courtyard as the final carriage comes through the gates. My heart lifts at the sight of Trey, one of my advisors, descending from it. His broad shoulders carry the weight of our pack's troubles, but the familiar determination in his expression feels like an anchor amidst the chaos. His coat, worn from travel, hangs heavy on him, but as our eyes meet, his gaze softens.

"Your Majesty." He bows deeply.

"Trey," I say, stepping forward to clasp his arm. "It's good to see you."

"And you, Queen Sloane," he replies, his tone formal and respectful. "The journey was long, but there's much to discuss."

"There always is," I say, a hint of a smile tugging at my lips. "But for now, let's focus on getting everyone settled."

He nods, glancing over his shoulder at the wagons being

unloaded. "The pack will need a strong presence from you in the coming days. We might've been preparing for this day, but facing the reality of it is something else entirely."

"I'll be here," I assure him. "Even in these lands, our people can count on me."

Trey's grey eyes darken and the slight wrinkles around them deepen as he looks around. "I hope so."

He moves on to help unload the transports, and I do my best to ignore the tightening in my chest. There will be those who think this is a bad idea, that merging with another kingdom is a mistake, and maybe it will be, but as I watch Aeson continue to work, I have hope.

The king has remained here all afternoon. Sweat glistens on the back of his neck, and streaks of dirt, likely from unloading the boxes my people brought with them, stain his once-pristine white dress shirt. His sleeves are rolled to his elbows, exposing forearms corded with muscles that pulse from the day's labor.

Despite my doubts, his presence and effort serve as a reminder. While I might have seen glimpses of things that give me pause, Aeson's actions today seem driven by genuine goodwill. For now, that's enough. At least until I have a better grasp on the things that still feel unclear.

As the afternoon wears on, I speak with more of my people, hearing their stories, their struggles, and their hopes. Each conversation strengthens my resolve, even as it chips away at my heart.

The last family to approach me is a young couple. Their faces are bright despite the weariness in their eyes, and their hands are entwined as if holding onto each other is the only way they've made it this far.

"Your Majesty," the man says, bowing deeply. "We can't

thank you enough for acting so quickly once the oasis emptied."

"You don't need to thank me," I reply, placing a hand on his arm. "This is what it means to be a pack. We take care of each other."

He nods then smiles down at his mate, his grip tightening on the bundle of belongings he carries. "Still, it means everything to us. To have hope restored so swiftly."

The words linger with me long after they've walked away. *Hope.* It's a fragile thing, but perhaps that's what we've all been missing.

By the time the last carriage is unloaded, the sun hangs low in the sky, casting long shadows across the cobblestones within the courtyard. Aeson approaches me, a streak of dirt now on his forehead as well.

"You've been busy," I remark, unable to suppress a small smile.

"It's what we do," he replies, his grin broad and genuine. "Your people are settling in well. They'll be comfortable here in no time."

The confidence in his words has an unexpected effect on me. The tension in my shoulders eases, just slightly.

"I agree, but I also need you to know how much I appreciate everything you've done," I say, and I mean it. Regardless of my wolf's reservations and the things I felt I was picking up on, Aeson is everything I hoped he'd be— kind, capable, and dedicated, following through on each of his promises without hesitation.

I can either choose to focus on all the good that's being done, or I can continue to look for the cracks. I'm choosing the former. That doesn't mean I'm ready to let down my guard, but today's taught me that it doesn't matter what *might* happen, only what is. Right now, my pack is safe and they're going to have everything they need for the time being.

Everything else will be handled as it comes, so there's no point looking for trouble.

Once the crowd disperses and the area grows quieter, the weight of the day settles over me. My wolf is restless and needs space. Hell, we both do.

"I'm going to go for a quick run," I tell Aeson, glancing up at the twin moons that are only half full tonight. "I'll be back for dinner, though."

"Of course." He squeezes one of my hands. "Do you want me to come with you?"

"No," I say quickly, softening the refusal with a grin. "I just need a moment to myself after the busy afternoon."

His gaze lingers on me, searching for something, but he doesn't press further. Instead, he nods and turns back to the remaining pack members, his focus already shifting back to the tasks at hand.

I'm surprised when he doesn't try harder to change my mind, but again, that's likely just my mind looking for a problem where there's probably nothing to worry about.

I head toward the back of the castle, the cool evening air washing over me. The faint rustle of leaves and the distant sound of a stream are a welcome reprieve from the noise of the day.

My wolf pushes to the surface of my mind, her eagerness to be free a palpable force. Without hesitation, I relinquish control, allowing the shift to begin.

The first ripple of energy spreads through me, and I gasp softly at the familiar sensation. My bones lengthen and begin to break before they're reformed, my muscles stretching taut as they realign. Fur erupts along my skin, onyx and silken, catching the silver light of the moons. The air sharpens, every scent and sound snapping into focus as my wolf takes over.

When the transformation is complete, I'm on all fours, the soft pads of my paws pressing into the cool earth. My wolf stretches, shaking out the tensions she's been holding onto. I expect her to take off toward the forest, to run as far and as fast as she can from the castle and its many burdens.

But she doesn't.

Instead, she turns back toward our new home, her ears pricked and hackles rising.

I try to guide her away, to urge her toward the trees and the freedom they promise, but my attempts are ignored.

Where the hell are we going?

CHAPTER FIVE

SLOANE

The night air bites through my fur, the twin moons lighting our way across the expansive castle grounds. My wolf's breath comes in steady puffs, her focus sharp and unrelenting as she drives us forward with an urgency I can't shake.

What are you doing? I push the question toward her, but she offers no response.

Our paws press firmly into the earth, the cool soil somehow calming me even as my pulse quickens. We move silently through the shadows, skirting the edge of the forest before cutting back toward the castle. Every instinct I have screams that we should be heading away from the imposing structure, not toward it. But my wolf doesn't hesitate.

What is it? What are you sensing?

Still, she gives me no hints at an answer, but her unease bleeds into me like a cold current. A low growl reverberates in her chest, vibrating through my body as I fight the rising tide of my own tension. I relinquished control willingly, trusting her instincts, but now I wonder if I've made a mistake.

Her ears swivel as we round the corner of the castle, its towering walls standing like silent sentinels against the moonlit sky. Shadows pool in the nooks and crannies of the stone, the silver light of the sky barely piercing the dense foliage clinging to its surface.

She barrels toward the wall, her speed unyielding. For a heart-stopping moment, I'm certain she's about to collide with the hard surface, her momentum too great to stop. My alpha power surges instinctively to the forefront.

Stop! My command echoes in her mind, firm and resolute.

Her muscles seize mid-stride, and the tension in her frame becomes nearly unbearable.

She lifts a paw hesitantly, trembling with restrained energy, but I've taken control now.

That's enough. My voice softens, though my frustration remains. *I know you can't speak to me, but you can at least give me some direction here.*

Her response is nothing more than a low whimper, her will pressing against mine as she continues to fight me, her desperation tangible.

Is there something near that wall you need? I ask, forcing patience into my tone.

In over three centuries of living as one, she's never behaved this way. This urgency, this raw intensity is foreign to us both. Whatever she's sensing, it's unlike anything we've encountered before.

She dips her head, a small, deliberate nod.

Fine. I ease my hold on her just enough to allow her to move again. *Proceed. Carefully.*

The growl that rumbles in her chest feels more determined than defiant, and she stalks forward, her movements slow and cautious. Her nose twitches, ears flicking at every sound, her senses tuned to something I can't yet perceive.

Until I do.

It's faint at first, but there's a ripple in the air, subtle yet unmistakable. As we inch closer, it grows stronger, an invisible pulse radiating from the castle wall. This isn't just power; whatever this force is, it's alive, humming with an energy that prickles along my skin.

The sensation is suffocating, like standing too close to a storm about to break. My breath catches in my throat as my wolf creeps closer.

We reach the bushes first, thick with ivy and shrubs. To any other eyes, it would seem unremarkable—a patch of overgrowth clinging stubbornly to the stone. But my wolf doesn't waver. She burrows her snout into the foliage, shaking her head until the leaves part and the wall is exposed.

The energy strengthens.

It thrums against my chest, a low, steady beat that resonates deep within me. My heart races in tandem, the rhythm erratic. Frantic. The air is thick here, weighted with a potency that feels almost conscious, as though the wall itself is watching us.

Every step closer makes it harder to breathe, the pull growing unbearable. It's magnetic, impossible to resist, yet saturated with an undercurrent of something dark and foreboding. My wolf trembles beneath the pressure, but she doesn't stop.

We reach a patch of deep purple flowers nestled against the wall, their petals trembling in the still air. My wolf sits back on her haunches, her eyes locking onto the bricks with unnerving precision. Her ears are flat, her gaze narrowed as she focuses on a single section of the wall.

She blinks and then…

We see them.

They're faint, nearly hidden beneath layers of dirt from years past and the ivy that's begun to creep up the walls. But there's no mistaking the soft glow—a whisper of light pulsing from the base of the wall.

These are ancient runes.

My wolf goes taut, her body rigid with a mix of fear and fascination. My own chest tightens as I stare at the symbols, the energy emanating from them crawling along my skin like tiny, charged needles.

Let me see.

She relents, and the shift back is almost immediate. My body tightens and stretches as the change overtakes me, the air sharp against my skin when it's over. I steady myself, smoothing my hands over my dress that clings once more to my body as I inhale deeply. It makes me cough as something rough, almost acrid, invades my lungs.

Something isn't right here.

I focus on the runes again, brushing away more ivy to reveal additional symbols etched into the stone. It's been over a century since I've encountered magic this potent, and even then, it was nothing like this. My palm touches the warm surface. This is…dark.

Repulsion moves up my spine and gets stuck in my throat. I want to vomit, to run, to tear myself away from whatever force is radiating from this wall, but my curiosity anchors me in place. My wolf was right to lead me here. Whatever this is, it's significant.

My hand trembles as I push more ivy aside, uncovering more of the faded symbols that seem to have been burned into the stone. The runes are intricate, their lines curling and weaving into shapes I don't recognize.

My wolf stirs restlessly, pacing in the back of my mind. Her instincts scream that this is wrong, dangerous even. Yet, neither of us can ignore the pull.

I lift my hand, hesitating for a heartbeat before pressing my palm against the largest rune.

The effect is immediate.

A jolt surges through me, piercing and unforgiving, racing up my arm and slamming into my chest. I gasp, stumbling back, but my hand remains glued to the stone as if some unseen force refuses to let me go.

The air thickens around me, heavy with energy that crackles like distant thunder. My pulse pounds erratically, my vision blurring as a heat unlike anything I've ever felt floods through me.

Then the images begin.

Chaotic and fragmented, they flash through my mind like shards of glass: a pair of piercing eyes, stormy and filled with anguish. Chains rattling in a darkness so absolute it feels suffocating. A voice—deep, raw, and drenched in desperation.

Help.

The singular word sends a shiver down my spine. The voice is unfamiliar, yet it resonates within me, intimate and undeniable.

"Who… Who's there?" I whisper, my breath hitching as the energy around me shifts again.

The glow of the runes intensifies, spreading out across the wall like veins of molten fire. The fervor is overwhelming, yet I can't bring myself to pull away.

My wolf howls within my mind, clawing for control. The force of her emotions is overwhelming—fear, confusion, longing.

The voice comes again, softer this time, but no less pleading, bordering on commanding.

Find me.

The pressure releases suddenly, and I collapse to the ground, gasping for air. My hand trembles as I press it to my lips, my heart racing as the glow fades, leaving only the hazy etchings of the runes behind.

I stare at the wall, trying to make sense of what just happened.

Help. Find me.

The words echo in my head, the desperation in them cutting deep. Whoever—or whatever—that was, I need to know why my wolf was drawn to them.

The pull I felt earlier hasn't lessened. If anything, it's stronger now, like a tether drawing me deeper into the unknown. But I've lived too long in this world to trust magic like this blindly.

My first thought is to go to Aeson, to question him about these runes and see if he has any answers. But even my wolf bristles at the idea.

I told myself I was done searching for cracks in Aeson's armor, but this discovery easily brings back my doubts—not that they ever really went away. I *want* to believe he's the gracious king he portrays himself to be, but I'm once again wondering what his real intentions are.

Alpha power rises within me, my wolf's doing, and I tilt my head.

You think he's using us to grow his stature?

Her replying rumble within my mind is all the confirmation I need. My thoughts reel. I've already wondered this myself.

With my pack joining his, Venaris will become the largest kingdom in Lunara. King Asher has always held the highest rank among the alphas, but if I share my energy with Aeson, becoming his chosen mate, that could all change.

I grip my head with both hands, a frustrated growl escaping my lips. "Damn it."

Am I once again searching for problems where there are none? These runes could be older than Aeson's reign. They're so hidden, he may not even know they exist.

Or he could be keeping secrets that might unravel everything.

I push to my feet, the air around me still heavy with the lingering energy of the runes. My chest tightens as I weigh my options.

I need to talk to Clara. Whatever lies behind these runes might not be friendly. It could be a monster—a vile creature locked away for good reason. The desperation in that voice could be a trap, a ploy to lure me into something far worse than I'm prepared to handle.

I clench my fists, resolve hardening to find answers.

With renewed determination, I head back toward the front of the castle, my steps purposeful despite the turmoil churning inside me. My intent is to go right to Clara, but then I remember the dinner I promised Aeson I'd attend.

It's not ideal, but perhaps it's an opportunity. I can poke around, see if he knows anything about Venaris's past—about these runes—without revealing what I've discovered.

I inhale deeply, steeling myself.

It's time for me to be the calculated queen I've always been.

My grin has my feet moving faster, and I can't deny the thrill that rises in my chest at the thought.

This is going to be interesting.

CHAPTER SIX

THE FATED MATE

She's here. I know neither her name nor her face, but I *feel* her. In every ragged breath I take, in the beat of my fractured heart. She's so close. Close enough to breathe life into the hollow shell I've become.

Years—or perhaps decades? Centuries?—have passed in this wretched darkness, but now, a flicker of light stirs within me.

A guttural roar tears from my throat, echoing through the cavernous void. My voice fills the air, raw and desperate, but no one will hear me. No one ever does.

My wrists bleed where the shackles bite into my skin, the chains never seeming to give way, no matter how fiercely I fight back. The links rattle as I pull against them, as I've done every day since being damned to this prison. The marks they leave are no longer wounds but scars, permanent reminders of the life stolen from me.

For years, I've wished for death, prayed for its mercy, but the gods haven't granted me that freedom. And now, when I'm finally resigned to my fate, I feel her.

She's so close.

I pull on my restraints as I've done many times before even though I know it's pointless.

The runes on the walls around me glow dimly in response, their magic tightening like a noose. My body tenses, the same frustrations I've fought for centuries rising once more.

I snarl, the sound primal and resonant, but the walls absorb the noise, mocking me with their silence.

Please. Don't turn away. Help me.

Her soul calls to mine, a tether forged by something greater than us both. I've sensed others close by before, but this is different. She's not just passing by. It's almost as if she's searching.

I close my eyes, focusing on the feeble thread of her presence. It's fragile, as though the magic binding me is trying to snuff it out. But even this darkness can't hide her light, not when it calls to me so intensely.

You're so close. I know you can find me.

The plea is silent, yet it ripples through the air, a desperate cry carried by whatever shred of power I have left. If she hears my words, if she feels me, then maybe—just maybe—there's a chance at freedom. After all this time.

But doubt claws at me. Will she even care? I know nothing of this woman except that she's my fated mate. She could be as despicable as the monster who trapped me here.

I slam my head back against the wall, the chains rattling. "No," I growl, my voice a guttural rasp. "She won't abandon me. She can't."

Because she's *mine*.

The thought burns, a fierce, unrelenting fire that refuses to be extinguished. My reason to fight for my freedom, harder than I ever have before.

I lift my head, scanning the runes as they fade once more. They might keep me trapped, their magic unyielding, but I have something now that they can't take away.

Hope.

The rhythmic click of my shoes echoes through the stone halls of the castle as I make my way to the dining room, alone. I told Clara and Trey to give us some privacy. I thought that might allow Aeson to be more forthcoming, but even as I wonder if that was the right choice, I know it doesn't really matter.

There's a precision to my stride that I haven't felt in weeks, a reminder of who I was before the haze of desperation settled over me. Of who I still am. I can do this, with or without them by my side.

The events of the evening cling to me, the pull of the runes and the voice that still lingers in the back of my mind.

Help. Find me.

My wolf had been desperate, drawn to something neither of us can fully explain. I expected to feel shame for being so easily lured into danger, but instead, there's a fire burning inside me, a resolve that's been missing for far too long.

I may not know what—or who—is trapped beneath this castle, but I refuse to be anyone's fool. Aeson included. I'm going to figure this out.

As I arrive at the dining hall, Dasha is waiting near the door, her posture rigid and eyes carefully downcast. "His Majesty is running behind, Queen Sloane," she says, her voice soft and polished but lacking warmth. "He asked that you please wait for him. He should be along shortly."

Her tone is practiced, her manner almost mechanical. Her meekness makes my wolf stir with irritation. If she's meant to be Aeson's right hand, where's her strength?

I offer her a polite smile that doesn't reach my eyes. "Thank you, Dasha. I actually need to speak to my advisor. I'll return shortly."

Her head dips in acknowledgment, her voice barely almost a whisper. "Of course, Your Majesty. I'll inform King Aeson if he arrives before you."

As I turn away, I can't help feeling that something about her is off. But Dasha's demeanor is the least of my worries right now.

"Where are you?" I reach out to Clara through our mental link, not wanting to waste time searching for her.

"My room," she replies almost immediately. *"But I can come to you if—"*

"I'll be right there." My stride lengthens, and I take the stairs three at a time, keeping my gaze focused.

Clara opens the door before I can knock, her expression already shifting to something between concern and vexation.

"What did he do now?" she asks, settling on annoyance. "Because if I need to cross a line, I'm ready. This kingdom doesn't scare me."

Her eyes narrow as she takes a closer look at me. Something changes about her—a flicker of realization.

"Oh," she breathes, her lips curving into a wide grin. "This is what I've been waiting for."

I arch a brow, confused. "What are you going on about now?"

"You've got the look again," she says, her tone bordering on smug.

"What look?" I ask, crossing my arms as I sink into one of the chairs near her fireplace.

"The one that's brought kings and queens to their knees. The one that tells me *my* queen is back." She places a hand on my knee and squeezes briefly. "I know you said you were done wallowing, but there was still a weariness holding you back. Whatever happened tonight has shattered the haze that was keeping you captive. Now, tell me everything."

I chuckle as I shake my head. This woman knows me almost too well.

"I found something."

Clara raises a brow. "Dead bodies?"

"Maybe worse." My voice lowers. "There are runes on the backside of the castle, and they're hiding something."

Her grin vanishes, replaced by a look of intense focus. "Do tell."

I recount everything that happened from the moment I shifted into my wolf form. She soaks up each word, leaning back in her seat as I speak quickly, knowing there isn't much time before I'll need to get back to the dining hall.

"And you think it's a man?" she asks when I finish.

"I do," I admit, leaning back in the chair. "The voice was deep, raw...desperate even. But that doesn't mean he's not dangerous. For all I know, he could be some kind of monster trapped down there for a reason."

Clara's lips press into a thin line. "Do you think Aeson knows?"

I glance out the window, my thoughts turning toward the king. "I don't know. I can't imagine if I found the energy so easily that he wouldn't know of its existence, but with the way it's been calling to me? Maybe he's in the dark."

Her eyes narrow, and her chest rumbles. "I don't like that you feel as though you have a connection to this thing."

She and I both, but there's no ignoring whatever this is. I need to understand it before I officially become part of the Venaris kingdom.

I stand, knowing I'm out of time, and Clara follows me. At the door, she reaches for my hand. "Be careful, Sloane. We can't afford to lose you. Not now."

I squeeze her hand briefly, offering her a small, determined smile. "I haven't lost a battle yet, and I don't intend to now."

DINNER IS SERVED IN ONE OF THE SMALLER DINING ROOMS—A more intimate setting than the grand hall used for formal occasions. The heavy wooden table is set for two, polished to perfection, the flickering candlelight casting soft shadows along the stone walls. A carefully arranged spread of Venarian delicacies is laid out before me, but I'm not focused on the food.

Aeson is already waiting when I arrive, his dark blue eyes lighting up as he stands to pull out my chair.

"Sloane," he greets smoothly, his voice rich with warmth. "You look radiant, my queen. Your run tonight did you good."

I don't let myself react to the casual possessiveness in his words, though my wolf bristles slightly at the familiarity.

"It did, thank you," I reply, settling into my seat. "You're as charming as ever."

He chuckles, that easy confidence rolling off him in waves. "Flattery will get you everywhere with me."

I'm sure it will. And I intend to use that knowledge wisely.

The first course is served—roasted meats, spiced vegetables, and a warm, fragrant bread I don't immediately recognize. Aeson gestures for me to eat first, ever the gracious host. We fall into an effortless rhythm, discussing the arrival of my people, their transition into Venaris, and whether they're adjusting well.

It's all very cordial. Very…kingly. But I'm not here for pleasantries.

Between sips of wine, I watch him over the rim of my glass. "Venaris is a beautiful kingdom," I say, swirling the deep red liquid thoughtfully. "But I've realized that I don't know much about its history. Have you fought many battles?"

Aeson's lips quirk into a half-smile, his gaze narrowing ever so slightly. "A few," he admits, setting his fork down. "Nothing like what Lunara faced during the Dark Wars, of course. Venaris has always been more…reserved. A kingdom that thrives on stability, rather than chaos." His eyes glint with something that makes me nauseous. "Much like Alcaris. It's one of the reasons I've admired you for so long."

"Quiet doesn't always mean safe," I muse, carefully keeping my tone neutral. "Polaris once thought the same. And yet, Queen Isla and King Asher were nearly destroyed when dark magic seeped through the cracks of their lands. Evil is clever like that. It waits, watching, until no one expects it."

Aeson lifts a brow, his fingers tapping idly against the rim of his wine glass. "Dark magic has never scared me," he says, his tone casual. "Nor has it ever been a problem for Venaris."

The words hang between us, thick with implication.

"Never?" I press, tilting my head slightly. "Not even a whisper of it throughout the years? I find that hard to believe. Even Alcaris carries the scars of those who thought they could wield such energy without consequence."

His expression remains carefully composed, but there's something in his stillness—a calculation behind his gaze. "Dark magic is like fire. It only becomes a problem if you allow it to burn you."

A shiver prickles up my spine, but I keep my face impassive. "An interesting perspective," I murmur, toying with the stem of my wine glass.

"Indeed." He smiles, lifting his glass. "To perspectives, then. And to our shared future."

I clink my flute against his, the sound ringing hollow in my ears. "A better kingdom for our people."

We resume eating, but my mind is already working through everything he's said. Before, I allowed myself to only see what I wanted and needed to. I let desperation cloud my instincts. But no more. I thought I was trying to see something that wasn't there, but it's those invisible forces I need to remain focused on.

I glance at him, feigning amusement as he recounts a story about Venaris's economic trade agreements. He's good at deflection. There's an ease to him that could almost be disarming. But I've played this game far too long not to recognize when someone is controlling the board. At least now that I have all my wits about me again.

I push my plate away slightly, leaning in as if I'm suddenly more interested in him than my meal. "You said Venaris has always been stable," I say, keeping my voice light. "Has that just been under your reign? What of the kings and queens before you? I feel as though I've been fighting my own war against the unknown in Alcaris, and I'm curious what battles other kingdoms have faced without anyone else realizing it. Maybe a war long ago fought in shadows or even enemies silenced before they've had the chance to become real threats."

Aeson studies me, amusement flickering across his face. "You wound me, my dear," he drawls, swirling his wine lazily. "You make it sound as if this castle might have a dungeon full of skeletons waiting to be uncovered."

I don't flinch, but I do hold my smile, raising a curious brow. "Does it?"

His grin doesn't falter, but there's a glint of something in his expression. A pause, just long enough to make me certain he's hiding something. Something I've already found.

"Of course not," he says smoothly, sipping his drink. "Our prior rulers have long understood the responsibility of power and wielded it wisely to avoid those sorts of circumstances."

"That's all very interesting," I muse, resting my hand over his.

Aeson's gaze sharpens. "You're intrigued by it, are you?"

I match his smile, resting my chin against my knuckles. "I'm intrigued by many things. Power, magic, history, how our world has gotten to where it is."

His smirk deepens. "I think we're going to have more in common than I realized."

At least he's going to think so. And that comment is precisely why I can't trust him.

As we finish the meal, silence stretches between us—not uncomfortable but laden with unsaid words. I smile when expected, nod when necessary, but beneath it all, my mind is working.

Aeson thinks I'm softening to him. That I've surrendered

to my fate, that I'm interested in what possibilities wait for me here.

As long as I can keep it that way, I'll be able to uncover the secrets this kingdom clearly has.

Aeson knows more than he's letting on.

I might not yet have the upper hand, but now that the veil over my emotions has been ripped away, I know a deceitful king when I see one.

Every move I make will need to be well thought out, and I might even need to give Queen Estee a call. If things go wrong, I need someone outside these lands to know that not all is as it seems in Venaris.

Aeson's gaze lingers on me as we rise from the table, his fingers brushing my cheek as he pulls me too close to his chest. "I hope you'll come to trust me fully, Sloane," he says softly. "We could be formidable together."

I meet his gaze head-on, a slow smile curving my lips. "I suppose time will tell."

As I leave the dining hall, I can't help but think…

Time will do more than *tell*. It will reveal. And when it does, I'll be ready.

CHAPTER EIGHT

SLOANE

Two more days have passed since that dinner with Aeson, and each minute within these walls has only made this place more of a puzzle. The pull to the runes lingers at the edges of my consciousness, a quiet hum in my bones that never quite fades. My wolf has grown restless, pacing within me, her claws raking against my control. She wants out, wants to seek what calls to us, but I keep her contained.

Aeson has kept a closer eye on me, though he's far too clever to make it obvious. It's in the way he lingers in the corridors when I least expect it. The way his eyes flick toward me in conversation, like he's trying to decipher something just out of his reach. My questions at dinner unsettled him, but I don't think it was in a bad way. If anything, he seems intrigued.

He thinks I might be more than he could've ever wished.

It's almost amusing how wrong he is.

We've spoken of how large and powerful our kingdom will be as of next week when we're bonded, how we need all the other alpha kings and queens present to witness our combined strength. All of it has me internally gagging, but I keep my grin in place, feigning excitement like this is the grandest of ideas.

But my patience is wearing thin. It's time for me to figure out how to get into the lower levels of the castle—with Clara's help.

With Aeson scheduled to be outside the castle this morning, Clara and I move quickly through the dim corridors of the southern wing, our footsteps muffled against the polished wooden floors. The early hour means most of the castle's staff are either preparing for their morning duties or still in their private quarters, almost ensuring we won't be disturbed.

The lights along the walls flicker, casting elongated shadows that stretch and twist like specters in the dark. The bare walls feel almost mocking, providing no information about the history of the Venaris lineage, like most castle hallways.

"This place has too many gods-damned corridors," Clara mutters beside me, her voice low but edged with frustration. "It's like a maze."

I exhale sharply, suppressing the growing impatience curling in my gut. "I assume that's the point considering the secrets that seem to be buried in these walls. Literally."

Clara glances over at me, her expression hard to read. "If we come face-to-face with a monster, and not a prisoner, don't be surprised if I let him eat you first."

I allow my grin to break through. "Noted."

As we descend another short set of stairs, the air thickens around us. It's not a physical thing, not something I can see, but rather something I *feel*. The magic saturating this part of the castle is dense, like an unseen mist winding through the halls, searching for escape yet unable to leave.

My wolf stirs at the sensation, pressing forward against my control.

I let her rise just enough to refine my senses. The pulse of power strengthens instantly, vibrating in my chest like a second heartbeat.

We're close.

The hallway curves to the right, and finally, there are paintings on the stone walls. Not many and completely out of place considering they're hidden in this alcove, not displayed proudly in the open. My shoulders tense as I look around, stepping more slowly.

There are six altogether. Most of them are smaller, landscape pieces showing the twin moons and the forest in all their glory, but there are two oversized paintings, one on the left and the other on the right.

My gaze travels over each one but lingers longest on the one to my left. It's an oil piece, depicting the kingdom as it must've looked centuries ago—its banners flying high, sentries patrolling outer walls that no longer exist, the castle looming in the background like an eternal guardian.

But something about it feels…off.

Clara steps closer, peering at it with narrowed eyes. "This doesn't match the rest of the castle's décor. The frame is almost brittle, too old, too…" She raises her head, fingers ghosting over the gilded frame. "Deliberate. Like no one would dare touch this for fear of damaging the stunning art."

I press my palm to the canvas, feeling the texture of the dried paint beneath my fingertips, moving slowly toward the edge until the wood casing brushes my skin. Sharp tingles cut into my skin, but when I pull my hand back, there are no marks.

Reaching for it again, I ignore the bite of pain and lift the picture away from the wall to peek behind it.

"Are you sure that's a good idea? What if you break it and then someone knows we've been here?" Clara asks, but I ignore her.

The stones start to glow as soon as they're revealed.

"Help me get this down," I demand, more eager than I probably should be to uncover whatever secrets are being held here.

"As you wish, my queen." Clara's formal tone has me pausing, but when I look over at her, she's grinning.

Sometimes I wonder why I've kept her as my advisor for so long, but the thought never lasts long.

She takes most of the weight of the painting, and together, we set it carefully on the floor, keeping it leaned against the wall a few feet away.

There are carvings in the stone. Some of them are the same as the runes outside, but around them, there's a long rectangle. I tilt my head, trying to understand what I'm seeing when Clara chuckles.

"There's the door we've been looking for," she says, pointing to a smaller circle on the right. "That's the handle."

"That's a drawing. Not a door. It has to mean something else." At least, I hope so because there's no way to open this, and I don't know enough about runes to understand what the symbols mean—or how to use them.

Clara shakes her head. "Oh, this is a door. There's no doubt about it. We just don't have the key. Not yet anyway."

"What do you mean?" I practically plead as my heart races. The need to get beyond this wall grows the longer we stand here. Pinpricks of energy seep into my skin, calling me forward, and it takes every ounce of self-control not to press myself against the wall.

Clara crosses her arms, staring intently at the glowing designs. "I've read about this."

I snap my gaze to her. "When? Where? What do you know?"

Her brows knit together, frustration flitting across her face. "I don't remember exactly. It was something I came across in my spare time when I was researching Alcaris's older texts—something about magic bound by sacrifice." She exhales loudly, stepping back. "I need to find that book."

"Then do it." I turn back to the markings, my fingers hovering just above them. "Maybe I can…"

A weightless sensation overtakes me—a hollowness spreading through my chest. My vision falters, the world around me spinning, breaking apart like shards of shattered glass.

I squeeze my eyes shut, willing the pain to stop.

When I open them again, I'm not in the hallway with Clara anymore.

I'm in a cave. Well, I think I am.

My body is shimmering, and if I look close enough, it's as if I'm transparent.

Holy shit, have I somehow projected myself somewhere? Or did I die?

I press my hands over my arms. There's still a solidness to my form. I'm not a ghost, so that's good. But I'm not sure if my spirit being forced out of my body is any better.

And I'm not alone.

A heavy dampness clings to the air, thick with the scent of earth, rock, and something else—something sharp, metallic.

Blood.

I stay in the shadows, my breath shallow as I scan the cavernous space. Stalactites hang from the ceiling like jagged teeth, and a faint trickle of water echoes through the silence.

Then, a pair of eyes—bright, piercing blue—snap upward, locking onto me.

A shudder rolls down my spine.

"You shouldn't be in here," he says, his voice low, rough—haunted.

I swallow hard. "Where is *here*?"

"My own personal hell."

Besides his eyes, I can't see much. The long tangle of hair and thick beard obscure most of his face, and the dim lighting does little to reveal more, but one thing I don't miss are the chains binding him.

Thick, blackened iron shackles bolt him to the rock wall, wrapping around his wrists with what I assume to be some sort of enchanted steel. He's trapped in a trench—water up to his waist, forming a circular pit around him, as if meant to cage him there forever.

Something in my chest clenches painfully.

I take a single step forward, my foot barely skimming the slick stone. The air around me presses in, forcing me to my knees, and it's as if my heart is being shattered into a million tiny pieces before coming back together.

My wolf howls, but this time, the sound isn't sorrowful. It's filled with the greatest joy I didn't believe we'd ever feel.

Mate.

"Don't look at me like that," the man pleads, his voice raspy as if he hasn't spoken in some time. "I thought I wanted you to find me, but I don't think I can bear to have you this close and not touch you."

The torture in his voice pokes at my defenses. I try to ignore his despair, but the mate bond is hard to ignore when his hurt is this loud.

His eyes remain downcast and his shoulders now slump as his chained arms settle back into the water. Tangled hair falls forward and every instinct within me wants to reach out and brush it back so I can see into his gaze, finding the truths I so desperately seek.

Yet, no matter how much I try to remain impassive, the agony rolling off him has tears filling my eyes. His pain is already becoming my own. It shouldn't be possible, but then again, the power of a mate bond isn't to be controlled.

It's meant to be accepted.

I could fight this. I could pretend I feel nothing, but that seems like a losing battle. Even now, when I still have so many questions.

Because in this moment, regardless of the lack of sense, I don't care how or why he became strapped to this wall. All I know is that I need him more than my next breath.

"I'm going to get you out."

His responding snarl sends a ripple of terror down my spine. "No. Leave. Now. Before it's too late."

"Too late for what?" I ask even though there's not a chance in hell I'm leaving my mate here.

The man looks back up at me, and I gasp. Now that I'm closer, his facial features…they're familiar. No, more than that. They're the exact same as the man I'm set to bond with in just a few days' time.

"Aeson?" I don't know how it's possible, but it's him. The man I had dinner with last night is right here. Only not the same. Has someone been impersonating him this whole time? Is this why I thought I felt a connection to him?

His lip curls, revealing pointed, almost feral, canines. "No."

My pulse thunders in my ears. "Then who—"

"It doesn't matter," he snaps. "You need to go. I don't want you here."

I laugh lightly and stand back up. "I don't think you're in a position to be making demands. I'm not leaving until I'm ready."

"You don't understand." His voice is laced with desperation. "He'll kill you if he knows you've found me."

"Who? The Aeson out there? I'm not afraid of…"

The hollowness returns just before I'm pulled back to the darkness that brought me to the cave. When I can see again, I'm in the hallway with Clara frantically shaking me. "Damn it, Sloane. What the hell just happened?"

"I found my mate." The words tremble as they leave my lips, my chest still heaving from the intensity of it all. My cheeks are damp, my entire body raw with the aftershocks of what just happened. What I felt.

I stagger toward the wall, reaching for the runes again, desperate to get back to him.

But nothing happens.

The magic remains silent, the connection is severed as if it was never there at all.

The void that follows is unbearable. A sharp, aching emptiness that settles in my chest like a wound that refuses to close.

"I have to get back in there."

"Absolutely not." Clara pulls me away from the wall. "We have no idea what's trapped behind there. It could be a trick. They might be able to manipulate you, and I won't risk your life until I know more about these runes."

"It's not your choice." I rip myself free, my body already moving back to the stone, hands slamming over the runes, but there's still nothing. No vision. No pull. The runes don't even flicker.

I press my forehead against the stone, a fissure inside my heart, but my resolve remains unshaken.

He's real.

And I will get him out. One way or another.

When I finally turn back to Clara, guilt crashes into me. She's pale, her breathing unsteady, but her hands are anything but weak.

She's holding a dagger, ready to fight me. "Don't make me restrain you, Sloane. I will for your own good, even if it means you hate me."

The sight of her standing there, weapon drawn, rattles something in me.

This is Clara—my closest advisor, my most trusted confidante, my fiercest protector.

And she genuinely believes I might lose myself to this.

I exhale, forcing my hands to steady as I step toward her, catching both her wrists.

"I'm sorry," I whisper, the words thick with exhaustion. "I let my emotions cloud my judgment." I shake my head, inhaling deeply. "I know you're worried. I am too. But I also know what I felt. There's no way that connection was fabricated." I press a hand to my chest, over my racing heart. "I still feel him, Clara. Even now."

Her eyes flicker with concern, likely for my sanity.

"It doesn't matter why he's down there," I continue. "I have to get him out. And if he truly is a monster, I'll kill him myself. But I have to know. After all this time, *I have to*."

Silence stretches between us.

Then Clara nods, her expression softening just enough. "I know, but please don't do this alone. Don't touch those runes again until I find that book. A lot of my belongings arrived yesterday. I'll go through them today. Just give me time. He's clearly not going anywhere, and neither are we."

She's right, and I hate how I reacted toward her, but all rational thought went out of my mind the moment I realized who this man is to me. The how and why will come later.

"Thank you for being my voice of reason," I tell her sincerely. "I won't come back here without you. I promise."

Her sharpened gaze pierces me. "Something tells me I shouldn't believe you."

I grin without any real humor. "Because you probably shouldn't."

If he calls out to me again, I don't know how I'll react, but denying my mate, even if he might be a danger, feels impossible until we know more.

Clara scowls. "I hate you sometimes."

"Only sometimes?"

With a final glare, she turns back to the painting, and together we put it back on the wall. I place my hand over the canvas, hoping for one more interaction, but there's nothing now. Not even the pull. Only the memory.

We head back to the main section of the castle, and I keep my face neutral. I can't give anything away, not even to passing staff. Whatever's been happening here, there's no telling how many of them know and what they might do to keep such secrets hidden.

We're almost to our rooms, but when we turn the final corner, Aeson is standing at the end of the corridor, waiting. His gaze sweeps over me, curiosity flickering behind his dark blue eyes. "Out for a morning stroll?"

I smile as I approach, letting my movements slow, become more fluid. "Exploring my new home. A queen should be familiar with the kingdom she's meant to rule, don't you think?"

His smirk deepens. "You are thorough, aren't you?"

"Always."

Aeson reaches for my hand, his fingers brushing mine. I let him take it, even leaning in slightly, as if drawn to him. His scent—an earthy spice and something distinctly *him*—

wraps around me, but it no longer stirs anything inside me.

I press my palm to his chest, angling my head closer. "You've been busy these last few days."

"As have you," he murmurs, his hand gliding to my waist.

The contact is possessive, but I let it linger as I feign excitement for what's to come. "Do you need any help with ceremony planning? It's getting so close now."

A glimmer of something indecipherable crosses his expression before he schools it back into a casual smile. "Our guest list isn't as full as I hoped it would be. Asher and Theo are claiming it's too short notice to attend."

"Oh, my king." I slide my hand down his arm slowly. "Estee owes me. Let me give her a call and see what I can do about that. We need them here."

And as an idea begins to form, I might need the other kings and queens now more than ever.

His smile turns approvingly. "You never cease to impress me."

I lift my chin, my voice dipping into something softer, more seductive. "You've only seen the beginning of what I'm capable of."

Aeson's fingers tighten slightly at my waist before he releases me with a lingering touch. "I look forward to seeing more."

I step back, offering him a final glance before continuing down the hall to my room, ignoring Clara's disgust at having witnessed that show until we're out of sight.

Aeson's starting to trust me more.

Now, I just have to make sure he never sees my next move coming.

CHAPTER NINE

THE FATED MATE

She shouldn't be here—she shouldn't have been able to break through those runes—but she did. And now, I'm coming undone. Her presence was a breath of air in lungs that have been starved for too long. A blade that slashed through the numbness, carving me open, forcing me to feel again. And it hurts.

Gods, it hurts so damn much.

Seeing her for those fleeting seconds was like staring into the sun after a lifetime of darkness. My body throbbed with the instinct to reach for her, to touch, to claim, to do anything but watch her vanish into the void once more.

My mate.

My wolf has been silent for years, buried beneath the pressure of magic and despair. But when she came into view, he roared to life, clawing at the edges of my mind, demanding I take what's ours…but I couldn't.

I can't.

She doesn't understand what she's done. What she's awakened. What finding me might cost her.

But I do, and I should've pushed her away harder. I

should've lied, twisted my words, made her believe *I'm* the monster.

Hell, I might be after all this time. I have no idea how much of my humanity is left. I've been caged in this pit for so long, bound in spells woven with malice, my body battered by unseen forces that would've killed any other man.

Yet, I'm still alive.

Maybe Aeson wanted it this way. To draw out my death in hopes I'd be too exhausted by the time my tortuous life ended to have any desire to be reborn, to return and take back what was never meant to be his.

The thought of my brother sends a deep, corrosive fury slashing through my gut. He who tricked his way into becoming king when it should've been my destiny, not his. I'd let it go, knowing he wanted the role more, but I should've looked deeper. I would've seen that his intentions were far from good, even when he was convincing me that he was making the *sacrifice* to take the crown for my benefit.

And now he has *her*.

I grit my teeth, my chains rattling against the stone as my arms tense. I pull against them, knowing they won't give but unable to ignore the need to fight.

He'll consume her.

Maybe not today, maybe not tomorrow. But Aeson doesn't let things slip from his grasp. He takes, he manipulates, he poisons, he conquers, and he'll continue to do so.

Unless I find a way to stop him.

CHAPTER TEN

SLOANE

As I spend the late morning in my room, I feel alive in a way I haven't in years. Every sense is improved, every thought electric. A determination has settled inside me, but unlike the doubt that's plagued me since signing that damn contract, there's only clear, deliberate focus.

Clara left me in my room to search her boxes, and I've taken the morning to write my thoughts out before burning them in the fireplace, leaving no trace of what I've learned beyond what's safe in my mind.

Coming to Venaris was supposed to be the saving grace for my people, but it's become my own. I'm still not sure this is where my pack will stay, but I know this kingdom is where I'm meant to be right now. Even though I know Aeson isn't someone I can trust. At least the version of him that's ruling this kingdom.

The man in the cave—my mate, who looks just like Aeson—remains at the forefront of my thoughts. Who is he? Is he the real Aeson? If not, how is he connected to Aeson? Who put him there? Why is he bound to that wall? How long has he been there? And what does all this mean for me and my pack?

So many questions now that I'm being directly influenced by the bond. Yet, the answers all elude me.

At least I know that my connection with Aeson was never real. I see that now. It was familiarity, a thread of recognition. Not love. Not fate. I'd been so desperate for answers that I'd let it mean something else when I should've known better.

Now that I'm seeing things for what they are—Aeson being up to something I don't yet understand and my mate trapped under this castle—it's easier to keep my emotions in check. My thoughts have quickly become more deliberate, focusing only on the facts. Not on what might be or what could be or any sort of emotion.

Even for my mate.

I meant what I said to Clara before. If the man in the cave is more monster than prisoner, I'll put him down myself. There's no more second-guessing who I am and what needs to be done.

But that doesn't mean I'm going to hesitate to free him. I need to know more. Especially why he seemed so hell-bent on *not* being set free.

Okay. Maybe my emotions aren't done taking a front seat here. I can't deny him pushing me away only made me want to know more. Vile creatures don't normally beg to be left captive.

I drag my hands over my face and exhale sharply. I can't do this alone. I need Clara to learn more about the runes, and I'm going to need help postponing the bonding ceremony. I can keep up pretenses as long as I don't have to tie myself to him.

That's a line I'll no longer cross. Contract be damned.

Which is why I'm now waiting on the phone to be connected to Estee.

We didn't get to spend a lot of time together when I was in Selaris, but it was enough that I believe asking for her help now isn't a risk to my plans.

Estee is unapologetically genuine and full of fire beneath her regal exterior. If there's anyone who'll gladly throw a dagger into Aeson's plan with me, it's her.

After several minutes of silence, she finally answers with an air of surprise in her tone. "Queen Sloane. To what do I owe this pleasure?"

I sit up straighter on my bed, holding the phone securely to my ear. "I'm not sure you'll think this is a *pleasure* once I tell you what I need."

Her laugh comes easily, rich with amusement. "Didn't you figure this out about me? I live for trouble. How can I help?"

"Well, first, do you know why Theo and Asher have declined to come to my bonding ceremony to Aeson?"

There's quiet then a low, warning growl that makes me grin.

This is a good start.

"What?" The rumble in her words is endearing. "I know nothing about this, but I assure you that's about to change. When is it?"

I grimace. "It's supposed to be in a few days, but if I can get all of you to agree to come, I'd like to use that as a reason to push things out a bit. Maybe give me another couple days to sort out my other problem."

"Are you going to leave me in suspense?" She says it lightly, but I know if I don't share everything, I could lose a valuable ally before I've even had her.

"You know the issues I've had with my land, right?" She offers a quick confirmation before I continue. "Well, Alcaris has officially run out of fresh water, and I've moved my pack to Venaris. I've been living in the castle for a couple weeks now, but it wasn't until these last few days that things have become more…suspicious."

"You have me intrigued already. How so?" she asks promptly.

"Well, for one, there are runes and dark magic within the castle. Ones I have a connection to. Or at least what they're hiding."

"Oh, Sloane." She laughs. "And here I thought you lived a rather quiet life. This sounds like my kind of fun. What did you find?"

There's no hesitation in my next two words. "My mate."

There's a pause before she lets out a long breath. "Considering you were just talking about bonding with Aeson, I'm assuming this is more complicated than it should be?"

"You're assuming right," I say solemnly. "The man I found, my mate, is chained beneath this castle in a cave-like setting that I think is placed in the basement. Even more confusing, he said that he doesn't want me to set him free. His exact words were: 'He'll kill you if he knows you found me.'"

"Well, that's ominous," Estee replies. "Though, if you're the queen I know you to be, I doubt that means much to you if he's really your fated mate."

"Correct." I switch hands and wipe my palm over my comforter. "I have no intention of letting my guard down, but I can't leave him there either. Not until I understand who the real monster in this castle is."

"What's that supposed to mean?" Estee asks with piqued interest.

I glance toward the closed bedroom door, using my senses to check for the third time that I'm still alone before answering. There isn't a heartbeat to be heard outside my room, so I continue. "Aeson isn't who he's portrayed himself to be. He's mentioned how large and powerful our pack will be once we're mated. His offer to help my people no longer seems as genuine as I once allowed myself to believe."

She scoffs. "Don't put any of this on you or the decisions you've made. As a fellow queen, there's nothing I wouldn't do for my people. You saw hope, just as anyone would have, and you took it. If Aeson isn't the honorable king he's supposed to be, we'll fix that before he even knows what's coming for him. You're not alone in this, Sloane. I'm glad you called, and I'll make sure we're there when you need us."

"Thank you, Estee." I breathe easier, relaxing back onto the pillows. "This means more to me than I can say."

"You were there for us when we needed it," she reminds me. "I'm happy to repay the favor."

Thankfully, I believe she truly means that. We firm up a few more details, and she promises to call Isla for me as well. Right after she has a conversation with her mate, who's currently hiding from her.

Smart man.

Now, it's time for me to help Clara with her part.

THE DAY SLIPS AWAY IN A BLUR OF UNPACKING AND SEARCHING. Clara and I sift through every box, each one a gamble—clothes, trinkets, old journals. Nothing useful. Aeson checks in more than once. His presence lingers like smoke, suffocating and impossible to ignore. He's watching me. But I smile each time, like a dutiful queen-to-be.

It isn't until after the sun has set that we finally find the books Clara believes will hold answers for us, their spines cracked with age, pages faded and brittle. Clara's breath hitches as she pulls the first volume free, fingers tracing the worn title. *Magic Bound by Sacrifice.*

"Here," she whispers, sliding the book onto the desk and flipping the cover open.

I move to stand behind her, heart pounding in my chest, when the door swings open.

Aeson strides in, his grin wide and eyes unnaturally bright. "There you are." He crosses the room in three long strides, arms looping around my waist as he lifts me clear off the ground. "*You* are going to be the most excellent queen."

I start to question him, but his lips crash over mine in a kiss that has my muscles tensing, that churns my stomach. It's quick, thoughtless, possessive.

"I don't know what you did, but King Asher and King Theo will be here in six days." His smile broadens as he sets me down. "That means we need to postpone the ceremony for a few days, but for a proper audience, I didn't think you'd mind."

My mind spins so violently it nearly knocks me off balance. It worked. Estee must've pulled the right strings. But I can't even savor the victory because my lips burn from his kiss, my wolf snarling beneath my skin like she's been scorched.

"Pretend you're happy and not disgusted!" Clara's voice slices through my mind.

Right.

I plaster on a radiant smile, my hands pressing against his chest as if to steady myself. "Of course I don't mind. Estee said she'd do her best to rearrange her schedule to get here on time still, but what's a couple of days in the grand scheme of things?"

He grabs my chin, still smiling widely. "Gods, I can't wait

until you're mine." He glances around the room before coming back to meet my stare. "Clara can handle the rest of her boxes. Let's go celebrate our success over dinner."

"I've got this," Clara speaks through our mental connection. *"Don't push him away when we're this close to answers."*

I hate that she's right, but I nod at Aeson's suggestion, forcing excitement into my tone. "As long as there's dessert, I'm yours for the evening."

His thumb lightly glides over my lower lip, his eyes darkening. "For you, there will *always* be dessert."

Don't vomit in his face, Sloane. Don't do it.

Clara coughs, but I can hear the laugh she's trying to hide. My *advisor* is going to enjoy my torture a little too much.

"Thank you, my queen, for your help today," Clara finally says out loud. "I'm glad to be getting settled in."

Aeson wraps an arm around my waist. "If you need anything for the rest of the evening, Dasha's available to you."

With those final words, Aeson guides me out of the room. I want to look back at Clara, to beg her to get me out of this dinner, especially with how touchy-feely Aeson is tonight, but this is part of my role.

Feign affection. Smile brightly. Lie my ass off.

Most importantly, don't get caught.

I need to make sacrifices to find answers, and if that means kissing a man who's been lying to me, my lips will just have to understand.

My wolf snarls within my mind once more, but her temper only flares briefly. Even she can't deny that if we're going to set our mate free, we need to keep Aeson's suspicions down.

He needs to believe that power is just as important to us as it is to him.

The hallway is quieter than usual, only the soft patter of our footsteps and the distant hum of castle life filling the space. Aeson keeps me tucked against his side, hand warm at my waist. It's meant to be intimate, but all I feel is confined.

"We should plan a dinner for the night of the kings and queens' arrival," I tell him, musing over a few ideas. "Clara and Dasha should prepare their rooms now in case they arrive early. And we'll need the finest carriages reserved to bring them from the docks to the castle, making sure to take the path through town, of course. Oh, and the kitchen should be stocked with their favorite foods. Everything should be perfect, and everyone should know that the other rulers of Lunara have made an effort to appear for our ceremony."

If I pretend there's a lot to do, maybe I can get out of this dinner sooner rather than later…

Aeson kisses the side of my head. "Oh, my queen. I love your eagerness to make our special day one that won't soon be forgotten. But don't you worry about any of that. I have this under control. All you need to focus on is being here in this castle and accepting your role as the Queen of Venaris."

My steps falter.

There it is.

The tightening of his grip, the edge in his voice.

Control.

This time, though, I don't hold back my discontent over his statement. There's such a thing as "too agreeable" and that's not who I've ever been. I won't pretend otherwise, even for this.

Just before we reach the dining room, I stop him and look directly into the blue eyes that no longer feel as welcoming as they once did. "I thought I made it clear that I'm an active queen, and I intend to stay one. If this is going to be a problem for you…"

He shakes his head before I can say much more. "Not at all. I was merely trying to remove any added stress from your life. Losing your kingdom can't be easy, even if we do have much to celebrate. If staying busy is what you need, please do so."

I don't miss the condescension hidden beneath his smile. He's trying to make me sound weak. Gods, if I didn't have to play nice... I switch the subject before I lose my temper. "Speaking of staying busy. More of my items will be brought over from the Alcaris castle over the next couple of days," I tell him, deciding to ruffle him right back. "I won't have enough room to store everything in the room with me, but I'd like to keep my belongings close. Do you mind if I utilize the attic or basement for things I don't immediately need?"

His jaw tightens and eyes darken, but only briefly. If I hadn't been watching for any signs, I might've missed them entirely as he leads us into the dining room, his hand burning into my lower back. "If you leave what you don't need right now in the foyer, I'll make sure it's safely stored."

I smile and nod as I take my seat to dine with him.

He didn't say I *couldn't* do it myself.

Checkmate, King Aeson.

CHAPTER ELEVEN

SLOANE

The castle feels colder tonight as I make my way to Clara's room. A chill runs down my spine and my wolf perks up, but when I look around, I don't see anything off-putting. Only the flickering of shadows thanks to the late hour and the sconces on the walls.

Squaring my shoulders, I continue, and when I enter Clara's room, I find her perched on her bed, cross-legged, surrounded by scattered books. Her hair is mussed from hours of reading, but her eyes are piercing as they lift to meet mine.

"I found it." Clara grins, holding up a leather-bound tome, its cover splintered with age.

The sight of the ancient book stirs something inside me—a mixture of hope and dread. I cross the room quickly, my chest tightening with every step. "Tell me."

Clara flips through brittle pages, her fingers gentle despite her urgency. "The runes we saw? They were traditionally used for two purposes: to cleanse a place of dark energy or to strip power from an individual. The spell itself doesn't choose. It only follows the intent of the caster."

My stomach knots. "So, it's not just about what the runes are doing. It's about *who* set them and *why*."

Clara nods grimly. "Exactly. They're either holding something dangerous back…or they were meant to destroy a being's power entirely."

I inhale slowly, trying to keep my thoughts in order. This confirms what I'd already suspected, but it doesn't answer the most pressing question: *Who's the true monster here—the man beneath the castle or the one ruling it?*

I glance toward the window, the moons hanging low over the distant treetops. If Aeson was truly hiding something this dangerous, why hadn't he been more careful? Why leave the runes exposed, where any curious wolf could stumble on them?

Clara slides out of bed, and I follow her to a table. She sets the book down, giving me an opportunity to peek through it as she grabs another. There are hundreds of pages here with information about runes—how to set them, what sacrifices are needed to do so, and the ramifications of using such magic—but there's nothing about how to break them.

"How are we supposed to get him out of those chains?" I ask, still not taking my eyes off the ancient text.

"Blood."

I tense. "Whose blood?"

She points to another book, this one frailer than the first. "Whoever cast the spell. We need their blood to open that door. I don't know if it will help with the chains, but it will get you physically inside instead of just projecting yourself into the room like before. Something I still can't explain."

She doesn't need to. I don't know how that happened either, but I know why, and that's all I can concern myself with for now. That man is my fated mate. I was drawn to him so I can find peace with my choices. Nothing more, nothing less.

"So, I need Aeson's blood." I close the book and cross my arms. "I could challenge him to a friendly sparring session, but I doubt he'd agree just days before our bonding ceremony."

Clara's eyes cast down, and I already know I'm not going to like what she says next. "You could bite him."

The suggestion slams into me like a punch. "Are you out of your mind?"

"Hear me out." She raises both hands, palms up in mock surrender. "If you bite him in the heat of the moment, he'll think it's instinctual, not premeditated. Let your wolf rise during...whatever you need to do, and no one will question it. Use your shirt to catch the blood, feign embarrassment, and get the hell out."

Revulsion twists in my gut, but I can't deny the logic. There's no way to stab him without raising suspicion and *asking* for his blood would be laughable.

"I hate that this makes sense," I mutter, running a hand down my face.

Clara reaches for me, squeezing my shoulder. "I'm sorry, Sloane. I can't imagine how difficult this is for you, but I know you can do it."

Gods, this sounds like the worst idea ever, but also like the only option. There's no way I can stab him and get away with it being an accident. Biting him seems the most logical, even if it's the most repulsive.

"I have to do this now," I tell her, beginning to pace. "We can't wait any longer. Not with the ceremony just days away. I need to talk to my...that man again before the others get here and getting through that door is the best way."

She grins at me. "It's okay, Sloane. You can call him your

mate. I'm not judging you, even if he turns out to be the monster. It's not like that would be your fault."

I'm not worried about her judging me; I just can't allow my heart to think of him as mine. Not until I have my answers, at least.

"Go back to your room and get into your pajamas." She points to my emerald dress. "You won't be able to soak up blood if you have to lift the hem. You need a loose shirt, preferably a cotton one."

My lips thin. "What if it's not Aeson? We have no clue how long those runes have been there. It could've been his father who laid that spell, or someone else who's no longer around to take blood from. If we're wrong, and I raise Aeson's suspicions too much…"

She grabs both my hands, her face stoic. "Something tells me he needs you more than you need him. Even if he questions your intentions, his end game seems to be power. Without your pack and bond, he'll be no better off than he was before."

"Unless he kills me and takes over anyway." It's a possibility I've tried not to dwell on, but one I know could happen. Well, I know he could try anyway. He's not the first man I've had to defend my place against, and he won't be the first to win either.

Clara's dark chuckle fills the room. "And how's that worked out for those who've tried before? You can handle Aeson. You're the Queen of Alcaris, an alpha who hasn't ever bowed to anyone. You're not going to start now."

No, I'm certainly not.

"Okay. If we're wrong," I tell her, "then we're no worse off than we are right now. Either way, we'll figure this out."

"There's my queen." She nods toward the door. "Now, go get sexy. You have a king to seduce."

"I hate you some days." My grumbles follow me all the way across the room.

"And yet you still keep coming back for my expert opinion," she teases. "Have fun!"

There's no way that could happen, but maybe, just maybe, making this man bleed won't be the worst thing to happen this week.

———

A QUICK CHANGE IN MY ROOM, AND I'M BACK IN THE HALLWAY, headed to Aeson's room. This time, I have no doubt someone's following me. I still can't get eyes on them, but the faint sound of a heartbeat never seems to get further away.

I could take this as a bad sign, but at least I know now. It will change my plans for when I leave Aeson's room. While I was hoping to go straight back to the painting, that will have to wait until I can be sure nobody is trying to trail us.

My heart pounds as I round the corner and spot Aeson's door. Every muscle tenses, but I don't try to calm myself. I need the flush in my cheeks, the quickened breath, the trembling fingers. He'll think it's nerves. Desire. He won't question it if I sell the act well enough.

You've survived worse, I remind myself, lifting my hand to knock. *You can do this.*

The door swings open faster than I expect. Aeson stands there, shirt unbuttoned at the collar, sleeves rolled up to his elbows. There's a flicker of irritation on his face, though it's replaced by curiosity in an instant. His gaze sweeps over me, and the corner of his mouth lifts in a knowing smirk.

"Sloane." His tone is indulgent, like he already knows why I'm here.

I push past him, brushing against his chest as I enter.

Let him think it's boldness, not desperation.

"I couldn't sleep," I murmur, turning to face him as he closes the door. "Dinner was…nice. Too nice. I tried to go back to my room, but all I could think about was you."

It's disgustingly easy to slip into the role. My fingers find the hem of my loose button-up shirt, toying with the fabric as if trying to steady myself. His gaze drops to the movement, heat flickering in his eyes. I force myself to look at his mouth, not his eyes. I can't risk seeing the darkness I know lurks there—the reminder of everything I'm fighting.

Aeson's hesitation lasts only a moment before he steps closer, sliding his hands around my waist to tug me against him. "I wondered if my kiss earlier had pushed you away," he murmurs, voice low and smooth. "But I see now it only left you wanting."

My stomach churns, but I lift my head, letting my lashes flutter. "It was exactly what I needed. It's just been so long since…" I bite my lip for effect.

His grip tightens, one hand tangling in my hair to pull my head back, exposing my throat. "Don't you worry about a thing, my queen. I'll remind you exactly what you've been missing."

I swallow the snarl rising in my throat. *He loves control. Let him think he has it.*

His lips trace a path down my neck, and I shudder, but not from pleasure. He reaches for the buttons of my shirt, working them loose with practiced ease. I groan softly, and his movements quicken, interpreting my discomfort as eagerness.

"Kiss me," I demand, voice low and rough, before I lose my nerve.

He obliges instantly, mouth crashing into mine. I lean

into it, letting my wolf snarl quietly in the back of my mind. *For the truth,* I remind her. *For us.*

The moment his tongue brushes mine, I let my canines extend, pointed and unforgiving. I moan loudly, tilting my head as if surrendering further, and he growls in response, fingers digging into my hips.

Now.

I snap my jaw closed, catching his bottom lip. Hard. The coppery tang of blood floods my mouth, sharp and metallic. He jerks back with a hiss, hand flying to his mouth as crimson streaks down his chin.

"Damn it, Sloane!" His eyes flash with surprise, not anger.

I stumble back, feigning horror, my hands flying up to cover my mouth. "Gods, I'm so sorry! I didn't mean to. I got carried away. I didn't realize my wolf—"

I reach for him, dabbing at the blood with the hem of my shirt, heart hammering. The cotton soaks through quickly, dark red spreading across the pale fabric. My hands shake, not entirely an act.

His gaze tightens, suspicion flickering there for the first time.

I duck my head, avoiding his eyes, playing the flustered lover instead of the scheming queen.

He catches my chin, forcing me to look up. His thumb brushes over my lower lip, smearing blood. "I like seeing you unravel," he murmurs, voice dark with satisfaction. "You should do it more often."

The revulsion crawling up my throat nearly chokes me, but I swallow it. "I—I can't," I stammer, stepping back, clutching the bloodied fabric to my chest like a lifeline. "I'm sorry. I thought I was ready, but it's too much. I need a moment."

Aeson's brows draw together, confusion clouding his expression. "Sloane—"

I don't let him finish. I spin on my heel, yanking the door open and practically sprinting down the hall, ignoring the low chuckle that follows me.

Let him think it's nerves. Let him think I'm weak.

Turning the corner, I catch a flash of movement. *Dasha.* Her pale face peeks from the shadows, lips pressed into a thin line. So it was *her* following me. Her gaze drops to the crimson stain on my shirt, and something like panic flickers across her face.

I ignore the meek advisor. She's not my concern right now.

Slamming my bedroom door behind me, I lean against the wood, chest heaving as I let the tremors take over. The taste of his blood lingers on my tongue, bitter and vile.

"I did it," I say to Clara through our mental link. *"But I'm being watched. We need to wait another day or two before we go back to the portrait."*

Clara's response is immediate, laced with worry. *"Are you okay?"*

"I am." For now, at least.

There might be consequences for tonight's show, but I have to hope they'll be worth it.

CHAPTER TWELVE

THE FATED MATE

Despair clings to me like a second skin, suffocating and relentless. Every hour since she appeared has stretched into an eternity, a cruel reminder of my fate. I'd convinced myself long ago that hope was a fool's indulgence, something to be gutted and left bleeding alongside everything else I'd lost.

But then *she* came.

My mate.

Even now, the phantom warmth of her presence lingers, a cruel imprint on my chest. Her scent—wild and fierce, like rain-soaked pine—still hangs in the stagnant air of my prison. It should've faded by now, like every other dream I've had in this forsaken hole, but it hasn't. It clings, keeping me tethered to sanity when I should've long since succumbed to the madness pressing in from every side.

My wolf stirred when she first appeared, snapping to attention like a soldier hearing the call to arms after centuries of silence. He'd howled for her, desperate to break free and claim what was rightfully ours. For the first time in decades, the crushing intensity of the chains around my wrists felt bearable.

But now…silence.

I grit my teeth against the void inside me, the ache where my wolf's presence should be. His energy had flared brightly, burning with the fierce recognition of our mate bond, only to dim once more when she vanished, leaving nothing but absence in her wake.

He's slipping away again.

Panic surges through me, swift and bitter. Without my wolf, I'm nothing more than a man bound by dark magic, stripped of everything that once made me powerful. If he dies, I die. Not just in body but in soul. There will be no reincarnation, no second chance at life or love. I will fade into nothingness, forgotten even by the gods who turned their backs on me the day my brother betrayed me.

Aeson.

The name tastes like poison.

My fists clench against the damp stone behind me, the rusted chains biting into my wrists. I used to think of him as my other half—the mirror image born beside me, a brother in blood and bond. But the thirst for power can't always be contained. It festers, corrodes, until crimson spills without hesitation.

He didn't just want the throne. He wanted me gone, erased, forgotten.

Something I nearly believed he'd succeed at until *she* arrived.

Like a damned fool, I told her to leave and forget about me, trying to keep her safe. Now, I can't think of anything but her.

Her fierce gaze lingers with suspicion, but is softened by something deeper. The delicate tremor in her voice when she vowed to free me, as though she already knew the weight of the choice she was making.

I slam my fists against the rock wall, the chains rattling like a cruel reminder of my powerlessness. If Aeson discovers her connection to me, there's no telling what he'll do. He's spent years ensuring I remain forgotten. My mate's existence changes everything.

You have to hang on for her, I tell my wolf, reaching into the empty space where his presence used to hum with quiet strength. *If you die, we both do. We can't leave her to face him alone.*

For a moment—barely a flicker—I feel something stir. A faint growl, more breath than sound, like the last ember struggling against the cold.

It's enough.

I lean my head back against the wet stone, closing my eyes as exhaustion weighs me down once more. The darkness presses closer, whispering promises of peace if I just let go.

But I can't. Not now.

Not when she's out there, and I have no idea what kind of danger she might be in.

But I know this: if fate is cruel enough to bring her to me only to tear her away, I will drag myself from the abyss of death and rip this world apart to find her again.

CHAPTER THIRTEEN

SLOANE

Gods, what did I do?

It's as if I've bathed in pheromones, and now I can't scrub them off. I've tried showering until my skin is raw, eating the most potent foods, and even drowning myself in unflattering clothes I own. Nothing helps. Since I went to Aeson's room, he's not left me alone for long, and I'm starting to go insane.

The next morning, he showed up at my door with a tray of breakfast, insisting we eat together in the privacy of my room. Clara, thankfully, burst in moments later, feigning an emergency with the pack. Aeson hadn't been pleased, but he'd left with a lingering kiss to my temple that made my wolf recoil.

Later, when I walked through the town to check on my people, he appeared beside me like a shadow, hand on the small of my back the entire time. Possessive. Controlling. My pack watched with carefully blank expressions, but I'd caught more than one wary glance at Aeson's public displays of affection. They didn't speak aloud, but through our mental link, I'd asked if there were any concerns, any whispers of mistreatment, anything they hadn't wanted to voice with Aeson present.

Nothing, they'd all assured me. If anything, besides the side glances, my people seemed more settled than they had been in months. Food was plentiful, their quarters comfortable, and the guards kept their distance unless invited closer.

From the outside, everything looked perfect.

Now, thirty-six hours after I'd bitten him and collected his blood, he's finally given me a sliver of space. Clara's still buried in the books, chasing down every lead she can find on those damned runes. And me? I'm suffocating.

I need out.

My wolf, caged for days, pushes against my control, her restless energy making my limbs twitch with the need to move. I stride through the castle's dimly lit halls, each step lighter than the last as the grand front doors come into view. The moment sunlight filters through the narrow windows lining the corridor, my chest loosens and my pace quickens.

Freedom.

We're nearly there when the world plunges into darkness.

Harsh hands clamp down on my arms, yanking me sideways into a shadowy room. The door slams shut behind us, the faint click of the lock sealing my fate.

For a breathless moment, all I hear is my own pulse thundering in my ears. Then, Aeson's scent hits me—dark spice and something colder beneath it, like snow melting over steel.

Instinct overrides thought. My wolf snaps to the surface, flooding me with raw, vicious strength. Canines extend, sharp and aching, while my fingers curl into claws. Before I can process the movement, my hand whips back, muscles coiling into a strike meant for his face.

Aeson catches my wrist mid-swing, slamming me against the wall with enough force to rattle the shelf beside us. My head pounds momentarily, but I blink away the pain, trying to process what's happening.

"Easy, my queen," he murmurs, voice smooth as silk. "It's just me."

I snarl, low and feral, the sound vibrating through my chest. My wolf doesn't care who he is. He touched us without warning. He *dragged* us into the dark like we were prey.

Predators don't take kindly to that.

I sweep my leg out, hooking his ankle and twisting. He stumbles, his grip loosening just enough for me to spin us around, slamming him against the cold stone. He might have six inches and fifty pounds on me, but I've taken down bigger threats with less adrenaline.

"Don't grab me like that again," I growl through gritted teeth.

His chuckle slides over my skin like acid. "Oh, Sloane. Come now. I was just trying to steal a moment alone with my mate. We've had hardly any time together since the other night."

I don't loosen my grip. If anything, my fingers tighten around his biceps, nails pricking through the thin linen of his shirt.

But I can't. Not yet.

I force a smile to my lips. "I know. But once our guests arrive tonight and the ceremony is complete, things will settle."

His expression softens into something dangerously close to affection, and that's what unnerves me most. He truly believes that I'm his prize, his queen, his perfect pawn.

He catches the fabric of my flowing green dress, tugging

me closer until his breath fans across my cheek. "We have right now, don't we?"

My wolf lunges forward, and it takes everything in me to hold her back.

I press a hand to his chest, keeping my voice low and teasing. "Did you see how close I came to ripping your throat out just now? I need to run, Aeson. To burn off the edge before I snap at the wrong person."

His lower lip juts out in an exaggerated pout. "I could give you a better workout."

Don't throw up on him, Sloane.

His grip tightens possessively on my waist as he nips at the sensitive skin just below my jaw. "My patience will only last so long, Sloane," he warns, his voice a breathy growl. "I hope you don't intend to keep teasing me."

I smile sweetly, even as dread coils like a serpent in my gut. "Of course not."

Finally, he releases me, stepping back with a satisfied smirk. Light spills into the room as he unlocks the door, and I realize we're in one of the smaller, unused offices off the main corridor.

"Sloane," he calls as I step into the hall, my heart already racing toward freedom.

I glance back, finding his expression wiped clean of charm, replaced by something colder. Emptier.

"I know you like running things your way," he says, voice measured. "But you're going to have to start giving more. After everything I've done for you, I expect a little more... *appreciation.* Do you understand?"

I swallow hard, my wolf growling in protest. "Of course, King Aeson."

He nods, satisfied. "Good." A pause. "I'll be unavailable this afternoon. Make sure you're dressed properly before our guests arrive. You should wear something fitting for the future Queen of Venaris." His gaze flickers over my simple silk dress, disdain curling at the corner of his mouth. "I'll have my choices laid out for you on your bed before I go."

On my bed.

My heart stutters. He's going into my room.

The room where I've hidden the bloodied shirt. Wrapped in plastic, drenched in perfume, stuffed between the mattresses, but still hidden in *my* room.

I force my lips into a tight smile. "That's really not—"

"I insist." His smirk grows, smug satisfaction oozing from every word. "Enjoy your run, my queen."

Like hell that's happening now.

He's not giving me space. He's hunting.

And if he finds what I've hidden, this game will be over before I've made my first real move.

Turning on my heel, I head outside as if his invasion of my privacy means nothing. As if the idea of him choosing my wardrobe is even remotely acceptable.

My fingers twitch with the urge to reach for my wolf, to let her tear through him and end this twisted game. But I force myself to walk—calm, composed, the picture of an obedient queen-to-be.

"Clara, I need you to run to my room and get the shirt," I command through our mental link. *"And move faster than you ever have. You might only have seconds."*

"On it."

Her reply is swift, and I feign joy and confidence to the people of the kingdom as I walk through the castle grounds toward the forest. I know this could go wrong, that I've just put my best friend in grave danger.

As the seconds tick by, my pace falters. I should turn

back. Should've pretended to forget something and returned to my room myself.

Clara is more than an advisor. More than a friend. She's family. If anything happens to her…

"*I want a raise,*" she pants through our connection, breathless but triumphant. "*That was damn close, but I think I'm in the clear.*"

My heart slams against my ribs as I pause at the tree line. "*What happened?*"

"*I got the shirt and hadn't quite made it to my room when he came around the corner. Instead of slipping inside and ignoring him, since he'd already seen me, I cracked my door open, dropped the shirt behind me, and kicked it away, acting like I was just leaving to find you.*"

Gods, I don't know what I'd do without her.

Her voice sharpens. "*He told me you were out for a run and that he was picking out your clothes for dinner. Then he said I'm to steam each item, shine your shoes until they glimmer like the gods damned stars, and make sure you're the picture of perfection' by sunset. How did we never see this side of him before?*"

"*Because he didn't want us to,*" I grumble. "*Now, he has the upper hand. Or at least he thinks he does. I'm going to take this hour to run, but we're not waiting any more, Clara. As soon as I'm back, we're going to that hallway again.*"

"*During the middle of the day?*" I can hear her disagreement, but I don't care anymore.

"*Aeson said he'll be unavailable this afternoon, and if someone wants to question what their future queen is doing in her castle, I wish them luck.*"

Clara laughs. "*Oh, I hope they do.*"

I call my wolf forward, and it doesn't take much before my bones are breaking and reforming into my animal half. "*You and me both.*"

With claws extended, my wolf takes off into the forest, a howl building from deep within her. She's mourning all the things we've lost and what we might not find when we get through the runes. I don't try to spin anything in a positive light—because she has a right to her own emotions, but also because I fear the same things.

If our mate isn't the good guy, if he's a monster who's been rightfully locked away and we're left with Aeson...

What the hell are we going to do then?

Less than two hours later, I return to my room, lungs burning and hair wild from the wind. Freedom clings to me like dew, but it evaporates the moment I see the gowns spread across my bed.

Three of them. Each one a deep purple, almost black, with intricate silver embroidery. The color of Venaris, of Aeson's reign.

His mark.

I spin around and leave without a second glance.

I'd almost forgotten the nightmare I was returning to. But Aeson, ever the calculating bastard, never misses an opportunity to remind me.

I never should've signed that contract.

The memory of that night burns brighter with each step I take toward Clara's room. I'd told myself to wait—to give it a moon cycle, to think with my head, not my heart. But then came the dream...

The one filled with strong hands, whispered promises, and piercing blue eyes.

Only now, with clarity realized by time, I understand the truth:

The man in the basement—the one shackled and broken —is the mirror image of Aeson.

Was my dream not of the king, but of the prisoner?

Hope flares, bright and treacherous, but I shove it down. Fated mate or not, I can't let myself believe in fairytales. Not until I have answers.

I need to stand before this man eye-to-eye. To hear his story, to weigh the truth in his words, not through the hazy veil of whatever it is I'm doing without knowing how.

Clara meets me at her door, looking every bit the warrior advisor I've always trusted. Her blonde hair is pinned back, her black slacks crisp, and her emerald blouse—*Alcaris green* —glows like a beacon against the drab stone walls.

The color of home. Of hope.

"Ready?" she asks, already locking the door behind her.

I nod then frown. "Where's the…key?"

She smirks, plucking at her loose blouse. The bloodied shirt peeks out from behind the fabric. "Safe and sound."

We move quickly, steps silent against the polished stone. I scan the hallways for Dasha. I haven't seen her since that night, but her absence only makes me more suspicious. She's watching and waiting, I'm sure of that.

But I don't care.

When we reach the southern wing's lowest level, the air thickens. The silence is absolute. Clara and I exchange a glance but say nothing as we approach the painting. The heavy frame looks undisturbed from the last time we were there, its centuries-old landscape depicting a Venaris long forgotten.

We work together to get the frame down, and as soon as the runes are exposed, they glow. My heart races, and I lift my fingers to touch them, but Clara smacks my wrist. "We need to use the shirt first."

Right. That's why we're here.

She unbuttons her blouse and slips the ruined pajama shirt free before covering herself again. I take the bloodied cotton and step forward. I hold my breath, my entire body tense as I raise a hand and press the heaviest spot of blood to the stone.

With bated breath, I stare, unblinking. There's a roaring in my ears as I wait for the drawing on the wall to become an actual door, but it seems sheer will isn't enough. Nor is Aeson's blood.

I glance at Clara, keeping the shirt in place. "Does it need to be fresh?"

There's a deep crease between her eyes. "It shouldn't matter—blood is blood—but maybe."

My stomach sinks. "Or maybe it's not Aeson."

Just a week ago, I told myself not to twist things into something they weren't, yet since finding the runes outside, I've continued to think the worst. Have I been painting the king as the villain without just cause? Sure, he's a misogynist, but he's also done a lot for my people. Does that give him an excuse to use his kindness against me? No, but that doesn't mean he's responsible for trapping a man beneath this castle either—even one who looks just like him.

A rumble builds in my chest. Gods, why is this so confusing?

"Sloane?" The concern in Clara's voice hits me just as my knees start to weaken and my vision falters. I'm thrust back into the darkness, but this time I know what's happening and there's no pain as I'm once again transported inside the cave.

My astral form stays standing, and I waste no time walking toward the water where he's trapped. His bright blue eyes are on mine as if he's been expecting me and his chest heaves as he struggles against the chains that bind him.

Water moves around his waist even once he stops moving. "You came back."

I cross my arms as if that will calm my pounding heart. "Did you think I wouldn't just because you told me not to?"

He smiles, and my chest tightens. The pulsing of our shared bond wraps around my heart, demanding I touch him, but I remain where I'm at, near the water.

"I'm glad you didn't because I was wrong." He stands taller, pulling against his shackles. "I'm getting out of here, and when I do, my brother's going to pay for what he's done and then I'm going to show you I'm not the monster he'll try to convince you I am."

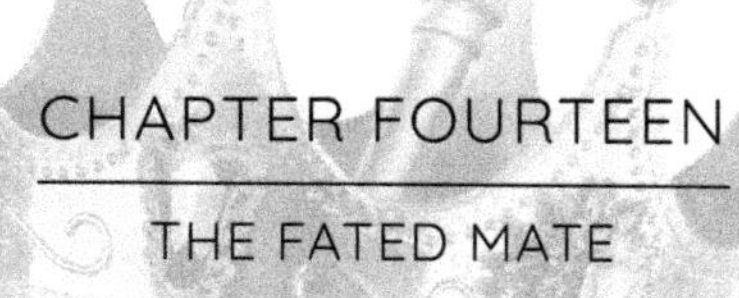

CHAPTER FOURTEEN

THE FATED MATE

She's back.

My pulse quickens, the dull ache of hopelessness retreating for the first time in what feels like centuries. The cave's shadows recoil from the light of her spirit form, as if even this cursed place recognizes her strength.

My mate.

Her scent lingers, faint but undeniable—a mix of pine and something sweet, like spring's first bloom. It stirs my wolf, weak but not yet gone. He growls low, more plea than warning.

Hold on, I tell him. *We fight for her now.*

Her gaze sharpens as she steps closer, the hem of her emerald dress brushing the damp stone. There's fire in her icy eyes, not the confusion I'd seen before. She's here with purpose.

Good. She'll need that intensity to survive what's coming.

"Who are you, and how did you get here?" she demands, coming as close to me as she can without touching the water that helps keep me trapped here.

"I'm Julian," I reply, but don't continue when she takes a small step back.

"Julian as in Aeson's brother?" Confusion fills her words.

"Yes."

Her brows knit together, disbelief flickering across her features. "That's not possible. He was killed centuries ago after murdering his brother's mate and was never reborn."

A bitter laugh escapes me, harsh and jagged. There's no hiding my disdain for the stories Aeson has undoubtedly shared over the years. "I didn't die, but I *am* dying. If I don't get out of here, my wolf spirit will continue to fade away, and without him, I'll be basically human. Once that happens, a few weeks without food and water and that's it. No reincarnations, just death."

I expect more of a reaction out of her, but she stays composed. Her hands clasp in front of her and her posture is straight as she stands before me in a stunning green dress that hugs her curves, teasing my resolve nearly to its breaking point.

Her ebony hair is loose and flowing around her shoulders, and her crown—elaborate twists that create seven distinct points—shimmers even within the darkness of this cave.

"How did you get here?" she asks again, her voice filled with determination.

I don't know how long we'll have this time, so I'm glad she's getting right to the point. I grip the chains at my wrists, the metal burning my skin. "Aeson. My twin. The King of Venaris that never should've been."

She doesn't flinch, but her lips press into a thin line. "What does that mean?"

"I am the first-born son," I say with confidence. "But Aeson had me convinced I didn't want the crown before we were even considered adults. I willingly let him take my place without realizing he still saw me as a threat regardless of what I did or didn't do."

There's no response from her, and I want to ask what she's thinking, but I continue instead. "He wasn't always this way. As boys, we were inseparable. He had the charm, I had the strength. Still, for him, it was always a competition. He was determined to make everyone see him as the flawless prince. A need for perfection that eventually began to rot his heart, making me realize too late that he wasn't the king I thought he could be."

"So, are you telling me you didn't kill his mate in a jealous rage, but you did try to take your crown back, and he locked you away for that?" she asks, her tone mostly even, but I can see the disbelief in her eyes.

I shake my head. "Not exactly. His fated mate Lira, she was as pure as they came. Her kindness knew no bounds. At least until she also started to see Aeson's darkness. I never wanted Lira, never lusted for my brother's mate as he convinced people I did. I was only trying to protect her, but Aeson came for me before I could stop the worst of his actions."

The memory claws at me, but I push through. My mate needs the truth before it's too late.

"He poisoned me. Something I could've overcome, but before I had the chance, I was trapped." I lift my hands and shake the chains. "They're enchanted to dull my strength, stealing my wolf's essence a little more every day. And the water is spelled, too. If I channel enough energy to shift, it reacts, sending an electrical current through me, strong enough to stop my heart."

"You haven't shifted in over two hundred years?" This time, the incredulity in her voice gives me hope.

"Not since the night he betrayed me."

I let her process this information, staying silent as she does, but my restraint only lasts for so long. I know she needs answers, but so do I.

"May I know your name?" I ask, not bothering to hide my desperation to know anything and everything I can about her.

She blinks and her fingers twist, but she stays still otherwise. "Sloane, Queen of Alcaris. Though, I guess that's not exactly true any longer."

A queen? What is Aeson up to? Gods, I hate that she's likely being used, but if she wasn't capable of thinking for herself, she probably wouldn't be here.

"What about Lira?" Sloane asks, her face paling as if she already knows the answer. "If you didn't kill her…"

"Aeson. She found him dragging me into the basement. He threatened to trap her here with me, but then he gave her a choice." My throat tightens as I remember the heartbreak in her eyes. "He told her she could die quickly as long as she vowed never to be reborn, or she could suffer alongside me for centuries. As I said before, Lira was pure. I knew her decision before she did. What I've endured, it wasn't something for her to survive. I just hope she's resting now and at peace with her choice."

Sloane's gaze narrows. "But there's no way Aeson could be sure she wouldn't choose to be reborn. That seems like a risk he wouldn't take."

"You're right. It would've been a risk, but only with anyone other than Lira. I don't know how she ended up fated to my brother, but when that woman gave her word, she meant it. There was no deceit in her. Something Aeson used to his advantage until the very end."

She goes silent again, gaze flickering away from me and

into the abyss of the cave. Shadows cling to her, swirling at the edges of her shimmering form like tendrils of doubt. I search her face for judgment, disbelief, *anything* that might mean I've lost her trust.

But there's none of that. Only sharp, assessing focus. Sloane doesn't flinch easily, and gods, if that doesn't make me want to fight harder.

"I don't know how much time we have, Sloane," I plead with her. "Do you know how you're getting into this room?"

When her eyes meet mine, my world turns on its axis. Her strength and determination alone make my heart race, but her beauty takes my breath away. I don't know how I'm getting out of here yet, but I do know that I won't ever stop fighting for this woman.

As she starts to talk, I've already forgotten the question until her words begin to take root.

"The mate bond," she says quietly, wetting her lips as if tasting the words. "That has to be why I keep finding you. It's the only connection strong enough to bypass dark magic like this." Her expression tightens. "But that's just the *why*. I don't know *how* I'm projecting here. All I know is that I took some of Aeson's blood to open the door we found, but it didn't work on the runes. Before we could try anything else, I was brought back here." She grimaces, but there's a hint of amusement in her eyes. "My advisor's probably strangling me right now for putting her through this again."

"Extend my apologies to her," I mutter, the corner of my mouth lifting despite the topic of the conversation. "But this is bigger than either of us. How did you get Aeson's blood? Does he know you're onto him?"

Panic coils tight around my chest. If he suspects her even *slightly*, he won't hesitate to crush her. And I'm chained like a wild animal, unable to protect the only person who's ever made me believe this life is still worth fighting for.

Sloane turns slightly, as if about to step back into the shadows but hesitates. She reaches for the long strands of her hair, her fingers twisting the soft strands in a gesture that seems almost…uncertain.

"You should know something about me," she says, voice quiet but steady. "I know you're my mate, but am I certain I can trust you? I'll be honest, no. I do believe what you're telling me has truth to it. Though, until I can be sure, I'm doing whatever I can to make sure I don't find myself falling victim to anyone who might not deserve my trust."

Her words pierce deeper than any blade ever could, but I nod. "As you should. I don't fault you for that, Sloane. Not in the slightest." The words are said in earnest even though they shatter my heart. I hate that she has to wonder if I'm the villain Aeson has painted me to be over the years. Though, that also means she doesn't believe in my brother, something I have to be grateful for.

"I'm supposed to bond with Aeson this week," she says abruptly. The words hit like a punch to the gut, but before I can speak, she adds, "He thinks I'm his doting mate. I stole his blood when I kissed him. A little too aggressively."

The world goes black for a moment as my wolf surges forward, fury eclipsing reason. I yank against the chains with everything I have, the metal biting into my wrists until fresh blood seeps down my forearms. The cave trembles with the force of my roar, echoing back at me like the gods themselves are mocking my impotence.

Not only because he's had the chance to taste her, but because if they have that ceremony, if he *claims her…*

What will that do to our bond? To her? To me? *To us?*

The thought is unbearable. My wolf howls, fighting the

numbness overtaking him, but the strain sends another bolt of pain through my chest. *I can't lose her. Not like this.*

I suck in a ragged breath, forcing myself to calm. She doesn't need my rage. She needs clarity. *Strength.*

"I'm sorry," I rasp, my voice raw with regret. "That wasn't meant for you. I'm not angry with *you*, Sloane. I don't fault you for doing what you had to. But you can't bond with him. Not this week. Not ever."

She watches me closely, like she's weighing my sincerity, as her arm lifts, almost as if she might try to reach out to me. Her spirit gleams faintly, light flickering like a dying star.

Time's running out.

"Sloane, please." I attempt to step closer even though I know it's not possible. "I'm not asking you to trust me blindly. Hell, I'd question myself too. But if you complete that bond, it'll tie you to his power. To his darkness. It'll make it harder for you to fight him or escape him. And if he realizes what you are to me?" I swallow hard. "I can't let you find out just how vile Aeson can be."

Her brows draw together but something in her posture softens. Slowly, she steps closer and reaches for me, leaning over the water. There are only inches between her fingertips and my face. Close enough that I swear I can feel the faint warmth of her presence, but if she stretches any further, if she slips…

"Please don't," I tell her with regret, moving away from her. "I don't know if the water can hurt you even in an astral form, and I won't risk it. I won't risk *you*."

The light surrounding her flickers again. She's fading. *Damn it.*

"Thank you," she says as she steps back. "If Aeson's blood won't work to unlock the runes, do you have any idea who else could've helped him?"

I rack my mind, sifting through hazy memories of those final days. Aeson already wore the crown. He had advisors, yes, but none he trusted enough to hold his secrets.

Except one.

"His council," I say, the realization hitting like a bolt of lightning. "Greggo—"

The rest of the name dies on my lips as the glow around her dims. *"Sloane!"* I lurch forward, the chains snapping me back. "Don't go. Not yet."

Her lips move, but the sound doesn't reach me. *No, no, no.* We're so damn close.

Desperation claws at my throat. "Don't bond to him!" I roar, voice cracking from my growing fear. "Promise me, Sloane. Please."

But she's gone.

The cave collapses into silence, thicker and colder than ever before. I sag against the wall, breathing hard, heart pounding like a war drum in my ears.

For a moment, all is lost. Despair creeps back, slithering into the cracks she'd managed to fill with her light.

And then, faint as a whisper on the wind, I hear her voice. *"I'll be back, Julian. I swear it."*

The words echo long after the light fades. And this time, the darkness doesn't win.

Hope burns brighter than it ever has.

Because my mate knows the truth. And Sloane doesn't strike me as a woman who breaks her promises.

The return to my body is jarring, like being ripped through space and slammed back to Lunara. My eyes snap open, breath rushing into my lungs as if I'd been close to drowning and only just broke the surface. My limbs are cold, my fingers tingling as sensation comes back in a slow, almost painful wave.

I lurch forward, bracing myself against the wall, my pulse hammering as I try to ground myself. My body feels like it doesn't quite belong to me yet, as if part of me is still down there, in the dark with him.

Julian.

His name lingers in my mind, foreign and yet familiar. Even my wolf's presence feels warmer just thinking of him, stirring with something dangerously close to longing. I squeeze my eyes shut, trying to process everything he's told me. Aeson's brother. The *rightful* King of Venaris. A man who was betrayed, cursed, and locked away in the depths of this castle, forced to endure centuries of torment while the world thought him dead.

And if he's to be believed, Aeson killed his own mate not

only to paint Julian as the monster, but so he could keep his secrets and have the throne unchallenged.

I press my palm to my forehead, exhaling sharply. *Gods, I was nearly bound to him. I still might be if I'm not careful.*

"Damn it," I breathe, starting to force myself to my feet.

"Sloane!" Clara's voice crashes through the fog in my mind, her hands gripping my shoulders before I can fully straighten. She's shaking me lightly, her green eyes wide with barely concealed panic. "You were out for twice as long. I was beginning to think something went wrong. I thought—"

"I'm fine," I cut in.

She scowls, her gaze appraising every inch of me. "You don't *look* fine."

I wave her off, forcing the tremor from my hands. "I'll *be* fine, then. What matters most is that I talked to him and got the answers we need. Well, most of them."

Clara's expression flickers between exasperation and intrigue. "And you're sure we can trust this person? I know he's your mate, but that doesn't always mean something good as we've seen in the past."

I don't fault her for questioning my judgement or Julian. In fact, I appreciate that she's going to dissect everything I'm about to tell her. Even though my gut tells me Julian should be the alpha of this pack, we need to be sure. Especially when I might start a war by trying to free him.

I go over everything with her in hushed whispers—who Julian is, what he said about how Aeson betrayed him, how he's been trapped in that hell for centuries. I tell her about the chains that are killing his wolf, and the magic in the water meant to keep him powerless.

And most of all, I tell her about the lie.

About Aeson's mate, Lira. About her sacrifice. About the

fact that the very man I considered bonding with *killed* his own fated mate to protect his place as the Alpha King.

By the time I finish, Clara's pacing the length of the hallway, her arms crossed so tightly over her chest I half expect her bones to snap.

"I knew he was bad," she mutters under her breath, "but *damn it*—this is worse than I ever imagined. Killing his own mate? Trapping his brother? He didn't just want power, he wanted to erase any threats to it. Likely still does."

I nod, jaw clenched. "And I could be next."

Clara stops pacing, turning to me. "So what's our next move?"

I open my mouth to respond, but a solid *thud* echoes from down the corridor. Both of us freeze.

My pulse spikes.

We stayed too long.

Clara's gaze meets mine, and without a word, we move.

She grabs the ruined shirt, stuffing it back beneath her blouse as I lift the heavy frame and position it back on the wall. My hands move quickly, my breath steady despite the tension coiling in my gut.

Once everything's back in place, we step away, assessing our work.

It looks untouched, but the air is thick with something unseen, something pressing.

"Let's get the hell out of here," Clara whispers through my mind.

I don't argue.

We slip out of the hallway, walking as fast as we can without looking suspicious, making our way back to my room without another word. I keep my senses on high alert, but no one stops us. There are no lingering shadows. No sudden figures stepping from the darkness. No heartbeats too close for comfort.

Still, my wolf doesn't settle until we're safely inside my chambers, the door locked behind us.

I exhale slowly, pressing my back against the cool wood.

"That was too close," Clara mutters, rubbing her hands down her face.

I nod but push away from the door. "We can't think about that now. The other royals are arriving soon, and if we're not there to greet them, Aeson *will* notice."

Clara curses but doesn't argue. She moves to the fireplace first, pulling the ruined shirt from beneath her blouse. Without hesitation, she tosses it into the hearth then strikes a match. Flames consume the fabric in an instant, curling around the bloodstained cotton before reducing it to ash.

I stare into the fire, bile rising in my throat. Aeson's blood wasn't the key.

And Julian was about to tell me who might've set the spell before I was yanked back to my body.

I grit my teeth, forcing the frustration aside.

Later. I'll deal with it *later*.

For now, we need to play the part.

As soon as the evidence is gone, we move quickly, changing into more formal attire. There are three purple gowns on the bed, and I badly want to ignore each of them, but I'm playing a game and now isn't the time to push Aeson. Not until I'm ready.

I nod toward the middle one, and Clara helps me into the dress. It's fitted around my chest and down to my waist, with intricate embroidery along the bodice. The full skirt is the least obnoxious of the choices and sways quietly around my feet as I walk to pick out my heels.

Clara disappears into her room for only a few minutes

while I touch up my makeup. She returns in a sleek emerald gown, and I smirk. She undoubtedly chose the Alcaris color on purpose. Even though I'm not ready to openly challenge Aeson, I'm not going to stop her from doing so.

Without saying a word, she steps behind me, her fingers deft as she weaves my hair into intricate braids and pins them around my crown, leaving most of the strands to cascade down my back.

She works in silence but tension rolls off her in waves as she asks, "Are you ready for this?"

I hold her stare, my back straight. "As long as you agree I'm right to believe Julian then absolutely."

Her mouth goes flat as she considers my words. "I've never liked Aeson, and now I know why. But I also don't like that we have no one we can trust to agree with or even counter what he's telling you. Yet…"

I hold my breath as she pauses.

"Considering he asked you to stay away and that he's worried about your safety with Aeson and when you got too close to the water, he stopped you, so you wouldn't be at risk of getting hurt. Maybe it's just wishful thinking, but those aren't the actions of a monster."

My shoulders drop as the tension melts away. *I thought the same thing.* But I also know the mate bond can twist emotions, make things feel more certain than they are. That's why I need Clara to help me be sure.

With her agreement that he's not likely the monster here, freeing Julian is now the priority. After that, after we know for sure who he is, I'll decide what we do next.

Clara and I head downstairs with only a few minutes to spare.

Or so I think until I see Aeson waiting for us.

His arms are folded over his chest, his face a mask of irritation. "You're late."

"I thought I was early," I reply smoothly, staying beside Clara.

"I just sent Dasha to retrieve you." His gaze rakes over me, a slow, assessing sweep. "They're coming up the drive now."

I wait for some kind of appreciation from him that I wore what he picked, but none comes.

Typical.

Instead, he strides toward the front entry, seamlessly stitching a smile onto his face before throwing open the massive double doors. His arms spread wide in welcome, his voice carrying over the courtyard even before the other royals have exited their carriages.

Gods, this is painful to watch.

"King Asher, King Theo," he announces, completely dismissing their mates. "My friends. I'm so glad you could make it."

The crisp evening air settles over my skin as I follow, keeping my head up. I wait at the end of the castle stairs, the weight of my crown light on my head, as Aeson greets our guests on his own.

The courtyard itself is sprawling, an expanse of polished stone framed by towering marble pillars. The banners of Venaris hang from the highest points, their deep purple fabric rippling in the wind. At the far end, the grand gates are closing now that the royal procession has arrived in an elegant display of power.

Their arrival is marked by sleek carriages adorned in their kingdom's respective colors. Isla steps out first, her blue cloak billowing as she lifts her chin, focused eyes scanning the courtyard with the confidence of an alpha queen. Asher is beside her, dressed in grey slacks and a long-sleeve shirt that matches Isla's cloak.

Next, Theo and Estee emerge, commanding the space around them. She's dressed in a rich maroon gown, dark curls framing her face, and she moves like the royalty she is, ignoring Aeson as he did to her and Isla in his initial greeting.

I barely contain my smirk as she marches past him. *Gods, I've missed her.*

Before I can say a word, she's in front of me, pulling me into a tight hug.

I tense for only a second before relaxing into it, wrapping my arms around her in return. "Estee." My grin widens.

"We have a lot to discuss," she whispers, holding on longer than I expect. "I'll be in your room tonight."

When we part, Isla quickly moves in, and there's no time to respond. Does Estee know something I don't? I told her enough, and while I appreciate her urgency, it sets me on edge as I hug Isla next.

The three kings walk toward us, and Theo's gaze sweeps the courtyard before settling on me as he adjusts his charcoal tie. His lips press together. Asher follows his line of sight, but his expression is less guarded, his irritation at being here clear as day.

I lift my chin, my smile firmly in place while I play my role as queen. "Welcome to Venaris."

Asher holds my stare for a long moment then inclines his head. "Let's hope it's worth the trip."

There's no warmth in the words, and I don't miss the way his fingers twitch at his side, as if he's resisting the urge to act.

I expected Estee to share what I told her with Isla, but I didn't consider the reaction of their mates. I hope it isn't going to ruin everything before I have the chance to free Julian.

Aeson moves next to me, sliding his hand around my waist with his usual grace. "Let's get you all settled before dinner. I hope you're hungry. We've prepared a feast."

His chuckle falls flat, an awkward silence filling the space for a second too long before I speak up. "I'm sure they're more tired than anything else, my king," I purr. "Dinner will be sure to brighten everyone's moods though. Dinner *and* drinks."

"Now you're speaking my language," Theo rumbles. "The seas were rough, but I'm sure an hour to rest will be plenty."

Aeson eyes me. I'm not sure if I've helped or not, but either way…

The game continues.

Clara and Dasha show the other royals to their rooms, and I attempt to sneak back to mine, but I don't make it two steps before I hear him.

"Sloane."

His voice slithers down my spine, smooth as silk but held together with something heavier. Expectation. Command. *Suspicion.*

I exhale slowly before turning toward him with a saccharine smile on my face.

Aeson still stands in the foyer, arms crossed over his chest, his blue eyes dark and nearly unreadable. But I see it. The sharp edge just beneath the surface.

He knows something.

I school my expression into one of mild curiosity and force sultry into my voice as I address him. "Yes, my king?"

His lips twitch as he strides toward me, closing the space between us with slow and deliberate steps. "We need to talk."

Aeson doesn't wait for an answer before gripping my elbow, guiding me through a side passage that leads to one of the smaller offices. The door clicks shut behind us, and all too soon, we're alone.

Just like before, but at least I'm not taken by surprise this time.

He says nothing at first, just watches me as he removes his gloves, flexing his fingers like a man considering his next move on a chessboard.

I lift my chin. "Is something wrong?"

Aeson's gaze tightens. "You were in the lower levels of the castle while I was gone this afternoon."

Shit. Someone *was* there.

I tilt my head, feigning confusion. "Lower levels?"

One dark brow arches. "Don't play games, Sloane. One of my staff saw you. I'd hoped you would be honest with me before I had to ask."

A slow breath. The tension of the moment settles over me, but I don't let it show. Instead, I shift, letting my expression soften—just enough.

Time to pivot.

I step toward him, deliberate in my movements, allowing my body to brush his ever so slightly. "Oh, in the south wing? I thought that was still part of the first floor. I was looking for extra space to store some of my things." I exhale lightly, letting my lips part just a little, and his eyes dip, just for a second. "There are still boxes being moved from Alcaris. I didn't want to burden you or have them in the foyer when our guests arrived, so I thought I'd find a place myself."

Aeson studies me, but I see it in the flicker of his gaze—hesitation. He doesn't want to believe me, but I'm vital to his plans. He needs me happy until we actually bond. Though, I'm not sure the cost of said thing is something he's decided on just yet.

Push him further.

I reach up, dragging a hand down his chest slowly, trailing my nails over the fabric of his shirt. "But..." I sigh, my lashes lowering slightly, inviting. "That wasn't all."

Aeson stays silent, but I can feel the shift. His grip on his control tightens, like a wolf caught between instinct and logic.

I lift my gaze, meeting his. "My wolf picked up on an energy in that part of the castle." I exhale again, slower this time, watching his pupils expand. "It called to me, settling over my skin like a warm summer's day. It was..." My fingers press against his chest, and I let my lips curve into something wicked. "Tantalizing. You've been holding out on me, my king."

Aeson's hand catches my wrist, but he doesn't push me away. He waits.

Good.

I step another inch forward, my voice dipping lower. "I wonder..." I let my breath ghost over his cheek before my lips barely skim the corner of his mouth. "What other powerful secrets are you hiding from me? Because I'm beginning to see the bigger picture here. More importantly, I approve."

His breath hitches.

He's falling for it.

Aeson holds onto my waist, his grip pressing in just enough to remind me of the power he thinks he holds over me. His voice is rougher now, thicker. "What is it you think you see?" he murmurs, meeting my heady stare with one of his own.

My fingertip glides over his mouth. "You're making us the strongest pack in Lunara. Something neither of us could've done on our own...but together," I scrape my lower lip with my teeth and let out a soft moan. "Together, we could be unstoppable. But only if we trust each other. Something you haven't extended to me."

His nose travels up my neck, and he nips at my ear lobe. "Trust, huh? That's not something I give easily. You might've signed that contract, but you've done little to show me just how invested you truly are in this partnership."

Gods, I can't do this. I can't let him continue to touch me like this. Not when I know Julian is so close, not when he's what I want above all else.

But I also know I have to. At least until I have a valid reason not to.

"Clara!" I scream for her through our mental link. *"I don't care what excuse you come up with, find us in the room nearest to the foyer and interrupt."*

"Be there soon."

Nothing will be soon enough, but I lean into Aeson's touch, playing my role. I can't crumble yet. I decided to play this game, and there's no backing out until I've won. No matter the sacrifices I must make.

Julian will understand if he's everything I'm beginning to believe he is.

Aeson angles his head, closing the space between us. His lips brush mine, making my wolf recoil, snarling and repulsed, but I don't flinch.

Instead, I let my hands slide higher, tangling in his hair, pulling him closer. Seconds stretch into what feel like minutes, and I let him ravage me. His dark scent assaults my senses, and the stubble on his cheek feels harsh against my exposed skin.

My heart hammers in my chest, and when he starts to unbutton his pants, I nearly lose the hold over my wolf as she attempts to take control.

"I've been waiting for this moment for decades," he

whispers into my ear. "We might not be mates, but you were always meant to be mine, Sloane. My only regret is that it took you so long to realize what I already knew." He grabs my chin, looking into my eyes, and I hope he can't see my revulsion. "I tried everything over the years, and my desperation to claim you only continues to—"

A crash echoes from the foyer. Aeson tenses for a second before opening his mouth, but then there are raised voices. Ones that will undoubtedly draw attention, and not the kind this king prefers.

Aeson jerks back, cursing as he fixes his attire. "Today of all days." His gaze snaps toward the door. "I'm done with interruptions."

Another shout. A woman's voice—Dasha.

What have I done?

I asked Clara to interrupt, but I didn't think she'd make a scene. Every hour, this situation becomes more complicated. I thought I could handle this, that I could play Aeson, but maybe Julian was right. I don't know what I'm getting into, and if Clara, or anyone else, gets hurt in the process...

Still, for the moment at least, I have to keep playing my part or things might get much, much worse.

I exhale sharply, smoothing out my gown. "What the hell is going on out there?"

Aeson growls under his breath, storming to the door without answering me. The moment he yanks it open, we're met with a scene I never would've expected.

Dasha has Clara pinned against the wall and both are red-faced with tightened fists, seeming ready for a fight. I have no clue what could've caused this, but I'm going to find out.

"I told you." Dasha's voice cracks with urgency. "You don't understand what you're doing—"

Clara scoffs. "What I understand is that you're trying to keep me from doing my job."

Dasha reaches for her, but Aeson grabs them both by the backs of their necks. "Enough!" His voice booms twice as loud as theirs. "The two of you are supposed to be leading examples of what it means to be an advisor and members of this pack. I should lock you in the dungeon."

Clara chuckles, but I step in before that's where she actually gets sent, or worse.

"I agree." This makes my advisor straighten. "Do you care to tell us what started all of this?"

Dasha keeps her eyes lowered as she answers. "Clara was trying to interrupt the two of you, and it was my job to stop her."

"And it's my job to inform my queen when a new pup is born into our pack," Clara sneers. "Promptly."

"Selene and Trav had a safe delivery of their young?" I ask, half because a change of subject might lighten the tension as Aeson still has a grip on their necks, but also because if this is true, it's not only a suitable distraction, but great news. The mates lost their last baby, and they'd been terrified throughout this pregnancy.

Clara nods. "Yes, a baby boy. The name has yet to be decided. If this is something not worthy of interruption any longer, I do apologize for my misstep."

The tick in her jawline tells me how hard those words were for her to say, but they seem to work.

Aeson finally loosens his hold and steps back to stand next to me. "A note will suffice in the future if we're indisposed. In the meantime, both of you will be punished for making such a scene, on today of all days."

I grab Clara's shoulder and shove her toward the stairs. "You'll spend the rest of the evening in your room, missing the royal dinner tonight. I won't risk this embarrassment continuing in front of our guests. Tomorrow, Aeson and I will inform both of you how you're to proceed moving forward."

Clara stiffens. I can practically feel the rage vibrating off her, but I shake my head slightly, wordlessly telling her to let it go.

Now isn't the time to push. Now's the time to retreat.

Aeson eyes me, but he doesn't counter what I've already commanded. He sends Dasha toward her quarters, and before I can consider what I've done, I'm alone with him again.

He runs a hand through his hair, jaw still tense. "My queen, I need a moment before dinner to compose myself. But after dinner..." He wraps his fingers firmly around my neck, but not tight enough to cut off my air as he whispers into my ear, "That's for *us*."

I can't hold back my shudder, but he at least interprets the loathing as desire.

"I'll see you shortly in your room so I can escort you to the dining hall." With that, he turns on his heel, heading for the corridor.

The moment he's gone, I grab the railing of the stairs and let out a long breath as I reach out to Clara. *"I'm so sorry."*

"I know," she replies quickly. *"This is only getting harder, Sloane. I'm not sure how much longer we can keep this up."*

She's not the only one thinking that.

"Was that argument with Dasha real? How did that even happen?" Aeson's advisor hasn't shown an ounce of strength since we arrived. I need to know what that was all about.

Clara's voice lowers, frustration and concern coming through loud and clear as she replies. *"She wasn't arguing with me, Sloane. She was warning me—no, pleading with me not to go where I don't belong. That there would be consequences."*

I narrow my eyes as I continue toward my room. *"From her?"*

"She kept looking at the door to the room you were trapped in," she says. *"Whatever Aeson has done, it has her terrified."*

Silence settles between us, and my wolf stirs.

The mention of consequences makes me think of Julian. Of his chains, the runes, centuries of torment, and the prospect of his death in the near future if I don't figure this out.

My throat tightens.

Does Dasha know that Julian's down there?

There's a rumble in my chest as I make my way upstairs. *"We need to find out what she knows."*

"I'll work on it," Clara promises. *"You just find a way to stay away from that creep while I'm grounded."*

That's something I'm not sure I can do, but I'm sure as hell going to try.

CHAPTER SEVENTEEN

SLOANE

I've barely had time to calm my wolf before Aeson is at my door. He doesn't knock. He barely cracks it open before saying, "Let's go."

Great. His mood hasn't improved, and neither has mine. This is going to be an interesting dinner.

I take my time adjusting the skirt of my gown, smoothing the fabric with steady hands. A flicker of irritation stirs in Aeson's gaze as I shift to double-check that my crown's aligned properly on my head. If he's in a rush, I don't care. I'm still the queen-to-be of this kingdom—at least in his eyes —and I'll walk at my own damn pace.

Finally, I turn, gliding toward him.

Aeson extends his hand. A silent demand.

I stare at it. Then at him. I should take it. That's what's expected of me. But seeing as he's not offering me any niceties, I don't either.

I sweep past him, my steps controlled, shoulders squared, as I continue without looking back. If he wants to hold hands like the doting mate he pretends to be, he'll have to show me some respect.

I make it three strides before pain shoots down my arm and my forward movements are halted.

Aeson grabs my bicep, squeezing unnecessarily hard. "You're either the most oblivious woman I've ever known or the smartest. I'm not yet sure which it is, and that isn't good for you." He grabs my hand, forcing my fingers to curl around his. "I came to escort you to dinner as my mate and queen, and that's exactly what I'm going to do. Afterward, you'll be joining me in my room for the night. No more interruptions."

My wolf snarls in protest, my stomach twisting with disgust. Like hell that's happening.

I allow him to keep my hand, but that doesn't stop me from reaching out to Clara. *"I know you're supposed to be sequestered to your room, but I need you to get to Estee or Isla. Now."*

Her tense confirmation comes as no surprise. *"What am I telling them?"*

"I need a reason not to be alone with Aeson tonight, and only another royal is going to get me out of this," I say. *"He won't want to slight them. We might be in his kingdom, but he isn't the most powerful alpha present, and he knows it. I need to use that to my advantage."*

"Understood. We have other wolves in the castle that I trust," she tells me, something I should've probably known sooner. *"If I can't get to one of them before you do, someone will. I promise."*

"Who's in the castle with us?" We're nearly to the first floor. There isn't much time left, and I shouldn't be bothering Clara with questions like that when I trust her judgement, but I can't help myself.

She doesn't answer, and at the last step, I act without thinking things through. I purposely miss and allow myself to trip. Pain rips through my ankle, a sharp, searing jolt that sends my body lurching forward. But Aeson is still holding my hand.

The act doesn't send me sprawling across the marble floor like I pictured, but it still hurts.

"Shit!" I hiss, bending down to clutch my throbbing joints.

Aeson doesn't move to help me. He doesn't kneel. He doesn't even ask if I'm okay.

Instead, he releases my hand slowly, deliberately, allowing me to fall back, hitting my head on the wall hard enough that black spots dot my vision for a few seconds.

He laughs at me, a low, mocking chuckle as he stares down, shaking his head. "You almost had me fooled, Sloane. Almost."

A chill races down my spine. His voice is void of warmth now.

Aeson crouches beside me, one elbow braces on his knee as he watches me like a predator watches prey. Calm. Certain. Smug.

"But it's too late for you." He leans in, his voice lowering to something just above a whisper. "You're mine. You will do as I expect. You have nothing without me. No home. No pack."

He smiles, slow and cruel.

"Don't you forget that."

There it is. All pretenses gone.

The mask has been shattered.

And finally, I see the real Aeson.

Good. At least the doubts I've had haven't been wrong.

I lift my head, baring my teeth in a slow, wicked grin, my voice cool as steel. "The funny thing about losing my land is that you're right, Aeson. I have nothing."

I shift, my weight pressing onto my injured ankle, pushing myself back up to my full height.

He stands with me, and I hold his stare as I add, "I have nothing to lose so I'll do as I damn well please. Don't *you* forget that."

His darkened gaze makes me question whether I've made the right move, but it's too late to go back. I won't be his pawn, and I'm certainly not going to be his mate. Though I can at least pretend I'm still willing.

"You knew who I was before I signed that contract," I tell him with certainty. "My inability to accept being your arm piece and my demand for respect shouldn't come as a surprise to you. I act with authority. You can do whatever you want as long as you leave me to do the same. I won't cower in your shadow. If you thought you could break me, you were wrong, and it's better we decide what we're willing to put up with now than to allow our mateship to fall apart later—an incident that would only reflect poorly on you, in case you're forgetting that."

He huffs and stands a little taller, so he can properly look down on me. "How so?"

"As you already pointed out, I have nothing," I remind him. "My land is dead. My pack is living in your kingdom. I can't change that. If we can't find a way to work around each other, I'll leave. Simple as that for me. But you? You'll be left here, dealing with wolves who might begin to doubt their king as they watch their queen walk away without a tear in her eye."

"Are you threatening me?" He steps closer, our noses nearly touching as his chest heaves.

"I'm merely telling you what I see as our options. You can take that as a threat or as an opportunity to find solutions to these issues before they explode any further."

He lifts his hand and settles it over my neck, his fingers splayed before tightening over my skin. He squeezes, nearly as hard as he did my arm. Still, I don't flinch. I don't even blink. I hold his stare, allowing my wolf to come forward.

If Aeson wants a challenge, I won't back down. Hell, I just might take his kingdom from him. I haven't thought about what happens once Julian is free, but I do know the man before me isn't going to control me.

His fingers twitch. His jaw clenches.

He lets go.

"You might be right, Queen Sloane." He extends his hand once more. "Let's go enjoy our evening."

I don't know if this is Aeson conceding or if he's trying to figure out a way to kill me now, but either way, I decide to keep playing the game, accepting his gesture.

As we continue toward the dining hall, my ankle strains with each step, but I don't falter, shoving any remnants of pain down. When we get to the open doors, I remember the task I'd given Clara. One it seems she followed through on.

Easton, one of my advisors, is standing there with a wry smile on his face. He bows appropriately as we approach. "King Aeson. Queen Sloane. I'm here to step in for Clara while she takes a brief reprieve from her role as lead advisor."

"Easton." I offer him a nod, holding back my grin. "I didn't realize you were staying in the castle."

I thought he was still in Alcaris. I guess this is what happens when I allow myself to be distracted by a mate trapped in a cave.

"Yes, Your Majesty. I arrived yesterday." There's a glint in his hazel eyes that tells me I've missed something but figuring out what is going to have to wait.

"How many advisors do you have?" Aeson asks tensely. "We really don't need more in Venaris."

"Let's save that conversation for later, shall we, my king?" I say with a little too much honey in my voice.

Aeson's jaw ticks, but he doesn't press the issue in front of witnesses.

Instead, he grips my hand tighter and guides me into the dining hall.

As we pass Easton, his presence nudges my mind.

"I spoke with Clara," he says. *"I was able to let Estee know you'd like her to arrange for a girl's evening promptly after dinner. Clara will also be temporarily resigning from her duties, passing them onto me."*

"While I appreciate you stepping in, I don't really think that will be necessary as of tomorrow." I trust Easton, but Clara's more than my advisor, and I need her at my side.

"She asked me to let you know that she won't be far," he replies quickly. *"Stepping back will allow her to do her research. Something she said you'd understand."*

The knot that had been forming in my stomach loosens. She's not abandoning me. She's giving herself more time to solve our problem of getting through those damn runes. Smart.

By the time we reach the long dining table, the others are already seated.

The chandeliers above cast fractured light across the sparkling silver place settings, the deep purple banners draped along the walls adding a regal contrast. It's elegant. Opulent.

And I hate it.

I force a pleasant expression, slipping into my role with ease. As I let Aeson lead me forward, Estee and Isla rise from their seats.

They march straight for me with wide smiles, effectively cutting Aeson off before he can pull out my chair.

"So, we were talking," Estee starts, grabbing my hand before Aeson can object, pulling me away without a glance in his direction.

Aeson isn't going to like this.

She leans in, lowering her voice just enough to sound conspiratorial. "Have you ever heard of a bachelorette party?"

I blink. "Um, no? Should I have?"

"It's a human thing," Isla answers, flipping her rose-gold hair over her shoulder. "But a fun one."

Before I can question what that means, they maneuver me into a chair across from where I should've been seated.

It's a subtle move. But effective.

The women on one side of the table. The men on the other.

Oh, Aeson's definitely going to hate this.

"Exactly," Estee continues smoothly, grinning as she settles beside me. "We'd like to treat you to one tonight. The fun begins right after dinner, as long as you don't have any pressing plans."

I barely part my lips before Aeson cuts in.

"Actually," his voice is low, edged with warning, "I had special plans for us."

Strain grows around the table, but Isla doesn't miss a beat.

She smiles sweetly, but her blue gaze intensifies. "Can't they be postponed? We're only here for a few short days, and I was promised time to get to know Queen Sloane." She pauses, tilting her head. "Something important for our future trade deals, wouldn't you agree, King Aeson?"

Silence.

Aeson's grip on his wine glass tightens.

For a second, I think he might refuse. Might insist on keeping me in his grasp for the night.

But then…he nods.

His smile is slow and forced. "Of course, Queen Isla. You ladies have your fun." His gaze flickers to me, flat and emotionless. "But stay in the castle. I wouldn't want any accidents to happen to my mate just days before our ceremony."

Right. That's why he wants to keep me close.

Isla grins triumphantly. "Excellent."

Estee squeezes my hand under the table. "We're going to have the best time."

Oh, how I wish I could mind-talk with these ladies. Waiting until after dinner to find out what they're up to just might kill me.

Then again, so might Aeson.

Well, he can try anyway.

CHAPTER EIGHTEEN

JULIAN

It's as if the darkness has grown teeth. It gnaws at the edges of my mind, devouring the scraps of strength I have left. Every hour that passes pulls me further into that abyss, my wolf a faint, flickering ember I can barely feel anymore.

But I hold on.

Because of her.

Sloane.

Her name is a lifeline, a whispered promise against the silence. I felt her hesitation when she last left me. The intensity of her uncertainty wrapped around my chest like a vise, but beneath it, there was something else.

Resolve.

She's not giving up on me. Which means I can't give up on her either.

I stare down at the blackened shackles cutting into my wrists, the skin long since rubbed raw. I've lost count of the years I've spent here, chained like a beast unworthy of sunlight, the magic embedded in the cables siphoning away what little power I have left.

A snarl rises in my throat, a guttural promise of violence.

When I'm free, I'm going to kill my brother. Slowly.

I'll shatter his bones one by one, tear the crown from his head, and make sure every single wolf in Venaris knows exactly who and what their king is.

A traitor. A coward. A murderer.

But first, I need to survive.

Pain has long been a companion of mine, a dull ache that's become part of me, but the weakness, the inability to keep my head up for long—that's new. My wolf barely stirs anymore, his spirit dimming like a candle running out of wax. If he dies before I'm free…

There won't be enough of me left to save.

But Sloane will come back.

She might not trust me yet, but she's too smart to fall for Aeson's lies. I saw that in the way she carried herself, in the way she spoke, even the way she tracked my every movement. It doesn't matter that we've admitted to being mates, if she decides I'm the monster she assumed to be locked away here, she'll end me.

That knowledge doesn't scare me. I know the truth, and I'll prove it to her.

If it takes a lifetime, I'll show her exactly who I am, who I should've been. Not just her mate, but the rightful Alpha King.

The cave's silence presses in around me, but I don't surrender to it. Not anymore.

I sit back against the slick, cold stone, breathing slowly, imagining her face. The slight crease between her brows as she listened to me speak and the defiance in her eyes when she challenged me.

The memory of her will be enough to hold onto, but as I

unwillingly drift off, I'm not sure my wolf is around to believe the same.

CHAPTER NINETEEN

SLOANE

Aeson ignores me for the rest of dinner, but I can feel the storm building beneath his skin, his silence more ominous than any threat he could've made. Every second of the torturous meal is spent with him preening, desperate to present himself as a king worthy to sit alongside Asher and Theo. The effort is almost painful to watch. The too-wide smile, the unnatural pitch of his voice, as if he's trying to sound relaxed and commanding all at once.

Asher and Theo humor him, polite nods and the occasional placating smile keeping the conversation from falling flat. But their civility is hollow, forced, and it's the women—Estee and Isla—who give me hope.

They barely touch their meals, their focus never straying far from their mates. Watching, analyzing, reading every shift in the air the way seasoned warriors do when they're waiting for an ambush. Sitting at that table, surrounded by two queens who see Aeson for exactly what he is, fills me with a rare sense of calm.

I'm not alone in this.

My fated mate is still trapped, his life slipping away with every hour that passes, and I'm expected to bind myself to Aeson in less than two days. But none of that worries me any longer, especially when I know I'm not the only one watching Aeson's every move.

We stand together at the base of the grand staircase after dinner. Asher and Theo keep a protective hold on their mates, their hands firm yet tender. In contrast, Aeson's grip on my hand is light, an afterthought. There's no affection there, no pretense of care anymore. He's angry, and I feel the thin veneer of control fracturing beneath his skin with every breath he takes.

It's not the lack of affection that chills me. It's the feeling that I've pushed him too far, that his careful mask is finally starting to slip.

He knows something is wrong.

He might not know about Julian yet, but the growing distance between us and my refusal to submit to his every whim has made him suspicious. And if Aeson feels like he's losing control, there's no telling how far he'll go to get it back.

A fresh wave of nausea rolls through me, the kind that has nothing to do with fear and everything to do with knowing that if Aeson ever discovers who Julian is to me, he'll kill him just to spite me.

I can't let that happen.

"I wish I could say we had something planned for you, Aeson," Theo says, his voice low and easy, "but a boys' night isn't exactly our style."

Aeson's laugh is a touch too loud, his smile stretched abnormally wide. "Quite all right. I'm sure I'll find something to fill my time while the ladies have their fun."

The way he says it sends an involuntary shiver down my

spine. There's an edge to his voice, a razor-sharp warning buried beneath the charm. He's going to be watching us tonight, of that I'm certain.

But when Estee's smirk deepens, my nerves ease just a little. Whatever Aeson has planned, I get the sense she's already prepared for it.

She stands on her toes to kiss Theo's cheek. "I'll see you later."

"Be sa—good."

I catch the slip, though it seems the others miss it. Whatever Estee told him about why they're really here, he's worried.

So am I.

Isla kisses Asher goodbye, and I turn to Aeson, my own smile plastered on like a mask I can't quite peel off. "I'll see you in the morning then?"

He steps in close, wrapping me in an embrace that's all steel beneath velvet. His hands press against my ribs, fingers digging just enough to remind me of his strength and temper. "Or sooner," he whispers, his breath hot against my ear.

When he pulls back, I school my expression, careful not to let him see the flicker of panic behind my eyes. I've pushed him too far already, stripped away too many layers of his act. He's not bothering to hide the monster anymore.

And monsters only know how to destroy.

Isla loops her arm through mine, her presence solid and grounding. "Let's head to your room, Sloane," she says cheerfully, her tone innocent but firm enough to leave no room for argument. She casts a glance back at the men and winks. "Don't wait up for us."

If only I could believe Aeson intended to sleep tonight.

We walk up the stairs together, Estee on my other side,

the three of us forming an unspoken shield around each other. The tension in my chest unravels, just a bit, with each step we climb. There's no denying the storm that's coming, but at least I'm not walking into it alone.

By the time we reach my room, my mind's already racing ahead, cataloging every move I need to make, every piece of the puzzle I still have to place before I can free Julian and end Aeson's reign.

The door clicks shut behind us, and Estee immediately pulls a vial of shimmering silver liquid from the folds of her dress. She holds a finger to her lips as she walks the perimeter of my room, carefully dripping the liquid along the walls.

The silver droplets glisten as they make contact with the stone then evaporate into nothingness, leaving no trace behind.

Once the vial's empty, she holds up her fingers and counts down from five. At zero, she grins. "Now it's safe to talk. This will last for the next eight hours or so."

"A cloaking spell?" I haven't seen one of those in years. I used to collect them when the realms weren't so separated, but after losing a couple of wolves to fights, I told my pack we were done using the portal to trade items with the other supernaturals.

Estee's grin deepens. "Leftover from the last Alpha King. He was into some seriously dark shit, but we salvaged a few useful tricks."

Isla steps in front of me, her expression unusually serious. "Before we start, there's something I need to say. I know you reached out to Estee for help, and that you and I don't really know each other yet. So, if you're at all uncomfortable with my being here, just say the word and I'll go."

"Absolutely not," I say without hesitation. "I know you

two are a package deal. If I had any reservations about that, I wouldn't have called Estee in the first place."

Isla exhales in relief. "Oh, thank the gods. Because I sat out of the last fight, and I'll be damned if I miss this one."

Her words pull a small laugh from me, the first genuine one I've had in days.

"Do you really think there's going to be a fight?" I ask, my brows pulling together as we all settle into the sitting area near the fireplace. The warm glow does little to thaw the growing tension in my chest.

"Seems like the only logical outcome," Estee says first, her tone blunt but not unkind. "Can you picture a scenario where Aeson willingly admits to his sordid plans, hands you back your freedom, and walks away?"

The thought is so ridiculous I can't help but laugh—a flat, humorless sound. "Not even a little."

"Exactly." Estee leans back, her fingers draped casually over the arm of the chair as she side-eyes her sister. "Which is why I have a plan. But *one* of you isn't going to like it."

Isla narrows her eyes. "What won't I like?"

Estee's grin is a little too mischievous for the situation. "Aurora."

Isla's entire body stiffens, her hands curling into fists. "That sleazy goddess isn't welcome anywhere near me," she snaps. "I don't care if she brought our mother back. She kissed my mate."

My head jerks up. "She did *what?*"

"Long story," Isla mutters darkly. "And not one I'm eager to revisit."

"Yeah, well, she's also the only reason either of us are still here," Estee reminds her sister, her tone gentler now. "We both owe her more than we want to admit. And who knows?

If we play this right, maybe she can even help restore Alcaris. Creation magic is her specialty, after all."

The thought sends a flicker of hope through me, sharp and bright. "You think she'd really do that?"

"Depends." Estee shrugs. "She's not a charity. She'll want something in return. Theo's power gave her something. We're not sure, but we've also chosen not to be worried about it. Asher…well, Asher's hot. What do you have?"

"Umm." I decide it's time to remind them of the most important piece of information. "I have a mate trapped by dark runes beneath this castle. One who should probably be dead but seems to be defying the odds by hanging on."

"Right." Isla frowns, sitting up a little straighter. "Estee told me about him. We dealt with dark objects in Polaris as well."

I exhale, running my fingers along the seam of my dress. "I thought Aeson's blood would unlock the runes, but it didn't. Julian tried to tell me who else it might be, but I was yanked back into my body before he could finish giving me names."

A pillow sails through the air, smacking me square in the face. "What the hell, Sloane?" Estee's mock outrage is softened by her grin. "You didn't tell me you were spirit-walking through the runes."

I bare my teeth in a half-snarl before tossing the pillow aside. "That's because I don't know what that is. So, I can't tell you how I do it. I just know it's happened twice. Well, almost three times. The first time I found the runes, we formed a connection. One that allowed me to hear him. That's when I went searching for more answers and was first pulled into the basement."

Estee's eyes widen, but it's Isla who leans forward, studying me with an intensity that sends a prickle down my spine. "That's rare. Spirit-walking is old magic. Most wolves can't do it without training, and even then, it's dangerous."

"I didn't exactly have a choice," I mutter.

Estee's fingers drum against the arm of her chair. "That settles it. I'm calling Aurora."

"Fantastic," Isla mutters, crossing her arms. "Wake me when the nightmare's over."

"You'll survive." Estee smirks. "I'll have our healer in Selaris summon her. They've got a direct link. That way, we're not tipping Aeson off to what we're doing. Sloane, do you have anyone here you trust to handle sending a message?"

"Clara," I say without hesitation. "She'll make sure it's done, even if she has to crawl through the walls to do it. But she's confined to her room right now. There was...an incident."

Isla perks up. "I knew I heard yelling earlier. What happened?"

Heat crawls up my neck. Gods, there's no hiding the lengths I've gone to. But if they're going to help me, they deserve the truth, no matter how humiliating it is.

I lay it all out. How I seduced Aeson to get his blood, how I faked my enthusiasm, how I've danced on the edge of danger every step of the way just to gather the crumbs of information I have.

By the time I finish, Estee's mouth is hanging open, while Isla looks equal parts impressed and horrified.

"Gods," Isla says, shivering in disgust. "He's even worse than I thought. And Asher had already painted him as a power-hungry prick."

"You're lucky to have Clara," Estee agrees. "But what about Dasha? Might she help?"

I recoil at the suggestion, my wolf bristling beneath my

skin. "Why the hell would I trust her? She's Aeson's top advisor."

Estee grins. "This is why you called me, Sloane. You're too close to the situation to see things as they are. You just told us that Dasha was trying to warn Clara and that she was following you, likely even knew you had Aeson's blood, but never saw that it was disposed of. If she was working against you, don't you think Aeson would've been more suspicious before today?"

My jaw clenches. "Or maybe she's playing both sides. Keeping just enough distance to look innocent."

"Or maybe," Estee counters, "she's the key to all of this. If Dasha's loyalty has even a crack in it, we can use that. She knows more than we do about the runes, about Aeson's plans. We'd be stupid not to at least find out."

My wolf growls low in my mind, uneasy. There's something about Dasha I can't put my finger on. Not yet. "We'll see," I say carefully. "But I'm not betting my life, or Julian's, on her."

"Fair enough," Isla says. "So, what's our next move?"

I lean my head back against the cushions, exhaustion settling into my bones. "Estee's message gets sent, we wait for Aurora. If she's willing to play, she'll be here tomorrow. If not, we find another way."

"Or," Isla says, her grin wide, "we let our mates overthrow Aeson and call it a day."

Estee snorts. "You just want to avoid Aurora."

"Damn right I do."

Their banter has me smiling, reminding me of my relationship with Clara, and for a moment, I let myself miss her. She would love to be here for this, but I can't risk her not being in her room tonight and Aeson finding out.

Estee's gaze sharpens again, her mischievous grin

returning. "You know, this whole 'bachelorette party' excuse was just supposed to get you away from Aeson, but since we're here…" She stretches, wiggling her fingers. "How much alcohol do you have, and have you ever played 'Never Have I Ever'?" She barks out a deep laugh. "That's a silly question. Of course you haven't, but we're going to teach you, and you'll thank us later."

Something tells me that isn't likely to happen.

CHAPTER TWENTY

SLOANE

I don't know what time it is, but all sense of caring went out the window about ten shots ago. Estee, Isla, and I creep into the hallway. Well, we attempt to. What we're really doing is giggling our asses off for no apparent reason, pretending we're being super sneaky while failing miserably.

"I have to pee," Isla whisper-yells, swaying slightly as she grips the wall for balance.

I point dramatically at a decorative vase overflowing with flowers. "Lift a leg. No one will even notice."

Estee collapses onto the floor, gasping for air, her hands clutching her stomach. There's barely any actual sound coming from her, which only makes it funnier. Either she's trying to be silent, or she's literally choking on my comedic brilliance. Both options are equally plausible.

Somehow, I end up sprawled next to her, laughing so hard my ribs ache, and tears blur my vision. It only gets better when Isla actually gathers the hem of her dress, crouching as if she's really about to water the poor flowers.

"What the hell are the three of you doing?" Clara's pointed voice cuts through the drunken haze, a shrill beacon of disapproval. Her footsteps echo down the hallway. "I leave you alone for one night, and you turn into feral pups. Gods, what a mess."

"Someone's in trouble," Estee whisper-shouts at me, her wide eyes far too innocent to be believable.

"You're *all* in trouble," Clara corrects, marching straight to me, wrapping an arm around my waist, and hauling me upright. "You need to get back to your room before someone—anyone—sees this disaster."

I shake my head vigorously, like a petulant child, and step away from her. "Nooo. I have to show my new besties how I spirit-walk!"

"How you *what?*" Clara's nostrils flare. "You're useless right now. All of you. Completely useless and drunk off your asses." She turns to Isla, crossing her arms so tight I'm surprised her ribs don't snap. "At least I don't have to clean that up."

Isla turns around and waves her hand over the puddle of pee she's left behind then grins back at Clara. "Clean what up? There's nothing to see here. I don't know what you're talking about."

Estee and I snicker, the puddle behind Isla still clear as day.

"Right." Clara reaches for me. "Let's get you three disasters to bed before you start a war or burn the castle down."

But I dodge her hand and do my best to run a few feet ahead. "I'm going to see my maaaate."

The announcement echoes loudly, full of drunken conviction and zero sense of self-preservation. My ability to stay balanced, however, is nowhere to be found. My feet betray me, and the floor comes rushing up, my skirt tangling around my legs as my crown tilts sideways.

Before I can even process the impact, Estee launches herself on top of me with a wild shriek. "I've got you, Beastie!"

"Don't forget me!" Isla war-cries then, as expected, lands directly on top of us, sending all three of us into a tangled pile of limbs and drunken giggles.

Clara stands over us, foot tapping with enough force to chip the stone floor. "You're all going to regret this in the morning."

I grin up at her, eyes heavy with mischief. "Not if I sleep until noon."

She pinches the bridge of her nose. "Impossible. Absolutely impossible."

We clumsily untangle ourselves, a process that takes far longer than it should, but eventually, we manage to find our feet again. Mostly.

"Come on, Clara," I croon, stretching her name out into a slurred song. "Come with us. Have some fun."

She watches the three of us swaying into each other like a wobbly wall of chaos. "Gods. *I'm* going to regret this in the morning."

Still, she steps in front of us like a general leading a haphazard army into battle. The world's best advisor, even when babysitting queens and their drunken new besties.

"I love you, Clara," I whisper conspiratorially. "I know I don't say it enough, but I couldn't do any of this without you. You're the best. The best advisor, the best friend. My wolf loves you. We both do."

She glances back, her expression conflicted. "You're buttering me up after I already agreed to this nonsense."

Estee waggles a finger between us. "She tells no lies, Miss Clara. Our new beastie here wouldn't shut up about you all night. Sister from another mister, ride-or-die kind of stuff."

"I don't even want to know." Clara raises a hand, cutting off any further drunken declarations. "If you three think you're getting near that painting tonight, you need to shut the hell up."

Isla moves her pinched pointer finger and thumb over her mouth then flicks her hand away. Estee does the same, and even though I have no idea what the action means, I follow suit. That's just what a good beastie does.

We creep through the castle's lower levels—or stumble, if I'm being honest. The air is thick, the shadows pressing in closer than usual. Still, somehow, we make it to the alcove.

"There's my mate!" I announce, pointing dramatically at the painting like it's the crown jewel of my life.

Estee drapes herself across my back, squinting at the artwork. "He's very…colorful."

"I don't think she means the picture," Isla says with exaggerated seriousness. "But if she does, we support you, Beastie. No judgment."

"I know I shouldn't ask, but I can't help myself," Clara grumbles. "Why do you two keep calling her *Beastie?*"

"Duh." Isla taps her on the forehead. "She's a beast. A wolf queen beast. And our new bestie. Our Beastie."

Clara shakes her head. "Just don't touch anything." She moves to lower the painting from the wall, and when the runes appear, my heart starts beating frantically in my chest.

"Julian." I whisper his name and step forward, but Clara shoves me back.

"No touching," Clara barks, her arm flung across my chest like a brace. "In your current state, we have no idea…"

Her words trail off, and I think I'm passing out, but then I'm pretty sure I'm going to vomit as my stomach roils. I try to breathe through the nausea but then panic because my body is missing. When I scream, the noise only echoes around me.

"Sloane!" Julian's voice booms so loudly I cover my ears.

Hey, I have arms again. Wait, not really. I mean sort of. *I'm spirit-walking!*

I stumble out of the shadows and chuckle to myself. Apparently, being tipsy doesn't discriminate between spirit form and my actual body.

"I'm okay," I say. "Mostly. I didn't actually think that was going to work."

"What happened to you?" His snarl rumbles deep, and for a split second, his eyes gleam too much like Aeson's.

I step back instinctively, raising a finger. "Nope. Don't do that. You look like *him* when you do, and that's a no from me."

His expression softens immediately. "Are you...are you drunk?"

I hold up my thumb and forefinger, squinting at the tiny gap between them. "Maybe just a smidge."

"That's not good, Sloane." His sigh is long and pained, almost identical to Clara's when I've pushed her patience to its limit. "You need to be able to protect yourself."

"Oh, I did." I smile proudly. "I've got backup now. Besties. New besties. They're amazing. My own personal warriors."

His brow lifts, but I don't give him time to ask. "I probably need a plan for tomorrow though," I continue, the thought smacking me in the face like an afterthought. "Aeson's mad. Like, really mad. I told him I'd do what I damn well please, and surprise—he didn't like that."

The low, warning growl that echoes from Julian makes me shiver, even in spirit form. It's less threatening and more...protective, like a wolf ready to rip out the throat of anyone who dares to touch what's his.

"Does he know you found me?" His voice is all gravel and heat, but the question feels like a blade to my heart.

"No," I whisper then hiccup. "I mean…I don't think so. But even if he does, screw him." I sway on my feet, spinning my finger in a lazy circle above my head. "I'm yours. All yoursssss."

The sharp edges of his expression soften into something warm, something devastatingly tender. "Hearing you say that is more than I deserve," he says quietly. "But Sloane, you have to be careful. Please."

"I am." I nod so hard my spirit form nearly topples. "Estee and Isla are here. They're badass queens, and they've got my back. We even have a plan. A goddess is coming. Aurora. She's gonna save the day."

Julian's face freezes, his jaw clenching tight. "The original goddess?"

The cave sways, my spirit flickering at the edges. "Dunno. Don't remember. Everything's spinning…"

"Sloane." He takes a step forward, the water around his waist rippling ominously. "You can't trust them. No matter what they offer, gods and goddesses always have their own games to play."

My stomach lurches violently, and my knees buckle. "Uh oh. I think I'm gonna—"

"Sloane!"

I can't hold it. The world flips upside down, my spirit slamming back into my body with all the grace of a falling boulder. My eyes snap open, and I immediately hurl all over Clara's shoes.

"Oh, gods." I wipe my mouth with the back of my hand, grimacing. "I'm so sorry."

Clara stands frozen, nostrils flaring as she glares down at her ruined footwear. "That better have sobered you up."

She shakes her foot violently, flicking chunks of vomit onto the stone floor before groaning. "Damn it. This I actually *do* have to clean up."

"No, you don't," a voice says from the shadows.

The four of us freeze, heads snapping toward the hallway.

Dasha stands at the edge of the corridor, her hands clasped tightly in front of her, a storm of conflicting emotions painted across her face. Guilt. Resolve. Fear.

Well, shit.

Dasha steps forward, the torchlight casting shadows across her face and highlighting the strain around her eyes and the tight line of her mouth. For a moment, no one speaks, the drunken haze clinging to the air like fog after a storm. My nausea retreats, leaving only the heavy sensation of knowing this isn't just some innocent run-in.

One that has me feeling not as drunk as I did just minutes ago.

"Dasha." My voice is hoarse. "What are you doing down here?"

Her fingers twitch at her sides, as if she's debating whether to fold her hands or ball them into fists. "I could ask you the same thing, Your Majesty."

Estee and Isla sober up faster than I would've thought possible, both of them straightening as their warrior instincts kick in. Clara steps slightly in front of me, her stance protective, but I touch her elbow. This isn't a fight. Not yet anyway.

"I'm supposed to be reporting your movements tonight

back to Aeson," she admits, voice softer than I expected. "But I haven't."

That catches me off guard. I exchange a quick glance with Clara, who lifts a brow. "Why not?" I press, unsure if I want the answer.

Dasha's shoulders slump, and she looks down, studying the uneven stone floor beneath our feet. "Because I've been pretending not to see things for a long time. If I reported every incident I noticed that might, even in the slightest way, threaten Aeson, half this kingdom would be dead." Her voice is thin, almost brittle. "And so would my brother."

"Your brother?" Isla asks, her brow furrowing. "What does he have to do with this?"

Dasha's eyes glance up, just long enough for me to see the flicker of fear she's been hiding. "Everything. Aeson keeps him close. Not as an advisor, but as a warning. Every day I follow orders is another that my brother gets to live. If I step out of line..."

The implication slams into me like a punch to the chest.

"Gods," Estee mutters. "That's twisted."

"It's Aeson," Dasha says bitterly. "Everything about him is twisted."

There's something raw in her voice, something personal. I step closer, my headache forgotten. "You're not surprised to find us here. You know about Julian."

Her breath catches, but she doesn't show any shock. "Of course I do," she whispers. "I've known since the beginning. I was there when he ordered the runes to be carved into the stones of this castle. I saw the magic they used to trap him. I held the chains that bind him. I saw it all."

My heart hammers in my chest. "And you didn't say or do anything? Why?"

If she tells me Julian did something just as evil as I know Aeson to be, my heart might actually shatter.

"What could I do?" Her voice cracks and her eyes glisten in the low light. "Aeson made it very clear what would happen if I intervened. To me. To my brother. To anyone I cross paths with should I dare stand in his way." Her gaze hardens, tears drying before they can fall. "So I did the only thing I could do. I watched. I kept my mouth shut. And I waited."

"Waited for what?" Clara asks tersely.

"For someone like you." Dasha meets my eyes, and there's a flicker of hope in hers. "Someone strong enough to stand up to him. Someone he couldn't just kill without consequence."

I almost laugh, but it dies in my throat. After all I've learned, there's no doubt in my mind that Aeson's already plotting my death, something to be blamed on anyone else, something that would garner him sympathy.

"Why tell me now?" I ask, trying to keep my voice even, but my words still slightly slur.

"Because you need to understand what you're up against," she says simply. "Aeson isn't just a king desperate for success. He's lost his true purpose as alpha. In his mind, power is the only accomplishment that matters, regardless of the cost. He can't even shift nowadays, his energy is so uncontrollable. And that makes him dangerous in ways you can't yet imagine."

I swallow hard, my mouth suddenly dry because I actually can.

"Just be careful," she adds. "I can't help you—not directly. Not without putting my brother's life on the line. But I can look the other way, pretend not to see things, like you stealing Aeson's blood or visiting Julian on multiple occasions." Her voice softens, her gaze flicking between all of us. "You don't need to consider me a threat, but I'm not your ally either. I can't be. All I promise is to protect your movements as much as I'm able, for as long as I'm able. But if it comes down to you or my family, I'll choose him every time."

"Fair enough." This is already more than I expected from her. "What about tonight? What will you tell Aeson?"

"As far as he knows, you're all sleeping soundly after an exhausting girls' night." She glances behind us. "I'll make sure this is cleaned up, and when the sun begins to rise, I'll let Aeson know that Isla and Estee have retreated to their rooms. After that, you're on your own."

Relief washes over me. It's thin, but enough for now. "Thank you," I murmur, the words feeling woefully insufficient.

"Don't thank me." Her expression turns grim. "Just don't get caught. Because if you do, there won't be anything I can do to save you."

With that, she turns and slips back into the shadows, her footsteps soft against the stone. We stand in silence, the weight of her confession settling over us like a heavy blanket.

"Well, that's sobering," Estee mutters.

"No kidding," Isla agrees, rubbing her temples. "I think I've sweated out half the vodka."

"We should go back upstairs," Clara says, her tone leaving no room for argument. "It's too risky to stay down here."

I nod, though my heart aches at the thought of leaving Julian behind. But Dasha's warning rings in my ears. If we're going to save him, we need to be smart. "Let's go."

We make our way back to my room in silence, the earlier laughter and chaos nothing more than a distant memory. By the time Estee and Isla head to their rooms and

I enter mine with Clara, exhaustion slams into me like a tidal wave.

"Try to sleep," Clara says gently, guiding me toward the bed. "I'll keep watch."

I want to tell her it's not necessary, but considering the room is spinning and I'm minutes from passing out, I'm more thankful than ever to have her.

"Don't forget. You need to get a message out for Estee." My eyes start to flutter closed. "Aurora. Their healer. Need help."

Her hand covers mine. "I'm already on it."

I think I nod, but my thoughts drift off within the next second.

Tomorrow will be here all too soon.

THE SUN PIERCES THE CURTAINS, EACH BEAM OF LIGHT A dagger straight to my skull. My head throbs with the relentless beat of my own pulse, and every sound—every footstep, every hum—makes me want to crawl under the covers and never come out.

"Drink." Clara's voice is soft but firm, and when I open my eyes, she's standing beside the bed, a steaming cup of tea in her hands.

I sit up slowly, wincing as the movement sends fresh pain through my head. "I hate you."

"I told you there would be regrets." She presses the cup into my hands. "This is my special hangover blend. Trust me."

The first sip is bitter enough to make me gag, but I force it down and then several more until the drink is gone.

Within moments, the pounding in my head eases, the fog lifting from my mind. "You're a witch."

"Just always prepared as you've employed me to be," she says with a smirk, handing me water next.

As I take the much-needed hydration, my thoughts become clear and the full weight of everything Dasha said settles within me. The gravity of what we're walking into. The truth that last night, with all its laughter and drunken bravery, can't happen again.

"We need to be ready," I say softly. "Did you get the message out for Estee? Aurora might be our only hope."

Clara sits on the edge of the bed, her expression serious as she nods. "We'll know soon enough."

"And if the goddess can't—or won't—help?" I ask, but the question is more for myself. My mate's life is on the line, and I'm running out of time. There's no more hoping things will work out. Action is needed, and it has to be today.

I refuse to mate with Aeson tomorrow, and I can't let him banish me from the castle before I've freed Julian.

"You always figure things out. Now won't be any different," Clara says with more faith than I currently feel.

"Not always. We still lost our land," I remind her with disgust for myself.

She shakes her head at me. "You were meant to end up right where you are. If you'd solved the problems in Alcaris on your own, you would've never learned about Julian. Would you prefer that?"

"Of course not." I sit up in bed, still dressed in yesterday's clothes. "I can't regret coming here, but our people, Clara." My frown deepens. "I've put them at risk. If this comes to a war… I can't let them die for me. I'm supposed to do that for them."

Her fingers tighten around my shoulder as she levels her

powerful gaze on me. "I know you had a long night, but today's going to be even longer. I need you to believe we're going to work this out. You don't need all the answers now. For the time being, we wait, we prepare, and we do our best."

I exhale slowly, setting the empty glass aside. "You're right."

Aeson won't beat me. He won't keep my mate from me. I need to grasp onto the confidence I feel when I'm standing up to him and never forget who I am.

I just hope the price won't be more than I'm willing to pay.

CHAPTER TWENTY-TWO

JULIAN

I've been staring into the darkness ever since Sloane left, solely focused on a singular spot. One that I'm certain is real and can no longer deny that something has changed.

When Sloane first found the runes, when I first sensed her close, there was a change in the air. I'd attributed it to my hope of finally being free and nothing more, but with this third visit, there's no denying that all is not as it has been for the last couple centuries.

The crack is so faint, I nearly think I've imagined it, but combined with the fact that the once-suffocating magic wrapped around this prison seems to be loosening, like a hand unclenching after years of gripping too tightly… I can't deny what's right in front of me.

My wolf stirs. His presence is fragile, far too weak for what he once was, but no longer fading either.

The crack is real. And however it formed, it's changed everything.

Sloane doesn't have to be the one to save me. She doesn't have to risk herself for me.

The runes carved into the cave walls pulse—a slow, flickering glow that falters every so often. Something I might not notice if I tore my gaze away for even a second. They've been unwavering since the day I awoke in this darkness, humming with the sinister magic that's kept me caged, siphoning my strength drop by agonizing drop. But now they stutter, as though whatever holds them together is struggling to breathe.

It has to be Sloane's presence, her ability to bring her astral form to me. The memory of her drunken smile makes my chest ache, but the fact that even in that state, she called herself mine keeps me standing.

My mate is doing what no one else has been able to do in centuries.

She's cracking the spell from the outside.

Water moves around my body as I allow myself to float in place, relaxing my muscles. I don't know how long it's going to take, but I'm going to get out of here, and when I do, I'm going to be ready. The chains may hold me now, rattling with every little movement as a reminder of my fate, but they'll break eventually. I feel the truth of it in my soul. In this new tremor in the walls.

Because if there's a crack, there's a way out.

The triumphant thought is almost eclipsed by the fire in my gut that won't be quenched.

Fury at Aeson.

Every time I think his name, my wolf stirs. My beast's presence might be a ghost of the strength I used to have, but he's still here, trying to claw his way back to the surface.

My brother did this to me. My blood. He took my life, my kingdom, my future. But this time, he made a mistake.

He lured my mate here, allowing her to find me.

And the moment I'm out of these chains, I'm going to tear him apart with my bare hands.

I don't care what it takes. I'll rip his throne out from under him and burn down everything he's built from the ashes of my suffering. I'll end him for what he did to Lira, for what he's done to Sloane, and for everything he's taken from me.

Another pulse shudders through the cave, this one significant enough that I jerk up out of the water, gripping my shackles as I search for any changes. The runes above me flicker again, their glow dimming for a breath before they return to life. My prison hums, charged with something unfamiliar—not dark magic, but something older, heavier.

Someone else is coming.

I don't know how I know, only that I do.

And it's not Sloane. Not this time.

This power is celestial, but not gentle. This is something with sharper edges, all radiant beauty wrapped around lethal intent.

Aurora.

I've never met her, only heard the stories of the creator goddess, the mother of wolves, the one who long ago abandoned us. When Sloane mentioned she was calling for her, I tried to caution her, but she either didn't remember or chose to ignore my warning.

Either way, it's too late.

The cave shudders again, a thin crack spiderwebbing through the stone beneath the runes. It's not enough to break them, but I feel the fracture like a heartbeat beneath my feet, the faintest tremor echoing through my bones.

The water around my waist ripples, shifting in subtle currents that have nothing to do with me. The shackles at my wrists hum, vibrating with the sheer force of what's coming. And then, light explodes into the cavern.

It's not warmth. Not hope. Not salvation.

This light burns. It cuts through the darkness like a blade honed too well, slicing through every shadow, swallowing what's left of the cave's silence until there's nothing left but blinding, merciless radiance.

A figure emerges at the edge of the cave, forged from that brilliance itself—a woman draped in liquid gold, her very skin gleaming like fiery sunlight.

Aurora's presence hums with divinity, and the air is so thick with her power it's suffocating. Her crimson hair flows like a river of flames, licking at the edges of her body without ever touching her. Her violet eyes glow with something ancient, both beautiful and terrifying.

She isn't just powerful. She *is* power.

Aurora tilts her head, those otherworldly eyes burning through me, dissecting me piece by piece, as if seeing not only my broken body, but everything that led me here.

"So, this is the lost prince," she says, her voice smooth, almost lazy, yet edged with something dangerous. "The wolf the world forgot."

Her ruby lips curve just enough to show amusement, like I'm something both fascinating and pathetic.

My instincts scream to kneel, to lower my gaze, to offer the deference the gods once commanded from our kind.

I refuse.

Instead, I straighten my spine, squaring my shoulders despite the ache, and meet her gaze head-on. "And you're the goddess who abandoned us."

Her laugh is soft, a melodic hum that shouldn't be terrifying but is. "Ah, you know not what you speak of, but I'm glad to see you still have a spine, even after all these years." She takes a slow step forward, each movement effortless, as if she glides instead of walks. "I see now why the others risked calling me on Sloane's behalf."

At the mention of my mate, my hands curl into fists at my sides. My wolf snarls within me, not yet whole, but stronger than before. "This is on me," I growl. "Not Sloane. She should be left—"

"Careful, little wolf." Aurora lifts a single finger, her expression cooling. "Before you say something I can't ignore, know this. Your mate is safe. For now."

My jaw clenches. "*For now?*"

She comes closer, her feet never quite touching the stone, her radiance bending the air around her like a living thing. "Your mate is clever, but she's reckless." Her gaze glides over the chains around my wrists, the spell-crafted metal glowing faintly beneath her scrutiny. "Though, she did ask for my help. I can't fault her for that when we all know it comes at a price."

The words hang between us dangerously.

I exhale slowly, carefully. "What do you want?"

Her smile tightens, the barest curl of her mouth, enough to feel like a dagger at my throat. "That's for me to know and you to find out, but only when I'm ready."

My stomach churns, but I don't back down. Aeson took everything from me once. I won't trade one prison for another. "You can't expect me to agree to a debt without knowing its cost."

Her eyes darken, the violet edges pulsing faintly. "Oh, but I can." The goddess's power hums through the cave, the very walls shuddering in response. "But that's not the point, prince. This deal isn't for you. Sloane called for me. She'll be the one to make the deal. I only came to decide if you're worth it."

I hate that my hands vibrate at my sides. Hate that I know the truth of this moment.

I don't get a choice here.

"And if you think you can talk her out of this, just know she won't be visiting today. She's busy preparing for her bonding ceremony to your brother." As my chest rumbles, she adds, "One that takes place tomorrow."

The world around me slams to a halt.

At first, I can't breathe. My lungs constrict as if someone's reached inside me and squeezed. The air feels too thin, too sharp. My wolf howls in agony deep within my mind, a sound that tears through my bones and leaves behind only rage and disbelief.

Sloane. My mate. Being bound to Aeson *tomorrow?*

I taste blood—real or imagined, I can't tell—as my jaw locks, grinding with such force I nearly shatter teeth. I thought I had more time.

My hands curl into fists, nails biting into skin, trying to keep myself present, to stop myself from shifting right here and now. The image of her in a gown, standing beside *him*, promising herself to that monster, burns into my skull. And the worst part is the fear. The sickening realization that I might be too late.

Though, Aurora is right about one thing. This isn't about me. It's about my mate.

If I don't convince this goddess I'm worthy, if I hesitate in accepting her help, I could lose everything.

My mate. My kingdom. My vengeance.

"What do I need to do to prove my worth?" I finally say, voice raw, low, and deadly calm because beneath the chaos brewing inside me, I know one truth:

I will *not* let her belong to him. Not now. Not ever.

Aurora watches me with patient, knowing eyes as she

stays perched at the edge of the water. "You already did. By surviving this hell that was meant to kill you long ago. You'll fit right in with Asher and Theo, but not yet. I have a few more things to do before I free you."

"What?" My snarl echoes around us. "You can get me out of here now, but you're refusing?"

"Patience, wolf." She flicks her long hair over her shoulder. "Be a good boy, and I'll be back before you know it."

"Don't do this, Aurora."

But she's already gone, vanishing in a burst of golden light, leaving only the scent of rain and scorched earth in her wake.

The silence that follows feels heavier than the chains on my wrists.

My chest heaves, rage boiling under my skin until it's all I can feel. My roar shatters the stillness, a sound so raw my throat burns with it, but I'm not alone.

My wolf howls inside me, his presence no longer faint or fading. He's back. Stronger, aware, and ready for battle.

I don't question whether this was Aurora's gift or my own fury reviving him. Though, I do test this new feeling.

His essence expands through my chest, up my arms, and down my legs. I tighten my fingers into fists and without thinking of the potential consequences, I call my wolf to the surface and pull on my chains.

Once, twice, and then...*freedom.*

My shackles break, and I stumble forward. The water pricks at my skin, angry that I've summoned my wolf's power, but there's no stopping me.

I trudge forward, hauling myself onto the rocks, then have to yank my left legs up the rest of the way as my pants get snagged. My chest heaves once I'm out of the harrowing trench, but there's a smile on my face.

Aurora might've left me here, but for the first time in centuries, I can breathe.

And when I do, I taste vengeance in the air.

Tomorrow, Aeson's reign ends.

CHAPTER TWENTY-THREE

SLOANE

Aeson doesn't show for breakfast the next morning. That alone is enough to make my stomach twist into knots. Every bite of food I force down is like ash on my tongue. His absence isn't a relief, it's a warning. Aeson thrives on control, on appearances, on his ability to loom over me like a storm cloud ready to strike. Him missing is far worse than him sitting across the table with that smug, predatory smile.

"Clara, go check the lower levels," I whisper through our mind-link, trying to keep the tension from my voice even though my heart's hammering like a war drum. *"Make sure Aeson's not near the runed door, or worse."*

The thought of him going to Julian, of him doing something permanent to my mate before we can free him makes bile rise in my throat.

Clara's answer comes quickly, but there's a thin edge to her tone. *"I'm on it."*

I trust her, but her assistance doesn't settle my nerves.

Dasha promised she wouldn't report what we did last night, but even that assurance came with conditions. She made it clear her loyalty isn't to me or to Aeson. It's to her own survival, to the safety of her brother, who's still tangled in Aeson's web. If the cost of keeping her sibling alive is selling us out, she will.

And I can't even blame her for it.

I want to swear off drinking with Estee and Isla, to promise myself I'll never get that sloppy again, but that would be a lie. Last night was the first time I've felt like myself in months. The first time I wasn't drowning in responsibility and fear, and if I get through this, I'll do it again. Only next time, Clara's coming too.

But first, I have to make sure we get through these next two days.

Tomorrow, at dawn, the bonding ceremony begins. Less than twenty-four hours until I'm supposed to be bound to Aeson, my soul tethered to his. Unless I find a way to stop it. Less than a day to either kill him, imprison him, or somehow take control of my own fate.

It feels impossible, like standing at the base of a crumbling mountain with nothing but my bare hands attempting to hold it all together. Abandoning this place would be the smart move. I could run to Polaris or Selaris, claim sanctuary with Isla or Estee, but my pack and Julian… they'd all be left behind.

I can't leave without my mate. And I can't lead without my people. So the only path to take is forward.

Clara's voice cuts back into my mind, soft but reassuring. *"The area around the painting is clear. No sign of anyone tampering with it."*

Relief flows through me, though it's thin and fleeting. *"Did Dasha clean up the mess?"* I wince at the question. It's humiliating enough that I puked all over her shoes, but leaving behind a physical trail that could lead straight to Julian's prison? I should've handled it myself.

"The area is spotless now, so someone did at least and no signs that anything was disturbed." Clara pauses. *"Though, I didn't linger. I didn't want to draw attention."*

"Smart," I reply. *"Do you think it's safe enough for us to head into the market today? I'd like to check on the new pup and his mother."*

My heart and mind might be fully focused on Julian, but that doesn't mean I've forsaken my pack. I still want to be there for them as much as I'm capable of right now.

Clara's answering smile comes through the link, even if I can't see it. *"I was hoping you'd say that. Let's make it look like you're playing the gracious queen-to-be, hosting your guests and mingling with the people. That should ease some suspicion."*

I glance across the breakfast table at Isla and Estee, both glow as if last night's chaos never happened. Though, their mates sitting beside them are looking more tense than relaxed. Theo's piercing gaze scans the room as though expecting an ambush, while Asher's jaw works tightly, his hand constantly resting on Isla's wrist like he's anchoring himself to her.

The palace workers move around us, refilling platters and polishing silverware, but at least two of them are watching us more closely than they should. Aeson's spies.

We don't have time to waste.

I set my napkin aside, smiling bright enough to mask the dread twisting my stomach. "How would you all feel about a tour of the market this morning?" I ask, voice chipper. "A new pup was born yesterday. I'm going to check on him and his mother after I pick up a gift. You're all welcome to join me for a walk through the town while we wait for Aeson to make himself available."

Isla sits up straighter, pushing her chair back. "A pup? Absolutely. Let's go."

I didn't expect her to be so eager. I hadn't even meant for us to leave this quickly, but I won't argue. The sooner we're out of the castle and away from prying eyes, the better.

The rest of the table rises, including Asher and Theo, though their wariness only deepens. Estee winks at me as she loops her arm through her sister's, and together, we leave the hall.

I feel the intensity of those two spying pairs of eyes on my back the entire way out.

The front doors of the castle open to the courtyard and Clara waits just beyond the gates, her hands clasped in front of her. There's a tightness around her mouth, the kind that only I would notice, and it's the only tell she's holding back nerves of her own.

We walk together, the cobbled path leading us through the outer courtyard and down toward the heart of the village.

The market is already bustling by the time we arrive. Vendors shouting their wares, children darting between stalls, the scent of fresh bread and roasting meat thick in the air. I let the chatter and laughter wash over me, grounding myself in the simple, fleeting joy of a community still willing to hope.

We stop at a few stalls, admiring carved trinkets and baskets of dried herbs. Estee and Isla ask questions, smiling at the vendors, while Asher and Theo keep close, never dropping their guard.

Then, from behind us, a voice shouts, loud and full of warmth. "Isla! Asher!"

A man jogs toward us, tall and broad-shouldered, his dark

blond hair catching the sunlight, his hazel eyes gleaming with joy.

Clara's grip tightens around my wrist, her fingers trembling.

"Holy shit," she whispers.

I turn to her, startled by the pallor of her cheeks. "What? What's wrong?"

Before she can answer, Asher steps forward, his brow furrowed. "Noen? What are you doing here?"

But Noen isn't looking at Asher, or even Isla, any longer. His gaze locks on Clara, and his entire body trembles. The man bows his head briefly, reverence mingling with disbelief, and then reaches for her hands, eyes lifting to hers.

Oh!

He shudders again and drops to his knees, right there in front of Clara, uncaring that dozens of eyes are on him. "I'm Noen."

"Clara," she squeaks, fighting a wild smile as a few tears fall down her cheeks.

I pry her other hand off my arm and give her a little nudge. "Why don't the two of you go talk, and we'll catch up shortly?"

Isla is crying more than Clara, and Estee is practically jumping up and down, which I find odd, but I have a feeling they'll explain momentarily.

Noen gets up and glances down at their combined hands, asking Clara, "Is this okay?"

She nods, no longer trying to hide her grin.

Slowly, they walk away from the crowded area, their steps quickening the further they get. And then…

The crowd around us applauds and cheers for them.

That has my throat tightening and my own eyes burning as I watch the closest person I have to family bury her head in her mate's chest as he wraps an arm around her, protecting her from further embarrassment. I have no doubt her cheeks are ten shades of red as the clapping goes on.

I raise my hand and turn toward the pack, smiling. "Witnessing a new mate bond being identified is certainly a special moment, but let's give them their privacy now, shall we?"

People nod and while some steal another glance, they go back to their shopping.

"I can't freaking believe that just happened!" Estee says, grabbing Isla.

"That was…" Isla can't finish as her sobs take over.

Asher reaches for her, holding onto his mate as he walks away with her.

Estee watches them go, her smile still intact, but then she turns to me, answering the confusion that's clearly written on my face. "Noen was Isla's best friend growing up. We were all close really, but they were closest. Probably because Noen was in love with her, but for Isla, it was always Asher. She didn't even know. When we finally made our way back to Polaris after, you know, being brutally murdered and banished to Earth, there was a brief time during which we thought Noen was the one to kill us."

My mouth drops open. None of this information had made it outside Polaris. All I knew was that their reincarnations had gone wrong. This is absolutely insane, though.

"After being wrongly accused," Estee continues, "he decided to take a break from our pack. We didn't know where he'd gone, and we've hardly heard from him in months. Running into Noen here was a complete fluke, but seeing him find his mate, Isla no longer having to feel guilty for breaking his heart… It's a lot on her. But she'll be okay."

"I can only imagine," I say, glancing at the shops. "Should we wait for them?"

She shakes her head. "Let's find a cute toy for the pup and move on." Her voice lowers. "There are things we need to talk about sooner rather than later."

Her tone makes my stomach twist. Gods, please let this mean Aurora has answered. Please let this mean help is actually coming.

I don't press her yet, though. Not here, where too many ears could catch the wrong phrase and carry it straight to Aeson. Instead, I let the moment settle, my fingers drifting over a few carved wooden toys and soft bundles of handwoven cloth at the nearest vendor's stand.

The green velvet blanket catches my eye. A deep, calming shade not unlike the forests of Alcaris. A small piece of home in a place that's anything but. I choose it with a grateful nod to the vendor then tuck it into the crook of my arm like a shield.

The homes sit just beyond the market square, clustered along a quiet lane lined with simple gardens and weathered fences. Most of the Alcaris wolves have settled here, trying to carve out a semblance of normalcy after everything back home turned to ruin.

I tap into the pack link, reaching out first to Trav, Selene's mate, to make sure they're up for visitors. *"Would a visit be okay with your family?"*

Trav's warm response is almost instant. *"Perfect timing. We just finished bath time."*

I smile at his easygoing nature. *"I'm bringing a couple of guests. King Theo and Queen Estee."*

"As long as they ignore the mess, they're welcome." His laugh is light, but there's something underneath it. Strain.

We turn onto the next street, but before I can ask which

cottage is theirs, Trav appears in the doorway of the third house on the left.

His smile stretches wide, warmth radiating off him, though there's a faint shadow of exhaustion under his golden eyes.

He bows low. "My queen. Your Majesties."

I clasp his hand in both of mine. "It's good to see you, Trav."

"Please, come in."

The cottage is cozy, the scent of woodsmoke mingling with something sweet, maybe the remnants of breakfast. Sunlight filters through the lace curtains, illuminating a small but well-loved living space.

Selene sits on the couch, her newborn pup nestled in her arms, swaddled in soft gray cloth. Her smile is warm and tired all at once. "Thank you for coming to visit, Queen Sloane. We weren't sure you'd have time."

I sit beside her, already mesmerized by the tiny wolf. His soft skin is tinged pink, a fine layer of dark hair already sprouting along his scalp. His eyes flutter as though he's fighting sleep, his tiny fists curling into his blanket.

"I'll always make time for my pack," I say softly, but the words stick in my throat, edged with guilt. Because I don't really know if I'll be able to keep that promise. By the end of tomorrow, my fate—and theirs—could be out of my hands entirely.

"Have you decided on a name yet?" I ask.

Selene blushes and glances at her mate, who chuckles. "This is a little awkward, given who's here, but his name is Theo. After my grandfather."

Estee gasps, nudging her mate with her elbow as she winks at him. "You better watch out. This little one might come for your crown one day."

Theo's rare grin spreads across his face. "I welcome the challenge."

The laughter that follows feels real, even if it's just for a moment. I set the velvet blanket beside the pup, brushing my fingers lightly over his impossibly small hand. "We won't take up too much of your time," I say. "I just wanted to show my love to the newest member of our pack."

The warmth in Selene's smile dims slightly as she exchanges a glance with Trav. It's subtle but enough to send a ripple of unease through me.

"Is something wrong?" I ask immediately.

Neither of them speaks right away. The silence stretches just long enough to make my pulse spike.

"You can speak freely in front of my guests," I assure them. "Whatever it is, I want to know."

Trav rests his hand on Selene's shoulder, his expression grim. "Do we still have a pack?"

The question hits like a stone to the chest. "Of course we do."

Selene's brow creases. "But are you happy, Queen Sloane? It's different here. We've been treated well, but it's not the same as Alcaris."

I hesitate, torn between the truth and the weight of what I can't yet share. "You're not required to stay," I tell them, choosing my words carefully. "None of the Alcaris wolves will be forced to live in Venaris. There are homes waiting for you in Selaris, Polaris, and maybe, one day, Alcaris itself, if we can rebuild. My only priority is making sure the pack is safe and happy."

Trav's next question strikes even deeper. "*Are* we safe here?"

I rise to my feet, keeping my smile steady despite the ice crawling up my spine. "I believe so," I say, and it's not entirely a lie. Aeson's cruelty thrives in the shadows, not the light. As long as no one gives him an excuse, the pack should remain untouched.

"But," I add, locking eyes with both of them, "if you see anything—anything at all—that makes you uncomfortable, tell me directly. No matter how small it seems. I'm still your Alpha Queen, and I will protect you."

Their relief is visible, though it's muted by caution. "Thank you, Your Majesty," Trav says, escorting us to the door. "We'll see you tomorrow for the bonding ceremony."

I nod, throat tight, forcing another smile I don't feel. The second the door closes, Estee grips my arm, her strength keeping me steady.

"They're going to be okay," Theo promises, his deep voice quiet but firm. "Asher and I have been talking, and we've stationed our most trusted guards throughout the kingdom. Aeson can't afford to make a mess, not with us here to witness it."

"Thank you," I whisper, my voice barely audible. "Calling you is the best decision I've made since I left my kingdom."

"Our packs should have always stood together," Estee adds. "We're stronger united. We always have been."

Their support is the only thing keeping me upright, but there's something else gnawing at me, something I need to know. "Have you heard from Aurora?"

Theo's expression shifts, the warmth fading into something harder. "She's here already."

The lack of celebration in his voice makes my stomach lurch.

"She hasn't shown herself to us," Estee adds, her brows knitting. "But Theo sensed her before sunrise. Clara's message traveled faster than we expected."

"Too fast," Theo mutters. "That kind of urgency doesn't usually mean good things when it comes to the goddess."

Panic prickles along my skin, cold and sharp. "Would Aeson have been able to sense her too?"

"It's possible," Theo admits. "This is his territory, after all. But I only recognized her because Aurora shared her power with me before."

A chilling thought roots itself in my mind. What if Aurora didn't come to us first? What if she went straight for the runes?

What if Aeson's down there right now because he senses a disruption? What if he knows I've discovered the hell in that basement?

What if Julian's already dead?

My heart slams against my ribs, and the world seems to tilt beneath my feet.

"We need to get back to the castle," I say, my voice hoarse but resolute. "Now."

CHAPTER TWENTY-FOUR

SLOANE

Clara's still with Noen when we head back to the castle, but Asher and Isla meet up with us, their expressions a mixture of apology and quiet urgency. Neither of them needs to say a word. Especially since I've asked all of them to stand at the center of my chaos, to stand between me and whatever fate I've dragged us into.

The five of us pass through the castle gates, and the instant my foot crosses the threshold, my pulse stumbles.

The air feels wrong.

There's a weight pressing down, thick and cloying, and I know without a doubt something has changed. My palm lands against the castle's front door handle, but instead of cool metal, it's warm. Unnaturally warm and not from the sun. It's something deeper, more deceptive.

I glance over my shoulder at the others, dread curling inside me like smoke. "This isn't right."

Asher closes his blue eyes, inhaling deeply. His brow furrows, tension pulling at the corners of his mouth. "It's Aurora," he says grimly. "Her energy is everywhere."

My stomach clenches, nausea threatening to overtake me. This is what we asked for. Help. Intervention. But the reality of it is so much heavier than I expected. My subconscious knew there were no guarantees when dealing with a goddess, especially one like Aurora, but the frantic part of me, the part terrified for Julian's life, hadn't allowed me to imagine this sort of scenario.

The moment we step inside, the silence is suffocating.

No clinking of dishes from the kitchen. No murmur of staff moving through the halls. No distant hum of conversations or footsteps echoing through the stone corridors.

Nothing.

The castle feels hollow, like the very breath has been sucked from its lungs. The air is thick with magic, the kind that prickles against my skin, seeping into my bones like cold water.

"Where is everyone?" Isla's voice is hushed, barely more than a whisper.

No one answers. None of us know.

I take a step forward, every nerve in my body on edge, my wolf pacing just beneath my skin. Each step feels heavier than the last, the burden of uncertainty dragging me down.

The deeper we go, the worse the sensation gets. It's not just the emptiness. It's the sense that we're being watched. Not by human eyes, but by the castle itself. The walls hum with faint energy, something ancient and predatory. Like the whole structure has become a living thing, bending to Aurora's will.

Except this isn't the first time since arriving at this castle that I've felt this way.

When I found the runes outside, it was similar. Maybe

this isn't Aurora. Maybe this is Aeson, and he's doing something to the magic long ago set into these stones.

Once again, my mind tells me I need to get Julian. I'm not waiting a second longer.

Asher and Theo reach for me at the same time. "We're not going to try to stop you," Asher says, "but we've dealt with Aurora before. At least let us lead."

I can't argue with them, mostly because I know if anything happens to me, if I do the wrong thing, there's a chance I won't ever see Julian again.

"We need to go down this hallway, toward the southeast section, and head toward the lower levels," I tell them, gesturing for them to go ahead.

Theo glances back at his mate then at me, his hand hovering near the hilt of the dagger at his waist. "Stay close."

That isn't going to be a problem.

Estee and Isla flank me, their presence a small anchor in the storm raging inside me. The five of us proceed with caution, but there's an urgency crackling in the air, a shared sense of impending disaster. Each step down the narrow stone staircase feels heavier than the last.

By the time we reach the lower levels, sweat beads along the back of my neck despite the cool dampness of the air. The castle breathes around us, thick with ancient power, and every nerve in my body is screaming that we're running out of time.

I continue guiding Asher and Theo, my senses tuned to the smallest flicker of magic or sign of life. The hallway stretches out before us, the narrow space leading to the painting, to the door hiding my mate.

I can't wait.

I shove between the two men and sprint forward, my heart slamming against my ribs, blood roaring in my ears. I know better than to rush headlong into unknown magic, but reason has no hold on me now, not when I can feel him. Not when my soul is clawing at my insides, desperate to reach him.

But when I round the last corner, I hit something invisible. Hard.

I slam into an unseen barrier, a wall of steel wrapped in pure, vibrating energy. I stagger back, my palms still pressed against it as the force vibrates up my arms like an electrical current trying to peel my skin away from the bone.

"Aurora!" I roar, my voice shredding the silence like a storm tearing through glass.

I don't care if she's a goddess or a curse in a pretty dress. If she intends to stand between me and my mate, I'll rip her apart.

My wolf surges forward, fangs bared, claws splitting through my fingertips, but just before I lose myself completely to the shift, my world flips sideways.

Julian steps into the hallway, and I freeze.

He's free.

My heart lurches painfully, torn between elation and fear. He's here. He's breathing. But something's…off.

His fists are clenched at his sides, veins bulging along his forearms. His shoulders rise and fall with each heavy breath, his chest expanding like he can't get enough air. But he doesn't look up. Doesn't see me. It's like he doesn't even know I'm here.

A soft golden sheen coats his skin, shimmering faintly like sunlight trapped beneath the surface. It clings to him, ethereal and wrong, like something borrowed from a force far too powerful to belong to any wolf.

And then I see her.

Aurora.

She steps into view beside him, her hand curling around his bicep like she owns him, her lips brushing the shell of his ear as she whispers something I can't hear. Her body leans into his, far too close for comfort, and the possessive snarl building in my throat is nearly impossible to contain.

"What's happening?" Estee whispers beside me, her voice barely audible.

I can't answer.

Julian's entire form begins to shimmer, the glow intensifying until his head falls back, his eyes squeezed shut. His mouth opens wide, but no sound reaches us. The opaque wall between us absorbs everything, including his apparent agony and the lingering fury, leaving us helpless spectators to whatever Aurora is doing to him.

My claws gouge into my palms as I fight the primal rage building in my core. My wolf thrashes inside me, slamming into my ribs, begging for release. I grit my teeth, trying to hold her back, but the moment Julian vanishes into Aurora's energy, I lose the fight.

A feral roar tears from my lips, my bones snapping, skin stretching as my shift begins and not the smooth, fluid shift of my usual transformation. No, this is jagged and painful, like my body itself is resisting.

What the hell is happening?

"You wolves have no patience." Aurora's voice slithers through the air, smooth and mocking. "I honestly don't know why I keep coming back to this miserable realm."

My shift falters, pain surging through me as my body is forced back into human form with a jarring snap. My knees buckle, and I hit the floor, panting and shaking with frustration and pain.

When I can open my eyes again, Julian is standing there, whole and perfect and alive.

My chest cracks wide open, everything inside me spilling out in a flood of raw emotion. Relief, joy, fear, and rage—all crashing together until I can't contain it.

His eyes meet mine, and they shine with that bright, endless blue I've dreamed about. His skin is clean, glowing with health. His hair is no longer the uneven mess it was moments ago. He's even fully dressed in black pants and a grey collared shirt that clings to his heaving chest.

Every part of him healed and brought back to what I imagine he was the day he was cursed. Strong, powerful, and now…mine.

I launch myself forward, my body moving before my mind can catch up. His arms open just in time to grab me, holding me so tightly my ribs protest, but I don't care.

"Julian," I whisper, my voice cracking as I press my face into the warm curve of his neck. His scent—clean yet wild, and faintly metallic from the magic still clinging to his skin— floods my senses, slowly unraveling me.

His hands press against my back, fingers digging into my waist like he can't bear to let go. His chest rumbles, a sound halfway between a growl and a sob.

"I'm here," he murmurs, voice rough and thick with emotion. "I've got you."

Tears prick my eyes, but I don't let them fall. I can't—not yet. Not with Aurora standing there, watching us like an animal toying with its prey.

"I hate to break up whatever this is," Aurora says, her voice cutting through the fragile moment like a blade. "But we need to go."

I jerk back, still clutching Julian's hand. "We're not going anywhere. I have a pack to protect from Aeson."

Aurora's lips curl into something that might be a smile, but there's no kindness in it. "That's not my problem." Her tone is bored, dismissive. "You asked for my help, and now it's time to repay me. We leave now."

"No." My voice shakes, but I hold my ground. "I—"

The floor shifts beneath my feet, the stone falling away like sand slipping through my fingers. My stomach lurches, Julian's grip tightening on mine just as the world tilts and collapses in on itself.

And then we fall into an abyss.

CHAPTER TWENTY-FIVE

JULIAN

Aurora had said I needed to be "properly prepared." I didn't fully understand what that meant until her hands landed on me.

Her touch was cold and sharp, her energy sinking into my skin like barbed wire laced with starlight. I hated every second of it, hated the way her magic clung to my bones, reshaping me in ways I couldn't see but felt deep in my marrow. I wasn't sure I'd still be me by the time she was done.

But then the shield around us shattered, and I felt her.

Sloane.

The moment her scent hit me, the entire world narrowed to the space between us. The grime, the cold, the years of silence, all of it dissolved in the face of her. My mate. My salvation.

Holding her was like breathing after drowning, like sunlight after eternal darkness. My arms locked around her before I could think, my muscles trembling with the strain of holding on too tightly, afraid that if I loosened my grip even for a breath, she'd vanish like a cruel hallucination. My wolf howled inside me, fierce and eager, a chorus of pain and joy all tangled into one unbearable knot.

Her scent filled every hollow part of me, earth and storm, wildness and warmth. It wrapped around my heart, soothing wounds I hadn't even realized were still bleeding.

My mate. My mate. My mate.

The words looped through my mind like a prayer, a lifeline keeping me tethered to reality.

Her body molded against mine, real and alive, and my knees nearly buckled beneath the intensity of it. After two centuries of nothing—no touch and no connection to the world above—this was everything. She was everything.

But there was no time to truly cherish it all.

The moment the castle disappears around us, Sloane's quickening breath is the only sound I hear before the world fractures.

A kaleidoscope of colors bleed together, shimmering with liquid brilliance and folding in on themselves, like reality is caught between living and collapsing before we're whole again.

The ground we arrive on—if it can even be called that— flickers beneath my bare feet, half solid, half mist, as though it can't decide if it wants to exist at all. There's a lightness here, like we're standing on air, but every step feels weighted. Above us, there's a pristine white palace floating effortlessly on a bed of clouds, its walls reflecting the endless horizon in perfect, yet unnatural, stillness.

The air is heavy, every breath scraping against my throat, thick with magic so potent I can taste it. Not the wild, untamed energy of wolves or the earth beneath our paws. No, this is pure power, ancient and indifferent, filled with secrets most supernaturals aren't meant to know.

I tighten my hold on Sloane, pulling her closer without

thought. Her heart slams against my chest, her fingers digging into my arms, almost as if she, too, is afraid I'll vanish should she let go.

"I've got you," I remind her, my voice rough from disuse and the storm of emotions clawing their way to the surface.

Her gaze snaps up to mine, and for a heartbeat, the entire realm fades. No gods. No traps. No threats looming just out of sight. There's only us. The mate bond pulses between us, a living thread of heat binding me to her soul, a reminder that even after centuries of torment, we've still found our way to one another.

But then Aurora's laugh slices through it all, shattering the fragile moment.

"Oh, how sweet," she drawls, gliding ahead of us, her gown of liquid gold trailing through the air like smoke. "As much as I'd love to give you two all the time in the world to stare into each other's eyes, I didn't drag you here for a honeymoon."

Sloane stiffens against me, her breath hot on my neck as she whispers, "I don't care if she freed you, I hate her already."

My chest rumbles with a low sound of agreement, but the truth is, it doesn't matter. We're in Aurora's realm now. Whatever strength I've reclaimed, whatever power I've fought to regain since the moment I was freed from my chains, it means nothing here. We need to follow her, so we can hopefully get the hell out of here, and I can do what I swore—end my brother's existence.

Footsteps scuff against the cloud-like surface behind us, and I turn to find four more people with us. I don't know them, but Sloane doesn't hesitate to catch me up.

She points at each one, speaking quietly. "That's Isla with the pinkish hair, the man at her side is Asher. Estee is next to her with Theo. They're the other kings and queens of Lunara and have been helping us."

"Where are we?" Isla demands, her voice strong and laced with alpha energy.

"We're outside her home," the man I believe Sloane called Asher answers. "And we shouldn't keep her waiting."

Aurora glances back at us, her smirk almost vile. "Oh, Asher," she croons, her voice dripping with affection. "I'm so glad you remember our time together."

Her word eliciting a deep rumble from the alpha.

Reluctantly, or so it seems, the six of us follow the goddess into her home. There's no front door, just an open entry, leading into a white home. Everything is free of color. The floors, the furniture, the walls. All of it.

After years of darkness, it's overwhelming, but I do my best to adjust, knowing I can't lose focus here.

These gods can't be trusted.

"Good thing I'm a *goddess*, huh?" Aurora taunts, making me grimace.

Of course she can read minds.

"And much more," she adds with a sultry voice as she reaches for Asher.

He's already pulling away, but Isla jerks him back quicker, her fingers curling possessively around his wrist. "Watch yourself, goddess," she warns, her voice like ice, canines extending. "He's mine."

Aurora's smile hardens. "Yes, darling, I know *exactly* who he belongs to. That's why I need him." Without warning, she tugs Asher forward, ignoring the snarl Isla doesn't bother to hide. Aurora drags him toward the pristine couch placed at the center of the room.

"Bite me," she orders, her tone all business, though there's an undercurrent of something far darker. "Like before." She twists her head to the side, exposing her neck. The golden glow of her skin shifts, runes flickering just beneath the surface, ancient symbols older than language itself.

"I don't fucking think so." Isla growls, her body already coiling to lunge.

Estee grabs her waist, yanking her back before she can do something foolish.

"Let me go," Isla snarls, but Estee holds firm.

"How about we try to play nice first?" Estee suggests through clenched teeth. "Aurora, what are you doing?"

The goddess sighs, her fingers tracing the line of her own throat with idle curiosity. "I'm temporarily binding your powers to me," she says, as if it's the most obvious thing in the world. "The six of you owe me, and I intend to collect. I need to put some of the other gods back in check. You're going to help me do that."

"Like hell we are," Theo snaps. "We're not helping you start a war with them just so it can bleed through to our world."

"Remember, you wouldn't have that world without me," Aurora counters. "So, you'll do as I request, or you won't have a home to return to."

I expect more arguments, but everyone remains quiet, making the goddess grin. "As I was saying. There are forces within this realm that have gotten out of hand." She pauses, her gaze landing on Theo and Estee's hardened faces. "Much like Orix. I intend to beat them by taking the power of your alpha bloodlines and infusing it with my divine magic. Simple yet effective and completely unexpected."

Theo steps forward, placing himself protectively in front of Estee. "You've been using us."

"Using?" Aurora feigns offense, her violet eyes widening. "No, Alpha King. I've been saving your asses, and it's not as though I'm asking you to go to battle against beings who could chew you up in seconds. All you have to do is bite a few people and give over some of your blood." She grabs Asher's chin and squeezes. "Now, let's show your friends what I mean."

His jaw tightens, and I sense his wolf rising. "And if we refuse?"

Aurora shrugs. "I'll still get what I want in the end, but you six, I'll set you loose in the god realm and blow you a kiss goodbye as I leave you for dead."

I've left one hell for another.

CHAPTER TWENTY-SIX

SLOANE

The bond with Julian thrums within me like a livewire. His essence is nearly all I can focus on. At least until I hear Aurora's threat.

Not only does that have me straightening, but I can sense the shift in Julian. He's just escaped one hell and, because I asked for this goddess's help, he's now in another.

Even still, he squeezes my hand, almost as if he's reassuring me when it should be me doing that for him after all he's been through.

Aurora's smile is wicked enough to cut as she steps back from our small group, her presence looming, even when she's no longer in the center of the room. "Why don't I give the six of you some time to talk things over? While one or two of you are objecting, not all of you are as obstinate as some."

She casts a glance at a glowering Isla, then saunters toward the back half of her house but pauses, turning to point at Julian.

"You, the lost prince," she says, her eyes sliding to him with a dark glint of amusement, "have the most to lose. I would do your best to convince your friends here. Or you might never know what your fate always should have been."

Julian's jaw tightens, but he doesn't speak. Not yet. I feel the ripple of frustration through our bond, the truth of her words settling over him like a curse.

The goddess doesn't wait for a response. She takes a few more steps away from us, her gown of liquid gold flowing behind her as she vanishes into thin air, leaving us alone in the vast, colorless room.

For a few long moments, no one speaks. The silence is heavy, thick with unspoken fears and conflicting thoughts.

It's Isla who breaks first, pacing a jagged line across the floor, her hands clenching and unclenching at her sides. "I'm not doing it. I don't care if she saved each of us or that she's an all-powerful bitch—she's dangerous, and I don't trust her for a second."

I step forward, swallowing the knot of fear lodged in my throat. "Isla, none of us trust her. But what other choice do we have at this point? She's not asking us to fight her war. All she wants is a bite and some blood. We've done worse for our enemies. This isn't some massive sacrifice—"

"It's our mates and our bonds, Sloane!" Isla snaps, spinning to face me, her rose-gold hair practically sparking with her agitation. "An alpha's bite is powerful alone, but to combine that with our blood? Do you have any idea what she can do with that? We're talking ancient magic, combined with divine energy, and none of us have any clue what that even means!"

I hold her gaze, my fingers curling into fists to keep my hands from shaking. "I know exactly what it means." My voice softens, but I don't back down. "It means we get to go home, that we don't fall victim to another god who could be much worse than Aurora. It also means we don't spend the rest of our lives looking over our shoulders, wondering when she's going to yank us back here because we refused to pay our debt."

Estee crosses her arms, her gaze shifting between us. "I hate to say it, but Sloane's right."

Isla's head whips toward her sister. "Excuse me?"

"I didn't say I liked it," Estee clarifies, her tone calm but firm. "But look around us, Isla. Do you see any other way out of here? We're floating on a damned cloud in the middle of the gods' playground. We owe her. That's the deal."

Isla's nostrils flare, her wolf just under the surface. "There has to be another way."

"Isla," Estee's voice softens, but the firmness remains beneath it, "sometimes there isn't."

The men have stayed mostly silent, but finally, Isla spins toward Asher, her hands gripping his arms. "Tell them. Tell them we can't trust her."

Asher exhales slowly, brushing a thumb across her jawline before speaking. "Isla, love of my life, queen of my heart..." His voice is tender, but there's a finality in it that makes her still. "I know this is killing you. I know you'd love nothing more than to pluck that goddess's eyes out, but I don't think we have a choice here either."

She shakes her head, her lips parting to argue, but Asher doesn't let her.

"My purpose in life is to protect you," he continues, his forehead pressing briefly to hers. "And I would be failing at my job if I allowed you to refuse. We know she'll do exactly as she's threatened, and like Sloane pointed out, we're not fighting her war. Just helping to enhance the gods on her side. Let's just do this and go home."

Isla's shoulders slump, her fight slipping away, leaving only exhaustion behind. "I hate this."

"So do we," Theo says quietly, placing a hand on her back. "But we need to get back to our people. They're waiting for us."

The group falls into reluctant agreement. The air's still thick with unease, but I'm quietly grateful. This was never about making a choice. It's survival.

Aurora reappears the instant the decision settles, her smile bright and victorious. "Excellent." Her eyes shimmer with something almost feral. "Come along, my little wolves. It's time to meet the others."

Julian keeps me close, his hand a steady warmth amongst the chaos we've been thrown into. I notice Asher and Theo do the same with their mates, their fingers curling possessively around Isla's and Estee's waists. Normally, the sight of such instinctive protectiveness would clash with the independent streak I've carried my whole life—a refusal to be seen as anything but strong, capable, untouchable.

But not now.

Now, I lean into Julian's warmth, the solid weight of his arm a comfort rather than a cage. I let myself press closer, taking in his scent, the steady rise and fall of his chest, the way his fingers spread wide against my lower back as though reassuring himself I'm still here too. Because for the first time in my long, complicated life I understand something I never truly let myself believe: being strong doesn't have to mean being alone.

This man, this broken prince forged in darkness and chains, is my mate. My equal. My balance. He isn't here to tame me or silence my voice, he's here to amplify all parts of me. To fight beside me, to lift me up when I stumble, and to hold me together when I fracture under the pressure of everything I carry.

Mates were always something I admired from a distance.

I understood their importance, envied the connection I saw in others, but I never let myself want it. Not really. Not when wanting meant admitting how much I longed for someone to truly see me.

But standing here, with Julian's touch anchoring me and his gaze sweeping over me like I'm the only thing keeping him breathing, I finally understand the gravity of what it means to be bound to someone by more than choice or circumstance.

I may not know everything about him yet. I might not yet be in love with the man he is today, but I would die for him without hesitation. And I know, with bone-deep certainty, that he would do the same for me.

That's the magic of being a wolf shifter. We don't weave spells like witches or bend shadows like vampires, but we have something far rarer. We have our bonds. That unbreakable thread tying one soul to another, strong enough to weather centuries of separation, torture, even death itself. And standing here, I know I wouldn't trade that magic for anything across all the realms.

Especially when he glances down at me, the corner of his mouth lifting in the faintest smile—soft and a little amazed, like he can't believe I'm real either. My heart stutters painfully, skipping against my ribs, and the world around us fades just for a moment.

This. This is where I was always meant to end up.

Finally.

The momentary peace is broken when Aurora pulls us from existence without warning, the world disappearing for a brief second before we reappear in another part of the god realm. This one is nothing like the clouded expanse we arrived at. The landscape shifts with each step, the ground firm beneath our feet but ever-changing in texture and color.

Sometimes grass, sometimes smooth crystal, and other times soft sand. The sky above is endless, not blue but a deep indigo threaded with silver veins that pulse like a heartbeat. Floating islands hover in the distance, each one linked by shimmering bridges made of pure light.

On those islands, figures wait.

The gods.

They're not what I expect. Some have eyes that flicker like flames and skin that shimmers beneath the brightness of their world. Others appear more human-like, except they're draped in fabrics that seem woven from the stars themselves, their stares too colorful, their features too perfect to belong to anything mortal.

Aurora leads us to a central platform, where a towering god with sleek opal hair and skin like polished obsidian waits. His presence hums in the air, powerful enough that my wolf instinctively bows her head within me.

"This is Damaris," Aurora purrs, placing a hand on his shoulder. "One of you will bite him first."

The god's silver eyes flick toward Julian, his gaze heavy with curiosity and something darker. "This is the lost prince?"

Julian doesn't flinch under his scrutiny, his jaw tight. "I am."

Damaris steps closer, offering his arm. "I choose you and your mate."

Julian's nostrils flare, but he doesn't argue, and I breathe easier knowing we don't have to be so intimate with them, biting their necks as Aurora seemed to have Asher do when he was here last time.

"And I'll draw your blood," Aurora says coolly. "I can take all of it now, or a little at a time. I'll leave that up to you."

My laughter is dark and rough. "*Now* we get a choice?"

"Technically, you had one before." The goddess pulls a silver blade from thin air, inspecting my arm.

"Die or obey," I remind her, watching closely as she cuts my wrist. "I understand we owe you, and I appreciate that you freed Julian when I couldn't, but you don't have to taunt Isla like you do or be so crude."

Aurora's violet eyes level on me, her smirk firmly in place. "No, I don't have to, but it sure keeps things more interesting, don't you think?"

This conversation is pointless, so I fix my attention on Julian just as his teeth cut through Damaris's forearm. The god trembles, closing his eyes, and his skin begins to shimmer. When he looks at Julian again, his gaze is golden with fine lines of silver bleeding through, his expression otherworldly.

"Such interesting power," Damaris murmurs as Julian straightens again.

Before I can ask what happens next, Aurora places a cloth over my wrist and steps away from me, a bowl of my blood in her hand. "Drink. One sip is all you need."

The god doesn't hesitate; he laps at the crimson, and Aurora is forced to yank the bowl from his hands. "Careful, Damaris."

As he drags a finger over his parted lips, his teeth lengthen then claws slide from his fingertips. His entire form seems to ripple, something more primal waking inside him. Almost as if he's preparing to shift, but the transformation is halted, keeping him more man than beast.

"Magnificent," Damaris purrs, flexing his fingers. "The mate bond is truly unlike anything we could have predicted."

Aurora's smile is all sharp edges. "I told you." Then she glances at the others, further away and still perched on their islands. "Who's next?"

CHAPTER TWENTY-SEVEN

SLOANE

The process moves faster than I expect, a rhythmic cycle of blood and teeth, of the gods teleporting in, receiving our energy, and stepping back with newfound power crackling through their veins. Some of them stay to watch, most of them disappear quickly, and a few even try to demand more than their share. Thankfully, Aurora surprises us all when she shuts that down quickly.

She takes only enough blood from the queens so that each god can have one drink of the powerful crimson. Something I appreciate so that we're not left weak when we return to Lunara. Even my wolf doesn't reject the help we're offering, but something tells me that's only because this goddess gave us our mate.

Julian offers me a reassuring glance as he finishes with another god, then his eyes cast down to my wrist as if he's asking if I'm okay.

There's a thin, pink-tinged line there from the cuts, but it's nothing that will bother me later and won't even leave a scar. I offer him a smile in return as he starts to walk toward me.

Isla and Estee stand with their mates and I think we're finally done after having repeated the same process with over a hundred gods. Each time, their eyes shifting to gold, their forms flickering as the surge of wolf magic collides with their celestial essence. Even now, the air is thick with the energy, the scent of iron and divinity mingling into something potent, something unnatural.

But there's still only one left.

Aurora.

She eyes Asher first, her smirk slow and knowing, as if she enjoys stoking the fire of Isla's rage. But then, in a move as deliberate as it is calculated, she shifts her gaze to Julian.

"You. Come."

Julian doesn't hesitate. He steps forward, his expression unreadable, and I swear I hear Isla suck in a breath beside me.

The goddess lifts her wrist, extending it toward him like an offering. "Be a good boy and finish the job."

I almost ask why she chose Julian over Asher, but the words never leave my mouth. It doesn't matter. If anything, it's easier this way. One less thing for Isla to hate Aurora for.

Plus, this means we're almost out of here.

As Julian's teeth slice into Aurora's skin, the golden runes along her arm flare to life, shimmering like blazing stars, and something in the air shifts. The very fabric of this place seems to pulse, bending toward the moment as if the god realm itself recognizes the final piece falling into place as she tilts a bowl with my blood in it to her ruby lips.

And then it's done.

I almost expect some sort of jealousy, but there's only relief, even from my wolf.

Aurora pulls back, her gaze no longer violet but still just

as wicked as she turns toward us. "Well, that was fun," she drawls. "Now, let's discuss your departure."

I straighten, instinctively reaching for Julian's hand. "So, you're holding up your end of the bargain?"

She rolls her eyes. "What kind of goddess do you take me for?"

Isla snorts. "Do you want an honest answer?"

Aurora winks. "I'm well aware of your opinions, *Queen Isla*." She flicks a hand, the space around us shimmering. "You fulfilled your end, so I'll fulfill mine. You'll all be going home, and we are officially even. No debts. No obligations. None of you will be calling on me again. Our worlds have entangled enough."

I exhale, relief loosening my muscles, but there's still a lingering discomfort crawling beneath my skin. Something isn't right, and the sooner we return to Venaris, the better.

Aurora moves to open a portal, but the air shifts again. Heavier and more potent. Worse, even the goddess wears a look of shock on her face.

The ground quakes beneath us, and a sharp, electric pulse surges through the air. The once-still sky splits open like shattered glass, the eerie, endless horizon shifting as a shadowed force tears through the delicate balance of Aurora's island.

A voice slithers around us, low and insidious.

"Did you really think you could get away with this so easily, Aurora? *Such a waste.*"

And then the attack begins.

There's no warning. No time to prepare.

One moment, we're standing on the cusp of freedom, and the next, the god realm erupts into chaos.

Figures materialize from the fractured sky, wreathed in ominous, rippling energy that twists and bends unnaturally around them. They're gods, much like Aurora, yet utterly different. Darker. Older. Their presence alone makes my bones vibrate with unease.

The largest of them steps forward, a towering figure with onyx skin that seems to drink in the light. His eyes are twin voids, endless and devouring. "You gave our enemies a gift," he sneers at the six of us, "and now you expect to walk away?"

Aurora doesn't flinch. "Oh, darling, I expect nothing," she purrs, inspecting her nails. "Though, I was hoping you'd show up."

But he wasn't talking to the goddess. His punishment doesn't seem to be meant for her. At least not right now.

He wants *wolf* blood.

I barely have time to take a breath as the mayhem presses in on us.

One of the gods lunges toward Isla, his hand outstretched, fingers elongating into piercing tendrils of darkness. Isla dodges, her movements swift, her wolf flashing in her eyes as she rips free from Asher's grasp and slashes upward with her claws. The god snarls, staggering back.

Julian shoves me behind him, his body coiling like a predator ready to strike. But I don't stay put.

I can't.

This is what I was born for.

With a growl, I leap and shift in midair, my wolf exploding to the surface in a blur of sleek fur and snapping teeth. My claws sink into the nearest god's chest, tearing through celestial flesh that shimmers unnaturally beneath my touch.

Theo and Estee fight as one. Two figures weaving together, a sword he must have taken from one of the other gods slashing through our opponents while Estee shifts, her inner beast keeping Theo's back safe from further attacks.

Even with all of us pushing forward, throwing everything we have into the battle, we are outnumbered. *Severely.*

The gods we've just enhanced are nowhere to be seen, and these newcomers fight with an efficiency that tells me this isn't just a battle—it's an execution. Our deaths are their sole mission.

A god grabs me from behind, his grip like stone, heat searing through my fur. I whip my head around, sinking my teeth into his wrist, tasting the acrid burn of divine blood. He shrieks, throwing me in the opposite direction. I skid across the earth, my ribs protesting the impact as I collide with the twisted trunk of a tree.

"Sloane!" Julian's voice roars through the battlefield, and then he's there, his claws slicing through the god's throat in a single brutal strike. The body vanishes before it can even hit the ground.

As I stagger back up, I notice Isla and Asher taking down several more of the gods, each vanishing just like the last. Julian stands protectively near me, his gaze already seeking the next target. For the first time, hope sparks. *We might be winning.*

But then Estee screams.

My head snaps toward her. She's no longer in her wolf form. Her knees buckle, a dagger protruding from her side, its blade pulsing with fire that licks up the hilt and sears through her flesh. She gasps, her hands trembling as she tries to grasp the weapon buried deep inside her.

Theo is already moving, but he's too late.

The god responsible steps forward, his presence *wrong* in every possible way. His skin is almost translucent beneath the shadows that flicker around him, and his eyes are endless voids swirling with disgust as they remain fixed on Estee with nothing but detachment.

He grips the dagger and twists.

Estee's body jerks. A choked sound escapes her lips as the fire spreads outward, crawling across her skin in glowing embers. The moment he rips the blade free, she collapses.

A shrill cry pierces the battlefield—Theo.

But he doesn't attack. He stumbles forward, his hands shaking as he reaches for her, as if his touch alone might be enough to pull her back.

The god watches, head inclining. Then, with cold precision, he lifts the dagger and drives it straight into Theo's chest.

Theo doesn't cry out. He doesn't fight. He just falls.

Gone. Both of them.

The world narrows.

No, no, no.

A strangled sound rips from my throat, a cry of denial, of fury, of helplessness so raw it nearly shatters me.

Aurora's voice cuts through the madness, fierce and unwavering. "Enough."

A wave of power explodes outward, knocking everyone back—friend and foe alike. The gods recoil, most of them retreating, but it doesn't stop me. Not when my heart feels as though it might shatter.

Estee was my friend. I may not have known her long, but enough to know that her heart was pure, and she deserved so much better than this.

My wolf is back on all fours, our sights set on the god who took our friends. He reaches for the dagger still in Theo's heart, but it's too late.

I'm too close, canines bared and claws at the ready.

I've never come face-to-face with a god like this, nor do I

know how to kill one, but that doesn't stop me from acting to honor my friends.

My bite cuts through his neck, tearing away at the skin, spilling black, glowing blood that hisses in the air. My claws swipe at his guts, digging deep until every piece of this bastard has been shredded. I want his head, but by the time I refocus, his form is already vanishing.

Nooo! I scream in my own mind, my wolf's chest heaving with the desire for justice.

"They will pay for this," Aurora says next to me, but she's quickly shoved away.

"*You'll* pay for this," Isla roars, stepping in front of the goddess, eyes brimming with wrath and devastation. "We never put you in danger. Yet, you brought us here against our will, forced us to give what wasn't yours to take. Goddess or not, I'll fucking kill you."

Asher pulls her against him, his grip firm, but she thrashes in his hold. "It's okay, my love. Everything is going to—"

"If you say one more word, Asher, I can't promise I won't hurt you." Her voice shakes with grief, but her glare is unrelenting, still pinned on Aurora.

I shift back to my human form, my own emotions threatening to spill over as I stare down at Theo and Estee. Gods, this can't be real.

"Bring them back," Isla demands through her tears.

Aurora wisely keeps her distance. "Those gods will be back. It's not that simple."

"I don't care if it's the most complicated spell in the world or if it will take every ounce of your power." Isla's voice is pure venom. "You *will* bring my sister back to me. Now."

"Listen—"

"No, Aurora." She breaks from Asher's hold. "*You* listen.

I've tolerated you objectifying my mate and driving me to near madness, but this I won't stand for. You're the goddess of creation. You brought our mother back, and now, you'll do the same for Estee and Theo. No excuses."

Isla's strength is admirable. She stands toe-to-toe with the goddess, trembling with emotions I can't even begin to fathom, but I do know that none of them are fear. This queen knows what she wants, and she's not going to accept anything less. Not this time.

Silence crashes over the battlefield like a hammer, the weight of it pressing into my ribs. Julian reaches for me, his warmth holding me together, but even his presence can't soften the ache cutting through my soul.

Because I know right then that none of us are leaving this realm unscathed.

CHAPTER TWENTY-EIGHT

JULIAN

We're taken back to Aurora's house in silence, the acknowledgement of what we've lost pressing down on all of us like a suffocating force. Even the goddess herself, who seems to thrive on chaos, says nothing as she lifts her hand, tendrils of shimmering gold energy spiraling through the air.

With an uncharacteristic solemnity, she conjures a pristine sheet of white silk, draping it over Estee and Theo with a care I don't expect from her. The fabric glows faintly before settling over their forms, a final reverence to the warriors they were.

Isla doesn't thank her. She doesn't even lift her head. Her trembling fingers remain curled around Estee's hand, shoulders shaking with silent sobs. Asher kneels beside her, his jaw clenched so tightly I can see the muscle twitching from across the room. His darkened eyes track Aurora's every move, watchful, wary. But for once, the goddess seems respectful.

"If there's any chance of me doing as you've demanded, I need to go," she announces, her voice quieter than usual but still laced with authority. As she speaks, the golden silk of her gown starts to shift, the marks of our prior battle disappearing as the fabric changes colors. The once-radiant gold is now black as midnight, clinging to her like a living shadow as she adds, "My home is a fortress. You'll be safe here until I return."

No one responds. Not a word. Even Isla doesn't snap at her.

Aurora steps forward, pressing her palm against a ripple of light in the air, and then she's gone, dissolving into a shimmering veil that vanishes just as swiftly as it appeared.

A heavy sigh beside me breaks the silence.

I glance at Sloane, watching the way her arms wrap around her body, the tension still coiled in her frame. Her fingers tremble, just barely, but she presses them into her sides, as if physically restraining the emotions raging beneath the surface. The battlefield is behind us, but the war still lingers in her eyes.

I follow her gaze to where Estee and Theo lie unmoving, their presence still commanding, even in death. Isla's breaking apart before us, her pain bleeding into the room like an open wound, but there's nothing any of us can say to her. No words to fix what's been done.

I turn to Sloane. She's still standing, still breathing, still here. And while it might be selfish, that's everything to me.

I lift a hand to the back of her neck, pulling her closer, grounding us both in the warmth of our bond. She doesn't resist. Instead, she leans into my touch, pressing her forehead lightly against my chest, her breath warm against my skin.

"I was terrified," I admit, my voice quiet but raw. "Out there, in that fight, I thought I might lose you."

Her throat bobs as she swallows hard. "I thought I might lose you too," she whispers. "We weren't prepared for that."

"No, but you handled yourself as if you were." I slide my fingers into her hair, tugging gently until she lifts her gaze to mine. "I'm sorry I tried to shield you as if you couldn't protect yourself. I see your strength, Sloane. I feel it in every breath you take, in every strike you made on that battlefield. I hope you can understand that my actions weren't out of doubt or disrespect. They were instinct. Because you are, without question, more than I ever could have dreamed of." I let my thumb brush over her cheek. "My mate. My equal."

Her lips part slightly, and even though she doesn't smile, I see it in her eyes. That flicker of light, of something deep and unbreakable between us. Then her hand slides over my chest, resting over my heart.

"Thank you," she says softly. "I've spent too many years feeling like I had to prove my worth."

A growl rumbles from deep within me before I can stop it, the very idea of her doubting herself making my blood burn.

It earns me a small, breathy laugh. "Easy, my mate," she murmurs. "That's in the past now. Once we get back, everything's going to change."

The reminder of home makes my hands tighten around her waist. My voice is steady, firm. "I'm going to kill him, Sloane. I hope you don't have any objections."

She is the only one who could stop me now. The only thing between Aeson and his inevitable death. But she shakes her head without hesitation.

"I'll be right by your side," she promises, her voice steady, unwavering. "I know he made you suffer. But I don't care about vengeance, Julian. I just want him gone. So that this," she glances at Estee and Theo, her jaw tightening, "can one day feel like nothing more than a nightmare we've woken from. For all of us."

I let out a breath, pressing my forehead to hers. "No matter what happens, we end this together."

The moment lingers, taut and unwavering, before the air shifts once more. A familiar energy crackles through the space, pressing against my skin like a slow-building storm. Then, in a flash of swirling gold, Aurora appears.

But she isn't alone.

A young woman stands beside her, her presence an unsettling mix of mortal and divine. Hair like fresh-fallen snow cascades down her back, the strands almost too bright to look at directly. When she turns to us, deep violet eyes glimmer with an eerie, knowing light, centuries of wisdom encased in a deceptively youthful face.

If I didn't already sense her wolf, I'd think she was Aurora's direct descendant. Though there's something more. Something beyond any shifter I've encountered before.

A low growl rumbles from Isla as she surges to her feet, her stance tight with barely contained rage. "What the hell is Elyn doing here?" Her eyes flick to Aurora then to the woman at her side, suspicion sharpening her every breath.

Aurora waves a dismissive hand, as if Isla's outburst is nothing more than a mild annoyance. "She's here to ensure I don't die."

Elyn inclines her head slightly, her attention settling solely on Isla and Asher. "This is *god* magic," she says, voice steady, deliberate. "Something none of you are used to dealing with."

Isla's nostrils flare, her hands curling into fists at her sides. "But you are now?" she snaps. "I'm not in the mood for games. From either of you. So tell us the whole plan. No riddles. No half-truths."

Aurora exhales, her gaze lowering to Theo and Estee,

their still forms a silent demand. "The way they died—by the hand of another god—it complicates things."

Something cold slithers down my spine.

Aurora lifts her chin, meeting Isla's burning stare head-on. "I can bring them back," she continues, "but if I do so the way I did for your mother, there may be consequences. They may look like themselves, but there's a chance they won't remember who they are. That their bond may not even exist any longer."

The quiet that follows is suffocating. Isla's breath catches, her body going rigid. I see it, her absolute refusal to accept a world where Estee doesn't know her. Where she doesn't feel her mate's presence in every breath she takes.

But it's Asher who speaks first. "And Elyn's here because there's an alternative?"

Aurora's expression shifts slightly, something close to solemnity flickering beneath her usual bravado. "Correct. I can tie them to my essence," she says, pointing at Theo and Estee. "Their lives will be linked to mine. As long as I live, so do they. If I die, they die."

She shrugs, an edge of smug confidence creeping into her voice. "But let's be honest. I'm not going anywhere. I've lived thousands of years, and I'll live plenty more. It's far more likely they'll live out their natural lives, die of old age, and be reborn like normal, no longer connected to me once that happens." Her lips curve slightly, almost wry. "While not ideal, this is the only other option."

The tension thickens, heavy and unmoving. Isla doesn't speak. She studies Aurora, as if weighing the goddess's words, searching for deception. Then, finally, she turns to Elyn. "And you? What's your role in all this?"

Elyn doesn't falter under the scrutiny. She meets Isla's

glare with unshaken calm, her posture as steady as the goddess beside her.

"I'll be the anchor for Aurora," she says simply. "What she's doing for you is beyond reason. It's a risk to her power. A big one. I told her she shouldn't go through with this, but our goddess does as she wishes." Her violet eyes flicker with firmness. "Something you'd do well to remember as you stand here judging her."

Another stretch of silence. Then, Isla exhales, low and slow. "How can we help?"

Aurora smirks. "Funny you should ask." Her attention flicks toward me and Sloane, eyes glittering with mischief. "The two of you will be in charge of restraining her."

Sloane stiffens beside me. "Excuse me?"

Aurora gestures toward Isla. "If she interrupts my process, you're all as good as dead."

A growl tears from Asher's throat. "I don't really think threats are necessary."

The goddess lets out a resounding chuckle, one that lacks its usual edge of amusement. "Oh, darling. That's not a threat. You have no clue what I have to do next." Her expression hardens, and the air around her thrums with something deeper, something primordial.

"Here's an idea," she purrs. "How about everyone just does their best not to piss me off while I do this and then we can all go our separate ways and never suffer one another's company again?" Her smirk grows as her still-golden eyes glow. "Sound fair?"

Nobody says anything, no objections or agreements, but that doesn't seem to matter to the goddess.

A deep pulsing spreads around us. The room is heavier now, charged with something unseen but potent enough to make my wolf stir.

Aurora steps forward, her bright aura stretching outward, the dim light of her home bending toward her as if the entire house breathes in anticipation. Elyn follows, her movements fluid, almost eerily calm, like she's done this before.

Still, no one speaks as Aurora stops before Estee's and Theo's covered bodies.

"This is your last warning," she murmurs, her voice almost too eager. "What comes next isn't gentle or kind in any way."

The truth of her words settles over us. Isla flinches but doesn't look away. Asher's grip on her shoulder tightens, his knuckles paling.

Sloane shifts closer to me, her body rigid, and even though neither of us speaks, I feel her tension in the mate bond.

Aurora lifts her hands, and the entire room changes, the floor vibrating.

A golden light snakes through, creating cracks in the pristine white stone beneath our feet, branching out like veins in a living body. A gust of wind swirls and power crackles, hot and electric, lifting Aurora's hair from her shoulders in long waves of liquid fire.

She breathes out, slow and measured, then moves her hands in deliberate, circular motions, her fingers glowing at the tips, leaving behind trails of golden embers in the air. The runes on her skin ignite, spreading like molten metal along her arms, glowing brighter until the very air trembles beneath the weight of her magic.

And then the first sound breaks through the room.

A deep, resonant hum, low and elemental, like the voice of something long forgotten that's stirring awake.

It echoes through the walls, rattling the very bones in my body, sending a pulse of energy into my chest. Sloane inhales, clutching my wrist as the tune deepens, vibrating through the floor.

Then Aurora slams her hands against Estee's and Theo's chests, kneeling over them with her head bowed.

A violent blast of energy explodes outward, so fierce that my vision whites out.

Sloane stumbles against me, Isla lets out a strangled cry, but none of us move. We can't.

When I can see again, my eyes focus on the golden light seeping into Estee's and Theo's bodies. The magic burrows beneath their skin, tracing their veins like liquid fire. Their bodies jerk—once, twice, each more violently than the last.

Elyn steps in then.

She settles herself next to Aurora, her white hair glowing like an electric charge, eyes dark with something deeper than power. She presses a palm to the goddess's back, steadying her, anchoring her.

A new color seeps into the magic swirling around us, a deep, rich violet, likely Elyn's magic. It wraps around Aurora's, tightening the golden tendrils as if holding them in place, keeping the balance as the goddess works.

The runes on Aurora's skin darken, shifting, twisting into new shapes, something older, rawer, dangerous.

And just when I was beginning to think this wasn't so bad, it becomes the nightmare Aurora warned us about.

Theo and Estee scream. A raw, agonized sound, not of the living but of something dragged back through the veil of death itself.

The floor quakes beneath them, more cracks form beneath the table, spider-webbing outward as if the entire god realm is resisting what's happening.

Isla shrieks, reaching for her sister, but Sloane and I lunge forward, grabbing both her and Asher, holding them back.

"Don't let them go!" Aurora barks, sweat glistening on her brow.

"Let me hold my mate," Asher demands, his body coiled with tension.

I look at his face, searching for his control. I don't know this man, but that doesn't mean I can't see the agony pulsing through him as he watches his mate fall apart, knowing there's nothing he can do to stop what pains her.

Without needing to think twice, I release him as Sloane carefully passes Isla over to him.

Her breath is ragged, her body thrashing against his hold while the screams continue, louder by the second. "Please forgive me, Estee. I can't lose you yet."

Isla's eyes spill over with more tears as we all stand there, helpless to do anything other than watch. Minutes pass, and when the torturous sounds finally cease, I think the worst is over, but then the bodies begin to smoke, their skin darkening.

This time, it takes all three of us to hold Isla back as she roars. "What are you doing to them?"

Aurora, of course, doesn't answer. Nor does Elyn. If I didn't believe we could all die, I'd help Isla kill this goddess, but before I can further wonder if it might be worth it, the power thrumming through the room eases.

The four of us watch, my chest tightening with anticipation as I hold Sloane's hand, hoping like hell this will work.

First, Theo's back arches, his lips parting on a ragged, soundless gasp, his fingers twitching above the sheets.

Estee's body shudders violently, her chest rising too quickly, too erratically, as if her lungs aren't sure how to breathe again.

Then everything stops.

The energy collapses inward, slamming back into their bodies in a final burst of gold and violet light. The hum fades. The trembling walls still and cracks in the floors fade.

Silence.

A long, endless silence.

Then…

A single inhale.

A ragged, gasping breath, followed by a second one.

Theo's fingers curl, his chest rising and falling quickly.

Estee's eyes snap open.

The room erupts.

Isla breaks free, and this time none of us try to stop her when she launches herself forward. Asher moves with her, nearly colliding with the table as they reach for their family.

Estee blinks rapidly, her expression dazed, confused. "I—" Her voice is hoarse, barely there.

Theo groans, head lolling to the side.

Aurora staggers backward, her glow dimming.

Elyn catches her, pressing a steadying hand to the goddess's back. "It's done."

But Isla isn't satisfied yet.

She cups Estee's face, scanning her features, searching. "Say my name," she orders, desperate, trembling.

Estee's lips part. "Isla."

Isla chokes on a sob, pulling her sister into her arms.

Theo blinks, focusing on Asher. "What did we miss?"

Asher lets out a breathless laugh, his hands shaking as he grips Theo's arm. "You missed everything."

But then Theo looks past him, his gaze finding Estee.

His mate.

And there it is.

The bond.

I see it ignite between them, their energy twining back

together, reforging what had been severed by death. The way they stare at each other, breathless, overwhelmed but whole, is all the confirmation any of us need.

I feel Sloane exhale next to me, a breath of relief so deep it shakes.

It worked.

Aurora lets out a dramatic sigh. "Well, that was emotionally exhausting. Now, it's time for you all to leave and never return."

Sloane surprises me when she steps toward the goddess. "How did this even happen? What was the point of us enhancing your gods if they weren't going to be part of the fight?"

The goddess arches a brow and shakes her head. "All too often I have regrets about ever allowing your kind to evolve." Her gaze narrows and darkens. "What you witnessed was nothing more than a distraction. The real fight is happening elsewhere, where my people are being slaughtered without me there to fight alongside them, because I'm here. With you. Saving two lives that mean practically nothing in the grand scheme of things. Now, I'm done wasting time here."

She flicks her fingers, and the air distorts, a portal tearing open before us. The energy around it shudders, rippling like a wound in reality itself. Aurora's knees tremble, barely perceptible, but there before she forces herself still. She rolls her shoulders back and lifts her chin high, refusing to betray any weakness despite the sheer magnitude of what she's done.

"Go," she commands, her voice lacking its usual lilt of arrogance. "All of you."

Though, she doesn't mean *all* of us. Elyn walks toward the back of the house as if she intends on staying.

Theo and Estee move first, their steps slow and uneven

almost, their bodies adjusting to life once more. Isla and Asher follow close behind, but before stepping through, Isla halts.

She turns to Aurora, locking gazes with the goddess. Her blue eyes are no longer filled with anger, but something closer to reluctant acceptance. A truce, fragile yet there.

"I misjudged you, Aurora," Isla says, her voice steady but not without weight. "I apologize for that. Thank you for saving them. We won't bother you again."

Aurora's eyes, violet once more, flash. Whether she intended to respond or not, Isla doesn't wait to find out. She steps through the rift, disappearing without another word.

I move forward with Sloane at my side, taking in the goddess one last time. Her power still hums in the air, but she's drained. There's no doubt she's not ready for another fight yet.

I meet her gaze. "Do you need me to bite you again?"

Her smile lifts, but it lacks its previous edge. "If you want to touch me again, just say so."

Sloane shakes her head but stays silent as I take Aurora's outstretched arm.

My canines extend, sinking into her wrist. Her blood is thick with power, scorching like liquid fire on my tongue. It thrums through me, vibrating with an energy I don't understand. It latches onto me, taking what it seeks before retreating to the goddess.

When I pull back, her eyes glow with renewed gold, and for the first time since meeting her, Aurora does something unexpected.

She nods appreciatively. "Thank you."

The words land heavily. Sincere. Real. A rare glimpse of the woman beneath the goddess.

Her gaze drifts between Sloane and me, distant, like she already sees the paths before us.

"Kill your brother and restore your kingdom." She tilts her head slightly, a flicker of amusement returning. "When you're Alpha King, everything will be right with your world again."

Sloane starts to speak, but Aurora lifts a hand, cutting her off as she points toward the portal. "I don't need more blood. Go. Now."

We don't hesitate this time, but when we arrive back in Venaris, I wonder if maybe we should have.

CHAPTER TWENTY-NINE

SLOANE

S tepping back into the realm of Lunara after being in the god realm should feel like a return to something familiar, something safe. But instead, it feels like suffocation.

The moment my feet touch the earth, the energy in the air coils around my lungs like roots, dense and choking. This isn't home. The land is warped. Off balance.

Worse, Estee and Theo are nowhere in sight.

I clutch Julian's hand tighter as we walk hesitantly forward, my grip bordering on desperate. After everything, I can't risk losing him now.

The bond between us pulses steady, and I use it like a lifeline as I scan the forest for any sign of our friends.

Before I can ask Isla or Asher where they went, my head is suddenly splitting.

"Damn you, Sloane!" Clara's voice barrels through my thoughts, wild and laced with fury. *"Where the hell have you been the last three days?"*

Three days?!

I stop dead in my tracks. *"We were only..."* I shake my head.

It doesn't matter now. *"We were forced to go to the god realm with Aurora. Without notice or I would have told you. What's going on here?"*

"Shift and go east," she says urgently. *"Don't stop until I find you. Not even for a second. He probably already knows you're back."*

There's no questioning her request or asking who "he" is. I knew things would be bad when we returned, but at the same time, I didn't expect days to have passed by either. This is going to be worse than anything I could have imagined.

"We need to run east," I tell the others. "Where did Estee and Theo go?"

Isla's brow tightens. "They needed time alone."

"Well, we don't have any." The words snap out sharper than intended, but I don't take them back. "We've been gone for three days. We need to regroup. Now."

A branch cracks behind us. The faint *thump-thump-thump* of paws slamming over the earth rips through the silence like a warning shot.

"Go. Now!" Julian snarls, just before he shifts.

His wolf explodes forward, bones snapping and reforming in a violent rush of power. He doesn't cry out—it's too fast for that. A deep chocolate wolf replaces him, muscles rippling beneath his sleek coat. He's beautiful and terrifying, but there's no time to admire the view.

I call my wolf forward just as Isla and Asher do. Isla's lets out two quick yips, and three more echo back. That must be her call to Estee.

Julian heads toward the incoming wolves then snaps his jaws at me when I follow, but I'm not going anywhere without him. And since we're not officially bonded yet, he can't yell at me in this form.

Though, he can run.

Now, what is he doing?

He takes off toward the east. The snarls coming from behind us are close, but instead of questioning whether we should stay and fight, having no clue just how outnumbered we might be, I follow Julian.

Isla and Asher are already ahead, and within moments, two more wolves flank us. One is slate grey, the other a midnight black. Theo and Estee.

Julian falls back to run beside me while the others surge forward to lead. Our pack of six tears across the landscape in a blur of pounding paws and beating hearts. The sounds of our pursuers fade, but that only sets me further on edge.

Why aren't they chasing us?

The trees blend together as we cross miles of dense forest and, later, open meadows and sloping hills. Sunlight breaks through the clouds, but there's no warmth in it. Not today.

"Turn north after the river," Clara says, cutting through my thoughts without warning. *"Not long after that, I'll find you."*

I don't know how she's tracking us, but sure enough, the soft rush of water ahead hits my ears. I push harder, passing Theo and Asher until I'm leading the way. My claws dig into the damp earth, propelling me forward faster than I've ever run. And strangely, it's easy.

I'm not tired. Not even winded. Julian's right behind me, his breathing just as steady.

Is this because we were in the god realm? Is this what Aurora's power did to us?

I don't know, but as long as this is the only side effect from our time there, I'll do my best not to question it.

Up ahead, Clara's blonde wolf is standing with another onyx one. They yip then turn left. The six of us follow them, catching up easily but then having to force ourselves to slow so we don't pass them.

The wolves lead us to a mountain base. Clara is the first to shift, her fur retreating in a shimmer of magic as she rises on two feet. She barely waits for me to do the same before she's throwing herself at me.

"Gods, I thought you were dead."

Her hug has my chest warming and my eyes watering. She holds on with everything she has, and I do the same. "I can't be taken down that easily."

My joke falls flat, and when she finally pulls back, she narrows her glassy eyes at me then shoves me back. "What happened to you?" She looks around then does a double take, obviously having seen Julian.

The way her gaze widens makes me chuckle. "Clara, meet Julian. My mate."

"How… When… What?" It's not often my advisor's left speechless, but I'm not surprised now is one of those times.

"Long story," I tell her. "How about you tell us what's going on here since that seems to be the most immediate threat?"

She nods. "Of course."

Noen is right there beside her when she steps back, and he offers me and Julian each a smile. "It's good to have you all back." Then he glances over at the others. "But there's something different about you."

"We were in the god realm," Isla says, her voice quiet but firm.

The sentence settles like fog over the group. Noen looks between us with growing curiosity, but wisely, he doesn't press. Estee pales at the reminder, and her fingers curl into Theo's sleeve as if just saying it aloud brings her closer to unraveling. We don't have time to unpack any of it. Not here. Not yet.

"I assume there are others out here with you?" I ask,

gently shifting the conversation. I gesture toward the mountain behind them, sensing my people near. "We should go meet them. I'm sure they'd like to know that they haven't been abandoned."

Clara grimaces, an apology already forming in her expression. "I had to tell the Venaris pack about Julian to gain their trust," she says, glancing up at him, uncertain. "Noen has been helping me get the truth out. I hope that was okay."

Julian's smile is soft. "Of course. If it kept them safe, it was the right thing to do."

She nods in relief then gestures behind her. "Come on. They'll want to see you for themselves."

Asher's already moving, bringing Isla with him. "Let's go, then."

Our group follows Clara and Noen through a narrow path carved between low shrubs and twisted trees, moving toward the right slope of the mountain. There's a jagged scattering of boulders ahead, as though a blast from above sent them crashing down long ago, sharp edges now softened by moss and time.

Noen climbs the rocks first, scaling them easily before turning to help Clara. He offers her his hand with practiced ease, and she grips it tightly as she pulls herself up and over.

"How far up are we going?" Isla asks, eyeing the steep incline with suspicion.

Noen grins, boyish and unbothered. "We're not. We're going *down*."

And just as he says it, Clara disappears. One second she's slipping over a rock and the next—gone.

Noen stays there, waiting for the rest of us to follow.

We're not exactly wearing proper clothes for this, all

three queens wearing dresses, but we manage, and when I reach Noen, there's nothing but darkness over the rock.

"It's a twenty-foot drop," Noen explains. "There are a few mattresses stacked on top of each other to soften your fall in case you don't land on your feet. Who's first?"

Estee steps forward before anyone can argue. Silent. Focused. She doesn't hesitate, just jumps. Theo follows a heartbeat later, the two of them swallowed by the shadows.

Isla exhales beside me. "I hate this. I hate that I can't fix it."

"They just need time," Asher murmurs, wrapping his arm around her. "We all do."

Noen's eyes flick to them, but Asher gives a small shake of his head, silently asking for space. Noen nods once and backs off.

Together, Isla and Asher take the plunge.

Now it's my turn.

I glance at Julian, a smile tugging at the corner of my lips. "See you at the bottom?"

He leans in, brushing his hand lightly against mine. "Right behind you."

I curl my fingers along the cool stone, resting against a patch of damp, bright green moss. Then, with a steadying breath, I step forward and into the dark.

The fall is quicker than I expect.

My dress flutters violently around me like the wings of a bird in panic, and then…*thud*. I land squarely on the mattress. My knees hold right until the heel of my shoe gives a little wobble, and I teeter back.

A strong hand grabs my elbow before I can fall.

"I got you," Clara says with a soft laugh. "I did the same thing the first time."

"I appreciate it," I say, finding my balance again.

I glance up in time to see Julian drop down with effortless

grace. He lands with a muted sound, knees bent, then straightens in one fluid motion. His eyes find mine instantly, and they flash with something warm and primal—*relief and desire*. As he steps toward me, I realize I haven't truly had a moment to breathe since he was set free. But now?

I'm taking this one.

Noen joins us, but I hardly see him. My stare is fixed on Julian.

For the first time since he was freed, we're no longer running, no longer bleeding. The air here is still, quiet. It's not peace, but it's the closest we've come, and in this fragile sliver of stillness, I feel it: the tether between us thrumming, steady and sure, anchoring me to him.

This is what it means to be mated. To feel the echo of your own heartbeat in someone else's chest.

"Leave us," I tell Clara through mind-speak.

She doesn't question it. Without a word, she guides the others away, their footsteps retreating into the shadows, giving us the one thing we haven't had since this nightmare began: space.

Julian says my name like a vow. "Sloane."

His voice brushes against my skin, softer than the wind, but it hits me like thunder. My pulse stutters. My breath catches.

And then I move.

I step into him, pressing my hands to his chest, palms sliding up over fabric and muscle and heat. His body responds instantly, like he's been waiting, no, *aching* for my touch. I trace the curve of his shoulders, reveling in the strength hidden beneath his quiet resolve, and thread my fingers into his hair, pulling him closer until I can taste the air he breathes.

He cups my face. "I've waited centuries for you."

Emotion swells in my throat, nearly choking me. "You don't have to wait any longer."

I rise onto my toes at the same moment he dips his head. There's no hesitation, no careful preamble. Our mouths meet in a kiss that sears through my soul like wildfire.

It's not gentle. It's ravaging.

He grabs my waist, pulling me flush against him, like he's terrified I might slip away if we're not touching everywhere at once. I part my lips, and he groans low in his throat, deepening the kiss, his tongue brushing mine, coaxing and claiming. My knees threaten to buckle, but his arms tighten around me, holding me steady as his mouth moves over mine with a desperation that feels like salvation.

The world falls away.

There's no war right now. No gods. No death waiting just beyond the next hill.

There's only him. His lips. His breath. His fire.

My fingers tighten in his hair as I kiss him back with everything I have, everything I've lost, and everything I still hope to fight for. My wolf hums in contentment, her joy wrapping around the bond like silk.

When we finally pull apart, it's only by a fraction, our foreheads pressed together, breath mingling in the quiet that follows.

Julian's hands stay on my waist, holding me together as his voice dips low, rough with emotion. "You're everything I never thought I'd have. I don't know how I survived in that hell for so long, but I know every second of loneliness was worth it, for you."

I graze the edge of his jaw with the back of my hand, my chest tightening with the sheer magnitude of him—of *us*. "You have me now. You'll never feel that way again."

He exhales shakily, and for a moment, the silence

between us says more than words ever could. It hums with possibility, with promises unspoken but deeply understood.

"Whatever comes next," he murmurs, "I'm not letting you go."

I rest my hand over his heart, feeling the steady rhythm of it, matching my own. "Good. Because we're not done yet."

His smile is small, but it reaches his eyes, warming something inside me that's been cold for far too long.

"No," he says softly, brushing a thumb across my cheek. "We're just getting started."

We stand there for another breath, suspended in the strength of a bond still forming but already unbreakable.

And for the first time since I realized I couldn't fix Alcaris, I feel like just maybe I'm right where I was always meant to be.

CHAPTER THIRTY

JULIAN

Clara and Noen return to lead us toward the others, but not before I steal a few more kisses from Sloane. Her taste lingers on my lips, sweet, intoxicating, and addicting. Kissing her feels like reclaiming something I never thought I'd get back: my life, my future, my sanity.

Her touch is full of warmth, her skin as soft as I imagine the clouds to be. Everything about Sloane makes my years of torture seem like a distant memory when I have her in my arms. But the time to truly appreciate all of her isn't yet. Not in this underground hideaway.

Or *sanctuary* as Clara calls it while she leads us further beneath the mountain.

Apparently, not everyone believed Aeson when he declared me dead. Some wolves, led by instinct and quiet resistance, never stopped questioning what truly happened back then.

That alone is more than I ever expected.

I thought they would've forgotten me. Or worse, remembered only the lies.

Yet this place, this hidden world carved into the mountain's bones, tells a different story. One of faith. One of survival.

The tunnels are lined with flickering lanterns, their soft glow bouncing across uneven stone walls. Fresh water glides along carved channels in the rock, humming a steady rhythm beneath our feet. Shelves and crates packed with dried food and roots line the walkways, and herbs hang in bunches from ceiling hooks, their earthy scent blending with wolf musk.

Sleeping quarters are tucked into nooks, filled with hay and folded wool blankets. There are signs of children here too. Small drawings etched into the stone and a pair of carved wooden toys tucked beside a sleeping pallet.

This isn't just a refuge.

It's a haven. A hidden heartbeat pulsing beneath the broken kingdom.

Still, my own pulse thrums unevenly in my throat.

They'll recognize me. They'll remember the stories, which include so many lies.

Sloane brushes her hand against mine, a quiet reassurance that keeps my heart from spiraling. One gentle touch, and I remember who I am. Who I've become.

A voice, deep and familiar, breaks the stillness. "Alpha King."

The title strikes like lightning.

I turn, breath stalling.

From the shadows steps a wolf I never thought I'd see again. Silver-haired and standing tall despite the weight of his years, he is still as sharp as a blade's edge.

"Garron," I whisper. The name stirs something within me. He was always more than just a soldier. He was a mentor and a keeper of history and honor. A wolf who fought beside my father, who taught me how to listen before I spoke, how to lead with more than just force.

He's dressed in black now, a blade strapped across each hip, posture straight and ready. Not the keeper of lore any longer. A warrior once more.

"I knew it," he says softly, voice thick with emotion. His pale blue eyes shine with something I don't quite understand—relief, maybe, or even hope. "I knew the truth would find its way back."

I steel myself, unsure what he means. Unsure how much he really knows.

Garron steps closer, gaze flicking over the rest of our group—Sloane, Isla, Asher, Estee, Theo, Clara, and Noen—before returning to me.

"My wolf knew," he says again. "The day you disappeared, the air turned rancid. It was wrong in so many ways. Aeson claimed it was *your* darkness, your betrayal, but my instincts said otherwise. I couldn't prove it. But I never forgot. The young prince I knew wouldn't fall to corruption. Not without a fight."

He gestures to the sanctuary around us.

"So I began preparing. Quietly. Carefully. Waiting for the day you might return. I didn't know if I'd live to see it, but I built this place anyway. For you. For all of us."

Emotion lodges in my throat. Not grief, not fear, but gratitude.

"Thank you," I manage. My voice is lower than I intend, but Garron hears it. "For remembering me when it would've been easier to forget."

He nods once then his expression sobers. "You came back at the right time. Things have grown worse, Prince Julian. Much worse."

Without another word, Garron turns and motions for us

to follow. We trail behind him through another branching tunnel until it opens into a broader chamber. Several wolves look up from the low-burning fires scattered throughout the space, their conversations dying instantly. Suspicion, curiosity, and cautious hope flicker in their eyes.

Garron glances back, catching me observing the other pack members. "They should know the truth. Your truth. Some won't need it, but others will. Especially after what happened when you all vanished three days ago."

"When the runes were destroyed?" Isla asks softly as we pause.

Garron nods solemnly. "The energy across Venaris shifted. Barely noticeable to most, but those of us who pay attention to our instincts, we felt it. Something otherworldly stirred. According to my contacts still inside the castle, Aeson felt it too. He panicked. Believed it was an omen. He called his inner circle, ordered them to prepare for war. But when he couldn't find Sloane…that's when he lost control."

Sloane's jaw tightens, and I reach for her hand, hoping she isn't taking on any guilt. We had no choice in leaving when we did. This isn't her fault.

Garron's lips flatten briefly as if reliving that morning. He turns away to continue walking down the dirt corridor but keeps speaking as we move together. "Aeson demanded the pack to bow before him. He didn't offer an alternative, which we all knew what that meant."

"Obey or die," Sloane mutters and then looks up at me. "My instincts told me he was evil. I felt it in my core, but besides his treatment toward me, I had no proof. It doesn't feel good being right about this."

I hold her tighter, whispering as we walk. "And that's why you're an incredible queen."

Garron continues, "I sent those I trusted most to rescue

as many as we could, but it wasn't easy. Aeson raved about betrayals. Said Sloane was conspiring with the other alphas to destroy Venaris from within. That the unity of kingdoms was a ruse. Most didn't believe it, but fear doesn't require logic. It requires control. So they followed him. Not out of loyalty, but to protect their families."

"How many?" Sloane demands, her grip on my hand nearly enough to crack bones. "How many did you get out before they were given no other options and what's happening to them now?"

"Just over three hundred," he replies stiffly. "But almost two hundred of the pack remain inside the castle grounds. A mix of both packs. Not all of them are trapped there, though most of them are confused. Some believe Aeson. Some think they were abandoned. All of them are divided."

Garron pauses and lowers his voice. "Those not willing to fight now that they're seeing this version of their Alpha King are being restrained, but most of them have agreed to stand by Aeson's side, preparing for a battle."

I grit my teeth, heart pounding. "I need to see the pack."

He lifts a brow as he glances back at me.

"I want to speak to them," I clarify. "The ones who are here. Let them see me. Hear the truth from my own mouth."

Sloane's shoulder rubs against mine as she counters me. "We need to plan first. If Aeson knows we're back, we need to be smart, and the pack needs to feel confident in our next moves. The only way to make sure of that is to have answers for them about what comes next."

Clara speaks up from just behind Sloane. "I've eased the worries of our pack members, and their belief in you is helping to keep the peace for now. Having some sort of hope to give them when you address everyone is good, though. They haven't had much of it in the last three days."

"Let's pause for a moment." Garron turns away from us, guiding the way down the dirt corridor.

This tunnel is darker, tighter. There are no lanterns here, only the distant flicker of firelight at the far end. My wolf doesn't hesitate, his enhanced senses coming to the surface as my eyes adjust quickly. The walls scrape against my arms, the passage narrowing enough that we're forced to turn sideways to continue.

Then the corridor opens into a private room.

It's small but warm. A shallow fire pit crackles at the center, surrounded by four worn chairs. A table rests against one wall, a modest bed tucked into the far corner. Small, hand-painted images line the stone walls. Drawings of moons and wolves, even one with a crown etched in shaky brushstrokes.

Garron has lived here. Not just prepared this space but lived and hoped in it.

Everyone finds a place. Some choose to stand, while the rest settle onto seats. Sloane and I remain together, standing directly across from Garron.

He studies me, the evidence of age and wisdom deep in the creases around his eyes. "You're no longer part of the pack. This could pose a problem. With neither you nor Sloane technically ruling over Venaris, the wolves won't have a connection to you."

"But you're still part of the pack," Asher says from the other side of the fire. "You've earned their respect. Wouldn't they follow your lead?"

Garron tilts his head. "Respect, yes. Loyalty in the face of fear? I can't be certain. Aeson still holds the crown. That alone demands obedience from some."

Sloane's eyes flash with unwavering purpose. "Then we do what we must. I'm still linked to Alcaris, and I'll lead those who will have me. If we do this right, we can reclaim what's been stolen with the least amount of bloodshed."

Their attention shifts to me. All of them waiting for answers I'm not sure I have. I've only just returned. For years, I didn't think I'd survive, let alone lead. I'm not sure what they want from me.

"I'm not your Alpha King," I start, voice rough. "I don't have that power anymore. But I can stand beside Sloane."

Theo's voice cuts in, firm and sure. "That's not enough. You can't hide in her shadow. I tried to do something similar in my pack, and it failed. People don't need perfection, they need the truth and for you to show that *you* care. If you're here to fight for your people, they need to see you, they need to hear you. Not as a ghost from their past, but as the king you were always meant to be."

Hiding wasn't what I had in mind, but I can see his point. If Garron has been able to convince even part of the pack that my return is a good thing, I have to find a way to be the leader I never thought I would be.

"Sloane should still act as the Alpha Queen in charge," I say, knowing my lack of connection to the wolves will be a problem regardless. "But I'll do my part by her side."

She offers me a gentle smile, but there's a tightness in her voice. "I can do that, but your speech to them is what's going to bring everyone together. Aeson has convinced most people that he's the epitome of kindness and strength." Her eyes darken, and I hate that she's been caught in all this. "From the outside looking in, Aeson's done everything right for this kingdom, even for mine by inviting us here. His ulterior motives have either been overlooked or well-hidden. They need to hear what he did from you and decide for themselves what they want to believe."

"I can do that," I say. "I'll share my story, but as Garron

pointed out, I no longer have ties to the pack. Nothing I say will change the fact that I'm not an Alpha King."

"Not yet," Asher cuts in, his tone calm but unwavering. "But you will be. We all sense it." His eyes lock with mine, filled with something between challenge and belief. "I can't imagine what you endured down there, Julian, but at some point, you need to realize this was *always* meant to be yours. You didn't lose it. It was taken. And now, it's yours to reclaim. This kingdom, these wolves, they're all waiting for someone to fight for them, even if some of them don't realize it yet."

His words land with an unexpected force. I feel them dig past the scars and silence I've lived in, right down to the marrow. He's right. I was born to lead—not because of blood or title, but because I never stopped fighting, not even when I had nothing left.

I know I have a long way to go, but I can't allow the past to dictate the future. Long ago, I let Aeson convince me that this wasn't the path I wanted, but I'm not the same man I was before. I can't be. Especially not when so many people are relying on me. I'm the rightful Alpha King, and I'm Sloane's mate. I want to be better for her. For all of them, but mostly her.

She needs someone strong by her side. I need to hold on to the fight I had in that cave, to remember that giving up was never an option before, and once I kill Aeson, my job here is far from over.

My wolf rises to the surface, his strength pulsing through me with approval. This is where we were always meant to be. With our mate, surrounded by other alphas, doing whatever it takes to keep our kingdom from falling.

Clara leans forward, her voice cutting through the silence. "Then I suggest you speak to the pack soon. We'll need them unified before we strike. Tonight, if we can. Every day Aeson rules, the darkness spreads. Whatever he's doing back at the castle isn't just tyranny. It's something worse."

"He's killing his wolf," Estee says softly, startling the room with her first unprompted words since returning to life.

Everyone turns toward her.

Her voice is calm, but her eyes are still shadowed. "When Theo and I were...gone, we weren't together. But I wasn't alone. I spoke with my ancestors. My great-grandmother—an Alpha Queen from the time when dark magic was wielded freely—told me that what Aeson's doing by using those runes is unnatural. He's sacrificing his wolf to remain in control. He needed a strong mate, one as powerful, or even more than himself, to balance out the dark energy he's absorbed. Sloane was the only one known in Lunara without a mate that could do that. An Alpha Queen. She was the perfect choice to balance out the monster he's becoming. Without her, even if we don't kill him, he'll eventually destroy himself."

A sharp gasp escapes Isla, and she moves instinctively to her sister's side.

They share a glance, silent but full of understanding. When Estee continues, her voice wavers. "The more desperate he becomes, the more reckless. Aeson's aware that his time is running out. And that makes him even more dangerous."

I clench my fists. "That doesn't change the outcome. There's only one ending for Aeson, and I'll be the one to give it to him."

Estee nods solemnly. "Just remember, we all have something to lose. He doesn't. That makes him unpredictable. We need to end this quickly. Cleanly."

Looking at Sloane, I know Estee is right. My vengeance

isn't worth losing my mate, but that doesn't mean we can wait him out, either.

"Then we use all our resources." I look at Garron again. "You said you still have wolves within the castle?"

"I do. Soldiers in line to protect Aeson."

Sloane turns toward him. "What about Dasha?"

He raises both brows and shakes his head. "I'm not sure what you heard, but she's Aeson's advisor. She's the last person we want."

"No, she's the first if you can convince her that the risk is worth the consequences. It would be worth reaching out to her through your pack connection and at least trying," Sloane explains. "Her brother is being used as a pawn, but Dasha wants free of Aeson just as much as all of you. I promise you that."

Garron strokes his jaw. "If she's truly an ally, that changes things. I'll send word—quietly. If we can get her, and a few guards on the inside, we stand a real chance."

"How do you plan to take the castle?" Isla asks, arms crossed. "Because we're not walking through the front gates like we're expected."

Garron's smile is thin. "I thought we'd bring him to us."

But when his gaze lingers on Sloane, something primal rises within me. I step between them with a low growl, chest rumbling. "You will *not* use my mate as bait."

"Yes, he will." Sloane's words slice through the air like steel.

I turn to her, stunned.

Her expression is unflinching, fierce. "If it's the only way to draw him out, I'll do it. This isn't just your war, Julian. It's *ours.*"

Her bravery both guts me and strengthens me.

Because she's right.

But that doesn't make it easier to accept.

I know what Garron is thinking the moment he says we should draw Aeson to us. And he's right. This is the best way to cause the fewest casualties for the pack, and I'm the perfect person to lure him. I'm the one prize he's desired, and I've just slipped right through his fingers. If I can convince him he has a chance to get me back, that I think Julian is the real monster here, then we stand a greater chance at ending this nightmare swiftly.

Julian turns toward me, and everything else in the room disappears. His gaze crashes into mine like a wave, filled with emotions too complex to name. I reach for him, taking both his hands in mine. They're shaking, but I hold tighter.

"I spent two centuries in a prison I never deserved," he says, voice low and rough like gravel. "I survived by letting go of everything—hope, revenge, even my purpose—but then you came. I sensed you, and for the first time through all that hell, I remembered who I was. What I wanted."

He pauses, pain etched along the corners of his mouth. "I first tried to keep you at arm's length because I didn't want you hurt. But now that I have you? Putting you in the path of destruction goes against everything in me."

I open my mouth, ready to explain why I have to do this, how I'm not afraid. But he keeps going.

"I see you, Sloane," he says, his palm pressing over my heart. "I feel your strength in the way you speak, in the way you lead, in the way you love. You're a warrior, through and through. Brilliant and terrifying in all the best ways. My fear isn't rooted in doubt. It's in the truth that I'm still learning to accept." He leans closer. "You've become the most important thing in my world in the span of days. After everything I've lost, I can't lose you too."

Tears prick my eyes, but I don't let them fall. "And you won't." I lift his hand from my chest and place a kiss over his knuckles. "You'll be close, all of you. Waiting for the right moment to strike. We have a plan. We know what needs to happen. If Aeson suspects anything, he'll burn everything down just to take one of us with him. We can't risk that kind of devastation for our people."

Julian's expression hardens, but not with anger, with resolve.

"I'll be careful," I tell him. "And I won't risk what we've found. I won't ruin the future we both deserve. I need you to trust me on that."

He presses his forehead to mine, a long breath escaping his lips. His energy is steady now, rooted in the trust we've slowly been building toward since the moment I somehow spirit-walked into the prison-cave.

"I do," he says quietly. "I meant what I told you before. I don't doubt *you*. I know I shouldn't let fear speak louder than truth, and I'll do my best to focus on that because Aeson's already stolen too much from me. I can't give him more by letting it poison what we have."

I nod against him, our bond pulsing warm and strong between us. "We'll finish this."

He lifts his head slightly, eyes fierce now, a storm behind them. "Together."

Someone clears their throat behind me, dragging me back to reality. We're not alone—of course we're not—but I can't bring myself to feel embarrassed. Not after everything we've endured. If these wolves are going to fight beside us, they should know exactly what we're fighting for.

I turn toward them, still gripping Julian's hand. "So," I begin, my voice steady, "the plan is simple. We spend the afternoon preparing. Then I'll leave alone, heading toward the castle. When I start to sense Aeson's guards, I'll stop and call for him. The rest of you will already be ready and waiting. Once the signal is clear, we move."

There's no reason to elaborate on what comes next. Not only because of the many variables we can't prepare for, but because we all know where it leads. Chaos, blood, and our hopeful survival.

I glance over at Estee and Theo. A part of me wants to offer them a way out. They've already walked the edge of death and returned. But the fire in Estee's eyes and the quiet resolve in Theo's expression says enough. Whatever they saw and suffered in the god realm hasn't weakened them. It's strengthened them.

I nod once. I was right to trust them, to trust all of them.

"We'll still need the two of you to speak to the packs," Garron says, pushing himself upright with a wince that betrays more pain than he's let on. "I'll gather everyone into the main cavern. Clara and Noen can guide you there when you're ready."

As he exits his room, the rest of us face one another. A thick silence blankets the space. But it's not from hesitation.

It's resolve. The kind of quiet that settles in right before the storm. We all feel it. The surety of what's coming. The responsibility that we carry not just for ourselves but for every wolf waiting for us to be the leaders they need.

We're not fighting for revenge. We're fighting for peace.

For the kingdom that's been strangled by lies for too long.

"We'll need some time," Asher says, slipping an arm around Isla's waist, "but we won't go far."

Isla gently steps out of his hold and crosses to me. Her embrace is sudden and fierce, her arms wrapping around me with bone-deep warmth. "I wish I'd known you sooner," she murmurs, voice tight with emotion. "But even now, I can say this with certainty. You're the kind of queen we should all aspire to be."

Her words cut through me with unexpected force. I blink fast, pushing back the sting in my eyes, and pull away just enough to meet her gaze. "Thank you, Isla. Truly. And thank you for standing with us. It means more than you know."

She gives a small nod, the glimmer of respect in her eyes unmistakable. "Greed and darkness affect us all," she says before returning to Asher. Together, they slip into the hallway.

Estee steps forward next, her smirk tempered by grief but fierce nonetheless. "What she said," she adds with a shrug. "My sister's always been better at the mushy stuff, but don't worry. My dying in the god realm is no reflection of my skills here. Aeson won't win this fight."

She and Theo follow Isla and Asher, leaving just Clara, Noen, and Julian with me.

Clara looks exhausted. Not physically but soul-deep. Her shoulders are stiff, her mouth tight, and her eyes...haunted.

"I would've argued with you earlier," she says quietly, "but Julian beat me to it." She flicks her gaze to him, assessing. "Be prepared for her stubbornness. And don't be afraid to push back. She needs someone to put her in check at least once a week."

Julian offers a brief grin. "I'll do my best."

Clara gives him a once-over. "I know you will, or I wouldn't trust you with the only family I have left in this world." Her gaze turns lovingly toward Noen. "You're more than family."

He chuckles. "No offense taken."

Clara turns back to us. "Are you ready to speak to the pack?"

I glance up at Julian, and what I see there tells me everything I need to know. He's still worried, possibly even afraid, but he's also healing. He's no longer the man who came out of that cave shaking with barely controlled rage. He's standing tall, eyes steady, with purpose etched into every line of his face.

He squeezes my hand. "Let's do this."

The path to the main chamber winds through several corridors, the stone cool beneath our feet, the air damp and earthy. I feel the pressure from Julian's hand on mine the entire way, steady, firm, and real.

When we step into the wide cavern, over a hundred wolves are already gathered, each of them falling silent as we approach.

Children tucked against parents. Elders gathered near the fire. Warriors and caretakers alike, all staring at Julian and me, their expressions ranging from awe to disbelief to tentative hope.

Julian hesitates beside me for only a breath. Then his spine straightens, and his voice cuts through the hush like a drumbeat. "My name is Julian," he begins. "Some of you know me. Some of you may not. Though by now, you've likely heard whispers. Maybe that I was the prince who died or the traitor who vanished. Either way, it's time for you to know the truth."

The room is still. Tension coils in the air, thick and ready to snap.

"For two centuries, you were told I was dead. That I betrayed the crown. That I turned my back on the pack I once called my family. But that's not what happened." His voice deepens. "I was imprisoned beneath the castle by my own brother. Cursed. Silenced. Forgotten. Aeson did it to keep the throne for himself, and for two hundred years, he ruled with lies. I was nothing more than a memory to him. A threat he intended to leave buried."

A murmur ripples through the pack, several wolves shifting on their feet. Eyes widen. Nods pass between some of the older ones. Garron stands near the edge, his arms crossed, jaw set in grim pride.

Julian reaches for my hand again before continuing. "But I survived. And I've returned to make things right, because it wasn't just my life stolen all those years ago. You might find this hard to believe, and I won't fault you for doubting what I'm about to say, but I do ask you to consider the possibility of it."

I'd forgotten about Lira, but it seems Julian hasn't. I didn't expect him to give the whole truth, but it seems there's no hiding any part of this reprehensible past.

"Aeson will have told you I murdered his mate. That in some jealous rage, I killed Lira. But that's another lie. She witnessed what he did to me, how he chained then cursed me. And for that, she paid with her life. Not by my hand, but by his."

The silence turns taut. Some wolves glance at each other. Others drop their gazes, ashamed or afraid.

"He twisted the truth into a weapon. And he wielded it against all of us." Julian's voice softens. "I'm not here to demand your loyalty. I won't even ask you to fight beside me, but I do ask that you don't stand in my way."

I step forward beside him, letting my voice join his. "I'll be fighting alongside Julian. I know my pack has heard, but for the rest of you, when I arrived here, I began to sense Julian's presence. I didn't know who he was, but once I found him, chained beneath the castle, I knew what I'd found. Not only did I learn that Julian is my mate but why I'd had my own reservations about Aeson."

Murmurs move through the people, but nobody has outright interrupted, so I keep going.

"Your king is good at what he does—convincing others he has only the best intentions—but every decision he makes always connects back to helping him acquire more power. Very little has stood in Aeson's way. He's been patient, calculating, waiting for the moment to execute his plan in becoming the most powerful Alpha King. Which he thought would happen once our packs joined, but that all came to halt once I learned the truth and refused to bend to his will."

My eyes flash up to Julian's. I know he'll ask about my time with Aeson, but that's not information he needs to live with. Neither does the pack need to know.

"I was threatened into submission, and if it wasn't for the alphas from the other packs, I can all but guarantee we wouldn't be standing here of our own free will today. Julian might not ask you all to fight, but I will. While we won't force your hand, especially when we know that your friends and family might be against us, we can certainly ask. I know this has been a lot for all of you, but I promise, as Alpha Queen, my intentions will always lie with the best interest of the pack. I will do whatever it takes to keep you all safe, and I know Julian feels the same."

The voices from the crowd get louder, and we wait them out. There's no rushing their loyalty. Not with so much on the line.

Finally, one sounds louder than the rest. "What's your plan if we agree to join you?"

Julian nods at me to continue, and I meet the gaze of the elder wolf I've yet to meet, along with several others, before I answer.

"I intend to draw Aeson out. Alone. He wants me, that much we all know. If he thinks I've turned my back on Julian and the rest of the alphas, he'll come for me. And when he does, we'll strike. Away from the castle. Away from the innocents."

Julian takes another step closer to the gathered crowd, voice compassionate but steady. "We're not just fighting Aeson. We're fighting for our future. For our children. For a world where no one has to live in fear of the crown."

There's a long silence.

Then someone steps forward. An older woman with silver in her hair, scars along her arms, and fire still in her bright gaze. "I remember you, as many do. While I might not have been among those trying to keep your memory alive, I know what I've seen over the years." She lifts her hand into the air. "If the rest of you think I got these scars because I deserved them, you're just as foolish as our current king." Then, she kneels, one hand over her heart. "I'll fight beside you, Julian, the rightful Alpha King."

A younger man joins her next then two more wolves then five, until the cavern is full of murmured oaths and bowed heads. Not all kneel. Some remain back, conflicted. But they're not shunned. No one is. That's what matters.

Julian nods. "We leave at sundown. For those of you who choose to fight, we'll welcome you. For those who cannot, we understand. We do this for all of you, whether you raise your claws in battle or not."

The crowd breaks into soft movement. A ripple of purpose. A hum of something long dormant now stirring to life.

Hope.

I feel it pulsing in my chest, just like the bond between Julian and me, alive with strength and certainty.

Tonight, everything changes.

CHAPTER THIRTY-TWO

JULIAN

Between Sloane's fierce loyalty, Asher's wisdom, and the voices of the pack echoing with belief instead of suspicion, I finally feel like I can breathe. Like I belong. For the first time in two centuries, I feel whole.

The energy inside the sanctuary is unlike anything I've ever experienced. It hums in the stone, ripples through every word spoken, every footstep taken. These wolves—our wolves—they've endured fear and uncertainty, but they haven't lost their strength. If anything, they've grown wiser in their silence.

And somehow, they've made room for me amongst them.

Aeson spent years convincing me I wasn't meant to lead. That I was too soft. Too impulsive. Too unworthy.

But now, I see how wrong he was.

I want this. The responsibility. The challenge. The honor. I want to be the alpha who protects this pack. I want to be the mate who makes Sloane proud. I want everything I thought I'd never have while locked in darkness, bones aching and soul unraveling.

My wolf stirs within me, no longer silent or fractured,

but alive and powerful. Ever since we left for the god realm, his strength has returned in full, surging through my blood like wildfire. He wants to run desperately, but we have more pressing things to attend to first.

I need Sloane to know how much I appreciate her and believe in her as the Alpha Queen. Not for the first time, I made it seem as though I was questioning her abilities, but that's the furthest thing from the truth. Fear is a powerful beast, and I can't let it rule my emotions any longer. I'm finally free, and I won't be trapped again. Especially not by my own thoughts.

Sloane and I are shown to a small, closed-off alcove carved into the stone. A blanket hangs from the entryway, giving a semblance of privacy.

"We should make rounds with the pack members," Sloane says as soon as we're alone. She's pacing the room, her arms crossed while her light blue gown floats around her ankles and her crown shimmers even in the dim light. "The pack needs to see us. It'll show strength. Unity. They've had too much chaos already—"

"Sloane," I cut in gently.

She pauses, blinking, clearly expecting a strategy question or logistical problem. "What? Did I forget something?"

I step closer, the firelight showcasing the tension in her shoulders. My fingers brush her hand then trail upward until they rest at her jaw.

"No," I murmur, holding her gaze. "But I did."

Her brow furrows slightly until I lean in and press my lips to hers.

It's slow at first. Just a whisper of contact, but then she exhales and melts into me like a dying star collapsing into gravity, and suddenly there's nothing else.

I pull her into my arms and hold her. Her body curves

against mine, her hands tangling in my shirt and her heart beating wildly against my chest, matching mine, like two beats of the same song.

Everything else fades.

The war. The fear. The consequences of tomorrow.

All that matters is this.

Her.

Us.

And the bond between us that not even gods could sever now that I've found her.

Sloane slides her fingers up my chest, curling them around the collar of my shirt as she presses her mouth more firmly to mine. There's hunger in the kiss now, and not just the physical kind, but one born of grief, of longing, of stolen time we can't get back.

I deepen the kiss, cupping her face with both hands as I pour every ounce of my devotion into her. My thumb glides over her cheek, catching the edge of a tear that takes us both by surprise.

"I thought I would never find you," she whispers, her lips brushing mine as she speaks. "I don't want this to ever end."

"It doesn't have to," I say, my forehead resting against hers. "Not for any reason. No one—not Aeson, not fate, not even the gods themselves—can take this from us."

Her eyes close, and when she breathes, it's like she's pulling me into her lungs. Like I'm the air she needs just to keep standing. I kiss her again, softer now, more worshipping than desperate. She sighs against me, her fingers tangling in my hair, holding us both together.

We lose time in each other. Touch, taste, breath, me and her, we're all that exists.

She traces the scar across my back, the one Aeson left when I was just a boy trying to survive, and something in me breaks open. But instead of the usual pain, I'm met with her warmth, her strength, her love woven into every caress.

"Sloane," I murmur, pulling her flush against me. "You remind me I'm still a man. Not just the ghost he tried to turn me into."

She lifts her head, nudging my hair back from my face with a gentle touch. "You could never be a ghost, Julian. I may not have known you before, but seeing how these people believe in you, I have no doubt that you've always been fire. I merely helped you remember how to burn."

My mouth finds hers again, slower, deeper. She melts into me, a soft moan escaping her lips, and I swear I could stay here forever. It doesn't matter that we're in an alcove, barely separated from the rest of the world. In this moment, there's only her and me. Every chance I have to revere her, every stolen second, I'll take. Not out of lust, but reverence. Gratitude. Awe.

And then—

"So, I was thinking that—oh gods!" Clara's voice cuts through the moment like a dull blade as she throws an arm over her eyes and spins back toward the entry. "I'm so sorry. I thought…"

I freeze, unsure how Sloane will react, but she surprises me by laughing softly, curling her arm around my waist and resting her head on my chest like she belongs there.

"It's okay, Clara. You can turn around," she says, her voice tinged with amusement.

There's a long, awkward beat of silence before Clara peeks over her shoulder, her expression caught somewhere between mortified and apologetic. "I didn't mean to interrupt, my queen."

"Really?" Sloane sighs, pulling back just enough to glance

at her. "We've rarely been formal with each other. Don't tell me you're going to start now."

Clara gives a sheepish smile, glancing between us. "I guess not."

"What were you going to tell me?" Sloane asks, her arm still warm around my waist.

Clara shifts uncomfortably, nibbling on the inside of her cheek. "I was just going to suggest we check on Estee. Might be good to ensure she's in the right headspace before we leave tonight."

I let out a slow breath, my grip on Sloane tightening instinctively before I force myself to let go. She straightens, smoothing her dress as she regains that quiet, commanding presence that makes her so damn powerful. So queenly.

"I'll be right there," she says gently.

Clara nods and retreats, the soft sound of her steps fading down the hall.

Sloane turns back to me, a smile blooming across her face like dawn breaking through the shadows. "Later," she promises, her voice a vow.

I step closer, pressing my lips over her forehead. "I'll hold you to that."

And gods help anyone who tries to keep her from me again.

CHAPTER THIRTY-THREE

Clara and I walk in silence, our boots scuffing quietly against the stone as the flickering lanterns cast long, dancing shadows on the cavern walls. We don't speak, but we don't need to. The emotion hanging between us is palpable. Thick with fear, determination, and the kind of understanding that only comes from standing on the edge of something life-altering.

War has a way of stripping everything down to its bones. It shows you what truly matters. And for me, it's not the title I wear or the crown on my head, it's the people who've fought beside me, bled for me. My mate. Clara. My fellow Alpha Queens. These women who were once strangers but have quickly become so much more. Sisters by choice. Warriors bound by shared purpose.

If anything happens to any of them because I made the wrong call, I'm not sure I'll be able to come back from that.

We reach one of the smaller caverns tucked deeper into the mountain. The air is warmer here, infused with the scent of soot and moss, the firelight flickering softly against the worn stone. In the center of the room sits Estee, cross-legged on a thick wool blanket. She's shed the remnants of her regal attire in favor of something practical—a charcoal sweater, black leggings. Her hair's still damp from a wash, pulled into a loose braid over her shoulder.

She doesn't look up when we enter, but I catch the smirk tugging at her lips.

"As wolf shifters, we're not supposed to fear death," she says, voice low but steady. "We're reborn again and again. Endless lives. Endless chances to start over." She finally glances at me, something fierce burning behind her eyes. "But today? That death almost became my last. And I'm so damn pissed about that."

My chest tightens. Not from sadness but recognition. I know that kind of fury. That bone-deep refusal to bow. Estee has been broken, burned, and reforged. And what's before us now is something sharper. Unshakable.

She isn't just surviving. She's becoming.

Isla's seated beside her, legs tucked beneath her, nodding slowly. "We didn't claw our way back from curses and god realms just to lose everything again. Not our mates, not our people, and definitely not each other." She reaches over and clasps her sister's hand.

The moment is quiet but charged, like the stillness of midnight.

Clara and I move deeper into the room. My gaze sweeps over the two of them, assessing, searching. But I don't see hesitation in either of their eyes. Only fire.

Still, the guilt gnaws at me.

"I don't expect you to join us tonight," I say, my voice soft. "You or your mates. You've already done more than anyone could've asked. If you want to sit this out, no one would blame you. I can go—"

"You've got to be kidding me," Isla snaps, her eyes narrowing into lethal slits. "Are you seriously giving us an out? As if we haven't earned the right to stand by your side?"

I open my mouth to argue, but she doesn't let me get a word in.

"No. You listen to me now." Isla pushes to her feet, moving toward me with the grace of a queen and the force of a storm. She grips my shoulders, steadfast and unyielding. "We were all in this the moment your kingdom started to fall. And maybe we didn't come soon enough, but we're here now. And we're not going anywhere."

Her words slam into me with the force of truth, of loyalty you can't demand, only earn.

She holds my gaze, unwavering. "Our kingdoms were never meant to be divided. *We* are Lunara. And when one of us suffers, the rest of us bleed."

Estee moves in right behind Isla, reaching for my hand. And before I know it, I'm wrapped in the arms of two women whose strength has carried kingdoms. Now, they're lending that force to me. Not in strategy or titles, but in something far more powerful.

Sisterhood.

Yet, something's missing.

I reach back without thinking twice, my fingers curling around Clara's wrist and tugging her into the embrace. Because titles don't matter in moments like this. Alpha Queen or not, Clara has stood at my side through every trial, every heartache, every impossible decision. She's fought for me, challenged me, and never once let me fall. She belongs in this circle—always.

She lets out a soft breath of surprise but doesn't hesitate to wrap her arms around us too.

"I don't say this enough," I murmur, my voice rough with

emotion. "But thank you. I needed this. I know what I'm fighting for, but sometimes knowing I don't have to do it alone is the difference between breaking and bending."

"You've never been alone," Clara says gently, her voice steady and sure.

I smile, pressing my forehead briefly against her shoulder. "You're right. But I've done a damn good job of pretending otherwise."

Clara lets out a short laugh. "Please. Like I would've ever let you get away with that for long."

Gods, that woman.

"So," Estee says as we pull back, though none of us move far. Her brows lift and there's a spark of steel in her eyes. "What now?"

I glance down at myself. The hem of my gown is torn and stained with dirt and ash. A symbol of the day's battles. A reminder of the chaos to come.

"Now?" I straighten, meeting their gazes. "Now I find myself something more appropriate to wear and prepare to make myself a target."

"You mean," Clara says with a gleam in her eye, "we need warrior garb."

"Hell yes, we do." Isla grins, turning toward the hall. "Where do we even find something like that around here?"

"I don't know," Clara calls, already halfway out the door, "but I'm going to find out."

I shake my head with a huff of laughter. "You don't have to do everything, Clara—"

"Sloane. Don't." Her smile is as sweet as fresh-picked fruit on a sweltering day. "This is what I do. And serving you? It's been one of the greatest honors of my life. Don't ever take that from me."

My throat tightens, and I manage a small, choked laugh as I nod. "As you wish."

She disappears into the corridor, her light footsteps fading down the stone hall, and I wonder, not for the first time, how I ever would have gotten by without her by my side.

"You're lucky to have her," Estee says quietly, and there's a wistful softness in her voice. "Leaving Isla when I went to Selaris…it nearly broke me. But she found her person to lean on, and I found mine. It doesn't take away from the love we have for each other, but it sure helps keep the world from feeling so heavy."

"There's nothing like the bond between women who truly see each other," Isla agrees, brushing a lock of pinkish hair behind her ear. "We've faced gods, curses, and war to have these lives. But having each other? That's what kept me sane."

"Especially when we all get together and drink too much wine," I add with a smirk.

Estee points at me with a wicked grin. "Now *that's* something we're definitely repeating once this mess is over."

A genuine laugh rises in my throat for the first time all day. That's something to look forward to. Right after I finally claim my mate.

A dull ache blooms in my chest as I think of Julian. No matter how grateful I am that Clara came to get me earlier, I haven't had more than a moment alone with him. And now, that longing is impossible to ignore. It hums beneath my skin like a second pulse, louder, needier, growing with each passing second. I glance toward the door, fighting the very real urge to abandon everything and run to him.

"Look at her," Isla teases, laughter coating her words like honey. "She's already gone for him."

"As if she had a choice," Estee mutters, feigning exasperation before fanning her face dramatically. "Did you see the way he looked at her when they first locked eyes? If I wasn't happily mated, I'd be a little jealous."

"Same," Isla chimes in with a grin. "You're lucky we're both taken, Sloane. Otherwise, you'd have some serious competition for that man."

Their teasing is light, playful—meant in good fun—but my wolf doesn't understand jokes. The possessive part of me surges forward, a guttural growl rising from my throat before I can stop it. "Mine."

Isla and Estee both take a step back, wide-eyed but grinning all the same.

"Easy, girl," Estee says with a smirk. "We were only teasing."

"Maybe we shouldn't joke about that until they've completed the bond," Isla adds, her hands still up in mock surrender.

"I think that would be wise," I mutter, my voice rougher than I intend, my wolf still pacing inside me.

"Sloane?" Julian calls from the corridor.

Estee snickers behind me. "Looks like she's not the only one struggling with control."

I ignore her—lovingly—and stride to the doorway, pulling back the blanket just as Julian reaches it from the other side.

His eyes are wide, searching my face with such intensity that I forget how to breathe for a second. "Are you okay? Did someone...?"

He cuts himself off as he notices Isla and Estee behind me.

"I'm fine," I say, placing both palms against his chest. "We were just talking."

Julian wraps his arms around me, drawing me close. His scent calms the restlessness in my chest. I could stay here forever.

"Okay," he murmurs. "I'll leave you to it then."

"You're not the only one who can't stay away," Asher calls as he stops behind Julian, followed closely by Theo.

The room fills quickly as the men enter to find their mates, arms wrapping around shoulders and gazes full of understanding. Suddenly, the space feels smaller, cozier, charged with something I can't quite name. Unity, maybe. Or simply the calm before the storm.

"You better not be plotting without us," Theo says, pulling Estee into his side.

"Always," she answers with a sly smile then glances around the room. "We should probably make the rounds. Figure out who's standing with us tonight."

I nod, having already been thinking about that earlier. "I'll start with my pack."

"We'll speak with the ones from Venaris," Isla says, her voice softer now. "Let them know that no matter what they choose, they'll have a home, whether in one of our kingdoms or yours."

"And no matter what role they choose to play," Julian adds, surprising even me, "we make it clear that every choice has value. The ones who stay behind will be just as critical. Protecting the vulnerable is just as noble as fighting on the front lines."

I glance up at him, pride blooming in my chest. He might not yet believe himself to be a king, but crown or not, he already is. It doesn't matter if he's spent the last two centuries locked away. His heart is exactly what these people need, and I'm going to make sure he never forgets that.

And as something powerful and unfamiliar settles deep in

my bones—hope, maybe, or a steady kind of determination—
I realize we're standing on the edge of everything.

One final battle.

One last chance.

But this time, we won't face it in fear.

We'll face it together.

CHAPTER THIRTY-FOUR

JULIAN

I've known since the moment Sloane found her way into my prison that I would never survive another day without knowing she was out there somewhere. But the more time we spent together, the more I realized it wasn't enough to simply know she existed. I needed to be beside her. Always.

Still, it wasn't until today, when I sensed her fear while she was with the other queens, that I understood the truth: this isn't just need. Sloane is my reason for breathing. If something were to happen to her, I would cease to exist in that same moment. I know this as surely as I know the sky is blue.

So, when I heard her getting upset earlier, I went to her without question. I had to see her, to feel the heat of her skin under my palms, to root myself in the rhythm of her heartbeat. She may not need saving, but I do. And she does so, again and again.

While I know she's perfectly capable of taking care of herself—gods, more than capable—reminding myself not to suffocate her with my fear is going to be a constant battle.

But as long as she looks at me with that fierce fire in her eyes, that steady belief in who I could still be, then maybe I can become the man she already sees.

Sloane deserves the best parts of me. Not the shadow Aeson carved out of my soul. And definitely not the fear.

So as we move through the crowd of gathered wolves, I walk tall beside her. I speak with confidence, meet eyes when they look at me, offer my hand when it's needed. Because this is my pack too. And if I want them to believe in me, I have to start believing in myself.

We've already spoken to a dozen wolves, many of whom carry old grief or uncertainty in their gazes. Some lost loved ones throughout the decades. Some carry fresh wounds from Aeson's rule. They're quiet but not weak. And they listen. That's more than I expected.

It isn't until we reach two couples standing near the back wall—one of them with a young pup clinging to the mother's leg—that everything truly sinks in.

This fight isn't just about vengeance or future peace. This is about the generations of people to come. Not only those who stand here today, but those who'll come after us. It's about the kind of future we'll leave behind for them based on our decisions today.

"Easton," Sloane greets softly, stepping forward.

The man nods. His mate, a woman with thick curls pulled into a loose braid, keeps a hand on their daughter's back as the child hides against her side.

"My queen," Easton murmurs. Then his gaze slides to me. "And King Julian, I suppose?"

A pause stretches between us before I answer. "Not officially, but hopefully soon."

He runs a hand through his auburn hair, a flicker of a grin ghosting across his face. "Most definitely."

"Julian, Easton is one of my advisors," Sloane informs me. "He's been part of my team for nearly three decades now." She glances at Easton again then at his mate and child, keeping her voice gentle. "And just because of the role you've held, that doesn't mean you need to fight with us. You have a family to consider, and your choice is your own. There will be no judgement from me or anyone else."

Easton wraps an arm around his mate and glances down at their daughter. "I appreciate that because I was nervous to tell you that I wanted to stay behind." His gaze lingers on his mate. "We agreed it would be better to stay here to protect the sanctuary and those unfit for battle."

His eyes meet mine then Sloane's. "But I want you both to know, I've been speaking with all the wolves here, not just the ones from Alcaris, and they agree that not everything is as it should have been in Venaris throughout the years. Aeson has ruled with a command that was merely coated with sugar to appear as if his actions have been for the betterment of the kingdom. As more things are questioned and brought to light, you'll find plenty of people who won't hold what happens tonight against you."

This is equally relieving and heartbreaking. I hate that I was the first to believe his lies and because of my misjudgment, these people have suffered. Maybe not outrightly, but nonetheless, this pack deserved better. I was supposed to be that for them.

While I can't change what's happened over the last two centuries, I can at least do my best for them with every decision I make moving forward.

"Thank you." I reach out and shake his hand. "Your support means more than you know."

"You have ours as well," the man behind them says as he

steps forward with another woman beside him. The man's jaw is tight, his mate standing proudly at his side.

"I'm Callen. This is Ree." The man's stance is firm, his eyes clear. "We were born in Venaris. Loyal to the crown all our lives. But something changed over time. We just didn't know how to name it. The bond with the Alpha, it weakened. Slowly and quietly. Aeson always looked like he was doing the right thing. But it never *felt* right."

Ree lifts her chin. "We stayed because we didn't want to abandon our pack over a feeling we couldn't explain. But now we know better. And we're not standing back anymore."

"I'm sorry," Sloane says gently, "that you were made to feel like settling was your only option. That's not what a pack is meant to be. When Julian takes the crown, wolves will be free to live wherever they choose. You'll never be silenced again."

"That's what we've been hearing whispers of tonight," Callen says. "And with your confirmation, comes ours. We'll fight tonight. For you. For this pack. For the kingdom we could have had and will have again."

"You're sure?" I ask, searching their faces. "We only want those who truly choose this."

"Absolutely," Ree says firmly.

Sloane stands taller beside me, her voice proud. "Then we're honored to have you with us."

We leave them with our gratitude, moving toward the next group. But for the first time since returning to this broken kingdom, I'm beginning to feel like the king Sloane keeps calling me.

I can do this for these people. I can bring them the hope they're searching for.

I glance at Sloane—the woman who freed me, the queen

who refuses to bend—and she looks back at me with something fierce and luminous in her gaze.

"Alpha King suits you," she murmurs.

I lift her hand and press my lips to her knuckles. "Only because you're standing next to me."

She smirks. "Then let's go find the rest of our army."

And this time, we don't just walk forward as warriors preparing for battle.

We walk forward as rulers. Ready to take back our kingdom.

CHAPTER THIRTY-FIVE

Walking among the wolves today is nothing like I imagined it would be. I've done it before, countless times in Alcaris, among my own people. But this is different. These aren't just wolves preparing for a shift in leadership or some change in law. They're wolves ready for war.

Most of them looked at me and Julian as if we're the spark they're clinging to. The one they're choosing to follow straight into the fire. Their eyes tracked us as we moved through the sanctuary. Some were cautious. Others reverent. A few looked as though they hadn't yet decided what to believe, but they're here. That's something. Hell, that's everything because they'll be safer in this mountain than nearer to the castle.

Even now, as we walk toward the room we were shown earlier, I sense the underlying peace, see it in their relaxed shoulders, in the way they nod when we pass. They're ready for what comes next, not because they were ordered, but because they believe in what we're trying to do. In what we're trying to protect.

And yet, every step I take brings the weight of their trust down on my chest. Half of these people are ready to fight, to bleed for their pack, maybe even die, all because I said this was the right thing to do. That's not the kind of responsibility I take lightly.

Julian brushes his hand against mine as we slow to a stop just outside the main cavern again. That simple touch steadies me, tethering me to the moment instead of letting my mind spiral toward what might go wrong. Because right now, we don't have time to fear. Only to act.

As if summoned by the shift in my thoughts, Clara appears, flanked by two younger wolves dragging several large crates behind them. Her blonde braid rests neatly over one shoulder, but her cheeks are flushed with exertion and pride.

"I knew if these people had built all this," she says with a wave of her hand, "they were likely prepared for many scenarios, including war, which means they'd need clothing fit for warriors. Though, I may have had some adjustments done to a few of them while you were busy. Between what they already had and what we could scavenge, I think you'll like what's been put together."

I raise a brow as she unclasps the lid of the first crate and flips it open. Inside, folded neatly and cleaner than I'd expect for having been made underground, are stacks of dark leather and reinforced fabric. Not royal garb, nothing flowy or gilded. No, these are clothes made for battle.

Armored corsets. High-necked, sleeveless tunics with reinforced stitching across the chest and spine. Leggings woven with protective threading and slots for blade sheaths. A belt already prepared with throwing daggers rests beside a set of leather bracers etched with the symbols for three of Lunara's kingdoms.

Clara looks up at me, smile soft. "I thought at least one item should reflect all of you. Not just Alcaris. You're fighting for more than one pack now."

Isla appears over my shoulder and lets out a low whistle. "Now *this* is something I can kick some ass in."

Estee walks in behind her, eyes scanning the crates. "Battle couture. I approve."

Clara pulls out a set from the crate and holds it up to me. "Outfits for all the queens and kings are ready. We didn't know how long we'd have, but there was no way I was sending you into a fight looking like you were headed to a coronation."

I take the clothes from her slowly, the material cool and dense in my hands. "Clara, you went above and beyond with these. You didn't have to do this."

She lifts her chin. "Of course I did. This is what you wear when you go to show the world who the hell is in charge."

I laugh, the sound soft but genuine. "Then I hope you brought boots too."

She grins. "Obviously."

Isla grabs her set next. "Damn, we're going to look terrifying."

"You don't need leather to accomplish that," Estee says with a wink as she runs her fingers down one of the embroidered bracers. "We're not just fighting for our people tonight. We're rewriting what it means to be queens in Lunara."

My gaze meets theirs—Clara's, Estee's, Isla's—and then Julian's, who's watched silently thus far. There's a coiling in my chest, tight and unrelenting. But it isn't fear. It's purpose and gratitude. The unshakable loyalty and love that roots me to this moment.

"We're not just rewriting it," I say, voice low but certain. "We're claiming it."

Isla closes the space between us and pulls me into a fierce embrace. "Damn right we are." She flashes a solemn smile. "I'm going to bring Asher his clothes and get dressed. We'll see you above ground soon?"

I nod, the knot in my stomach drawing tighter. "We leave within the half hour."

Estee steps forward next and wraps her arms around me without a word. We don't need them. I squeeze her back then watch as the two of them move out with the unspoken understanding that the next time we stand side by side, it will be to face our enemies.

Clara eyes the crate again then bends down before tossing items to Julian. "I hope you didn't think we'd left you out." She grins then turns to the two wolves flanking her. "Get the rest of these to the others as quickly as you can."

They move swiftly and without question.

Clara sets her gaze on me, all fire and steel. "Noen and I will also be watching your back tonight."

I open my mouth to object, but she holds a firm hand over my lips.

"Don't even start. You're my queen, and I respect you with every breath in my body, but this is non-negotiable." Her eyes simmer, her voice harder than iron. "I've been beside you through every rise and fall. I'm not stopping now."

She pulls back, and all I can do is smile because she's right. I can't take this from her. If something happened to me, she'd never forgive herself for not having my back. Just as I won't forgive myself if anything happens to her, but we can't live in fear of what might be. That's something she taught me long ago.

"We'll see you soon," I tell her proudly as she picks up the crate to continue passing out clothes.

Julian's at my side the second she turns away. He doesn't speak, just guides me down the corridor toward our room with his hand placed gently on the small of my back. The moment the curtain closes behind us, he takes the clothes from my arms, sets both outfits aside, and without warning, pins me to the wall with a quiet ferocity that steals the breath from my lungs.

His body presses close, his palm cupping my jaw, thumb brushing beneath my bottom lip. "Within the hour, you'll be using yourself as bait," he murmurs, voice rough.

I nod slowly. "It's the only way."

"I hate it," he says, resting his forehead against mine. "But gods, I've never respected anything more than what you're doing today. You're walking into the fire to end this for all of us. For them."

His fingers curl around my hip, anchoring us both.

"I believe in you," he breathes. "But I swear to the moons and the stars above, if something happens to you tonight—"

"It won't," I interrupt, wrapping my arms around his shoulders, pulling him closer. "You'll be right behind me. I'll feel you in every breath, every heartbeat. And when this is over, we'll have more than just these quick moments. We'll have time. All of it."

His kiss is fierce and unyielding. There's no hesitance, no uncertainty. Only fire. Only love.

His mouth moves with a hunger that borders on worshiping, like he's trying to memorize every curve, every sigh, every flicker of warmth. His hands are firm on my waist then they slide upward, curling around my ribs as if he's trying to anchor himself inside the space where my heart beats wildly, only for him.

The kiss deepens, and I surrender fully. My fingers thread through his hair, tugging gently as his body moves closer, heat radiating between us. He tastes like promise, like fire and desperation tangled with devotion. Every brush of his tongue against mine is a vow, unspoken, undeniable.

He holds me like I'm the last breath of air he'll ever take, like I'm his salvation and his ruin all at once. There's almost a hopelessness in the way our mouths meet again and again, like he's terrified of letting go, like he's burning this moment into his soul in case it's the last.

My back presses into the wall and his lips trail down my jaw to the hollow beneath my ear, drawing a shudder from my throat. My nails scrape lightly down the muscles of his back, feeling them tense beneath my touch. The way he holds me—possessive, protective, priceless—makes my heart ache with the depth of everything we haven't yet said.

When we finally pull apart, gasping and trembling, he cradles my face as he brushes his thumbs over my cheekbones like I'm something fragile. All the while, his kiss has just shattered me completely.

"Promise me," he says, voice low and thick with emotion. "Promise me we'll have more than this."

"We will," I vow. "There's no other future I'm willing to accept, or even imagine, now that I've found you."

His forehead rests against mine as he exhales. "Then I'll see you at the end of this. And when it's over, you're mine, Sloane." His voice breaks. "All fucking mine."

"Forever."

We stay like that for a moment longer, two warriors bound by something even war can't tear apart. His touch still lingers on my skin, the phantom warmth of his lips a constant thrum over my own.

Reluctantly, we give each other space to dress for the evening.

I turn my back, focusing on my pile of clothing as I listen to the soft rustle of Julian changing behind me. I know he's undressed, and it takes every ounce of willpower I have not to glance over my shoulder. Because if I do—if I see even one glimpse of the man who makes me ache in ways I never imagined—I'll forget the war outside this cavern. I'll forget the reason we're here. And I'll drag him into bed, this time to have more than just a taste of him.

I'll have Julian when this is over. No distractions. No interruptions. Just us. And that will be perfect because it's what we deserve.

The clothes Clara gave me are simple but powerful. A matte black top made of soft, fitted leather clings to my body like a second skin, sleeveless but high-collared, tailored with intricate silver stitching. The pants are equally fitted, allowing for full range of movement, with thick, reinforced panels along my thighs and calves. A wide belt cinches at my waist, and an elegant sheath for twin daggers rests over my hips. The boots come up to my knees, durable and whisper-quiet, made for a queen who doesn't just rule, but fights.

When I turn around, Julian is already waiting.

And gods, he's breathtaking.

His shirt is a deep, charcoal gray with faint silver embroidery extending along the chest and shoulders. It has short, tight sleeves, revealing the carved strength of his arms, and it's cinched with a dark leather harness across his chest to hold a sword. Black combat pants tuck into worn boots that he's just finished securing. His hair is slightly tousled, eyes glowing with determination and something softer, just for me.

"You look lethal," I tell him as I put on my bracers, tightening them into place.

He steps toward me, gaze sweeping from head to toe. "And you look like a queen even the gods would bow to."

I smirk. "Let's hope that works in our favor tonight."

We leave the room together, footsteps silent on the dirt floor as we retrace the path we took when we first entered the mountain. At the narrow corridor that led us inside, a ladder has been installed, replacing the sheer drop we were forced to jump during our arrival.

Clara waits for us at the base, arms crossed, one brow arched as she watches us approach.

"Convenient," I say, glancing at the ladder. "Would've been nice to have this on the way in."

She smirks. "Where's the fun in that? Consider the jump a bonding experience."

Julian just shakes his head, but I can't help the chuckle that escapes me.

"I'll see you at the rendezvous point," Clara adds, voice quieter now. "We've already sent scouts to clear the outer perimeter. Noen and I will be close."

"Thank you, Clara." I meet her eyes, letting everything I don't have time to say pass silently between us. She nods, and with one last glance at Julian, heads up to the surface.

When we follow suit, the rungs groan, likely from overuse tonight, but hold steady. Once I'm at the top, the cold night air greets me like an old friend, and I pull myself onto the rocky boulders. For a moment, I pause, inhaling deeply. The trees beyond the mountain rustle in the wind. The twin moons glow above. And the ground beneath my feet feels like it's alive, waiting and watching.

Julian is right behind me, and we follow the murmurs to find that there are nearly a hundred wolves waiting for us.

The sight renders me speechless as my heart explodes with appreciation. This fight won't be in vain. We're going to succeed and bring this kingdom back to the glory it always should have had.

Julian grips my hand once more and brushes a kiss over my knuckles. "Come back to me, Sloane. No matter what."

"I will." My voice is soft, but it holds the intensity of my promise.

I give the pack another glance. I see Clara with Isla and Estee, their mates by their sides, each of them dressed as Julian and I are. They meet my gaze and nod approvingly. I consider going to them, but our plan is already set. There are no more reasons to linger.

And this isn't goodbye.

We're not losing tonight.

We're ready for this.

I give Julian another kiss, but this time, I don't let it last. There'll be time for that later. There has to be.

"I'll see you soon."

He nods stiffly. "I'll hold you to that."

Turning my back on him feels wrong. Stepping in the opposite direction, putting space between myself and my mate is unnatural considering what I'm about to do, but I keep going. I don't have a choice. Going forward by myself is the best plan to lure Aeson out, to end this without putting too many innocents at risk.

Once I'm far enough away, I call my wolf forward. She explodes from beneath my skin in a rush of energy and fur, limbs lengthening, senses sharpening. The world turns vivid, every scent and heartbeat pulsing in brilliant detail.

She's tempted to look back but keeps the course. We both know we have a job to do tonight.

We run, wind streaming through our fur, paws pounding

against earth, every muscle moving with purpose. The forest blurs around us. Miles pass, and we don't stop or even slow until my wolf senses others up ahead, coming from the direction of the castle. They're drawing in, just as I knew they would be.

We skid to a halt in the open field that stretches before the last section of forest that leads to the main part of the kingdom. My wolf relinquishes control, and I shift back, my boots landing on cool grass as the wind dances through my hair.

I raise my voice, firm yet filled with vulnerability, a feigned need.

"Aeson! Where are you?"

It's time for me to see just how desperate this *king* is to have me.

CHAPTER THIRTY-SIX

SLOANE

Minutes tick by, slow and heavy. I stand alone at the edge of the field, my breath steady even as the silence thickens around me. The scent of damp earth and distant fire lingers in the air. No more rustling. No birds. No wind. Even the forest feels like it's holding its breath.

I shift my weight, hands loose at my sides, and try not to shake as my fingers twitch with anticipation. In hindsight, maybe the new outfit wasn't the best choice. The warrior's garb that once made me feel invincible might be working against me. It clings to my body like a second skin, showcasing my strength.

I don't look like a damsel calling for her king. I look like an assassin.

"Aeson, we need to talk," I say, projecting my voice just enough to carry beyond the trees. "I know what their plan is. I snuck off once I'd convinced them I would fight with them. I'm here to warn you."

The plan was always to lie my way into the castle, to

create a distraction. It just looks a little different than I anticipated.

I walk forward with my hands up. "I'm not here for a fight."

There's a rustling in the trees, but I keep going.

"It wasn't my choice to leave the castle the other day," I say, keeping as much to the truth as possible. "I was taken against my will—forced into a conflict I never wanted. When we returned, I was going to come straight back to you. I wanted to apologize for our last fight, but Clara called for me. She sounded scared. I couldn't ignore her. You have to understand that."

I'm nearly into the next section of trees, and the silence has returned around me, but not inside my head.

"Lie better," Clara says. *"but not too well. Julian already isn't handling this well. But don't worry. Asher and Theo are keeping a close eye on him."*

I can't even sense them, yet Clara can hear me? I don't know how that's possible, but I do as she requests.

"Listen, Aeson. We both know we were lying to one another before, but let's be honest now." I step into the shadows of the trees. "We knew what we were doing when we signed that treaty. We both had our reasons. Now, it's time for us to remember them and find a way to move forward. You need me to beat Julian. Like I said—"

A figure lunges from the trees. An arm wraps around my waist, a hand slams over my mouth. My body reacts instinctively. I drive my elbow into ribs, stomp down hard on a foot, and slam the back of my head into someone's nose. A grunt of pain follows, but it's quickly drowned out by the thunder of feet behind me.

More come. None of which are Aeson.

He's not even here.

I was wrong. He didn't take the bait.

Gods, I left them for no reason.

Yet, it's too late to go back. I have to figure this out. Most importantly, I have to survive.

There are more men than I can count now, dressed in dark armor, their movements precise and rehearsed. These aren't scouts. These are trained soldiers.

I snarl, ripping an arm free for a moment before two more pile on. I kick, claw, twist. One gets a fist to the jaw, another a knee to the gut. But I don't go for the kill. I hold back just enough to make the struggle real, to sell the ruse because I *want* them to take me.

If I can't bring Aeson to me, I can at least get inside and warn the others what they're walking into. That's better than this part of our plan being a complete failure.

Eventually, one gets a cuff on my wrist. The moment it locks, my strength wavers. Enchanted and not in a good way. I curse beneath my breath as they secure the other wrist then bind my ankles. They lift me off the ground and carry me like a slab of meat.

My wolf snarls beneath my skin, pacing furiously, but we both know the plan. We can't fight. Not yet.

The air shifts as we cross the threshold into the castle walls. My stomach clenches, not from fear but from the sheer *wrongness* that floods the space. The magic here is tainted. The castle has always been cold, but now it feels like it's decaying from the inside out.

They drag me past the courtyard, where I catch sight of the gathering.

Wolves. Dozens of them.

No—hundreds.

A sea of bodies in armor, some pacing, some shifting

restlessly, others swinging weapons. Nearly two hundred. That's what Garron said. And now I see them with my own eyes.

All of them ready for war.

The guards don't slow. I'm shoved through the old servants' passage then dragged into the great hall on the first floor. The room is lit with golden chandeliers, food spread across the long dining table like it's just another feast.

Aeson sits at the head of the table.

He cuts into a thick slab of roasted meat with calculated precision, chewing slowly, like the flavors are the only thing he's interested in savoring tonight.

I'm dropped into a chair, and I breathe a sigh of relief when the cuffs are removed, but it doesn't last long. I'm then bound to my seat with thick rope laced with silver threads. The sting is immediate, but I don't flinch.

Aeson doesn't look up right away. He dabs his mouth with a cloth napkin and finally lifts his gaze to meet mine. Those dark eyes…they're too calm. Too collected.

Like he already knows something I don't. Or at least don't want *him* to know yet.

"You look different," he muses, cutting another piece of meat. "More feral. I like it."

I don't speak.

At the edge of the opulent dining hall, Dasha stands like a statue carved from regret. Her arms are tightly crossed over her chest, jaw clenched so hard I can see the tension from across the room. Her gaze remains fixed on the far wall— anywhere but me. But her silence is its own language.

She's not with him. Not fully. But she's not with me either.

Aeson lounges in his chair as if he's a man at the head of a celebration rather than the edge of a war. The firelight dances off the wine goblet in his hand, casting crimson reflections across the stone table.

"Nothing to say now?" he drawls, voice laced with venomous amusement. "I thought you were here to warn me about Julian."

The way he spits his brother's name like it's a curse he's been choking on for decades sends a ripple of fury through me. My nails curl into my palms, but I force myself to remain still, to play the part.

"Excuse me for second-guessing my decision to do so," I reply coolly, giving just enough edge to my tone. "Considering the warm welcome."

Aeson's gaze slides over the ropes binding me to the chair, and a crooked smile curls his mouth. "You're right, but I didn't take you for stupid, Sloane. Did you really think just because I was willing to fuck you that I'd let you walk in here and threaten everything I've built?"

My stomach twists. Not at the vulgarity, but at how easily he weaponizes the agreement I signed because I was too desperate to see what was right in front of my face.

But even worse is the fact that I did think I could fool him. I thought desperation had made him weak. I thought he wanted me too badly to see through the act.

Clearly, I was wrong.

Still, I lean into the lie one last time.

"The others are bringing a war to your front doors," I say evenly. "They intend to take your crown and dismantle this whole kingdom. Julian tells everyone who will listen that he was wrongfully accused, but there's a darkness in him. The others have passed it off as anger, but something about him isn't right. Why did you have him trapped beneath the castle? Why not just kill him?"

Aeson's smirk deepens, his fingers steepling beneath his

chin. "Because killing him would've been a waste. Death is too easy. But also interesting that you mention his *darkness* to me of all people," he says, standing slowly. "You didn't sense it with me. Did you even try? Or were you too busy falling for the monster you thought you could tame?"

What does this man think he knows about what I've been up to?

Clara's voice brushes through my mind. *"Noen and I, plus one of the Venaris wolves, are near the castle. Are you okay?"*

"For now."

"Be careful," she warns. *"We were already attacked. We have no clue what Aeson and his people do or don't know."*

I grit my teeth and adjust my strategy.

I meet Aeson's gaze and let my voice harden. "I didn't think you were a threat. You were a means to an end. I came to be Queen of Venaris. You were just the steppingstone. Julian, on the other hand, he's reckless. Dangerous, even. I kept my eye on him because he didn't bother hiding his intentions."

Aeson laughs. It echoes around the chamber, hollow and sharp. "Oh, Sloane. You'll say anything to get what you want, won't you?" He leans across the table, his eyes gleaming with sick delight. "I wonder what you'd *do* to get what you want."

Clara again: *"He knows, Sloane. He knows Julian is your mate."*

A chill pierces my spine. I've walked into the lion's mouth.

"Dasha finally responded to Garron," Clara continues, her voice clipped. *"She said for you to get out. Aeson's plan is to force the bond. To mate you and lock you away like he did Julian."*

And still, I don't move as Aeson inches closer.

"Are you finally piecing things together, my queen?" He gets up and comes to me, stroking my cheek with the back of his hand. "I've always gotten what I wanted, and nothing will change that. Not you, not my brother, and not the ninety-eight wolves you have left to fight against my army."

He lowers and takes a deep breath at my neck, a low moan coming from the back of his throat. "Hmm, maybe you're smarter than I gave you credit for. You didn't fuck my brother the first chance you got. Maybe I can reward you just a little."

Aeson grabs my chin and smashes his mouth onto mine. It's not a kiss. It's a violation. Acid poured over my lips. His tongue forces its way past my teeth, and I jerk, trying to wrench away. Rage explodes behind my eyes, and I do the only thing I can.

I drive my forehead straight into his nose.

The crack is satisfying. Blood spurts down his face as he stumbles back, clutching his nose.

"You bitch," he snarls.

I smile, wild and unbroken. "Yeah. I might be. But I'll never be yours."

Energy builds within me like a storm caught in a bottle. My wolf thrashes against the confines of my skin, her energy clawing at the ropes that bind me. She's seething—wild and primal—and there's no magic strong enough to keep her caged when her fury ignites.

Then it happens.

The shift comes fast and hot, fire coursing through every vein as my body gives way to the beast inside. The magical bindings crackle then snap with a sound like dried branches underfoot. The ropes disintegrate into ash. My wolf surges forward, free and vicious.

I waste no time. My vision locks on Aeson, and we strike.

Our aim is true, my claws directly in line with his throat, but he's ready. He lifts his arm to block, and we slice into flesh, just not where I was hoping. For the briefest moment, I feel victory.

But then…

His blood hits my paw like boiling oil. He's become his own personal brand of poison.

He laughs, the sound a bitter symphony of pleasure and madness. "Haven't you learned by now?" he taunts, voice reverberating like a curse. "I'm not the same man I used to be."

I circle him warily, my wolf wounded but not broken. We'll recover, but we'll have to be smart about it.

The burning stops before it reaches my flank, and we can put some pressure on that leg, just not enough to charge forward aggressively a second time.

Aeson saunters toward me like he doesn't have a care in the world. "Are you understanding yet, my queen? Can you see how this ends yet?"

I'd rather be dead than his queen, but something tells me my death isn't his goal. At least not yet.

Moving as swiftly as I can, I lunge for him once again with jaws snapping. I go low, aiming for the flesh of his thigh, but he's faster than I expect for someone filled with toxins.

He dodges, seeming unconcerned that his wounded arm is still dripping, not healing as it would for a normal wolf. There's something unholy holding him together. It's not adrenaline. It's not instinct.

It's dark magic. Just as Estee warned.

Aeson shoves me back, and I skid across the floor, my claws scraping stone as I slow my momentum.

He comes for me again, the grin of a devil on his face as he raises his bloodied hand. Before I can react, he wipes two fingers across my right eye.

The effect is immediate.

Agony erupts through my wolf's head as the darkness soaks into my vision. My right eye goes blind. We howl in pain. I stumble, thrashing. For a terrifying moment, the world is lopsided. Sight and shadow merge, and I can't tell up from down.

"Shift!"

I hear the word, and I can't tell where it comes from or who said it, but I listen anyway before the poison can reach my brain, ending all this before it's even truly begun.

I change back, the magic from the transformation covers my body, slowing the shift. Its warmth seeps into me as if cleansing my body. By the time I'm on two feet again—well, on my knees—the burning has subsided, but my vision is still blurry in the right eye.

I clutch my face, fresh blood on my cheek that feels like tar. Is this my own or Aeson's? I reach for the tablecloth, yanking it toward my face even as dishes crash on the floor, and wipe furiously and just when I think I might be okay, a shadow falls over me.

"You didn't really think I'd let you touch me without consequence, did you?" Aeson taunts, his voice low and nearly as sharp as the blade he draws from his suitcoat pocket.

It gleams silver under the golden light, and I feel his intent.

My life is no longer safe.

He means to end me. Now.

He stalks closer, slowly, savoring it.

Then—

"Don't!" Dasha's voice shatters the tension like a lightning bolt. She's moving, fast and desperate, her hand clamping around his wrist. Her fingers shake, but they hold. "You *need* her, Aeson. If you kill her, you destroy yourself. You said it yourself. You needed her to balance…"

Aeson's glare is enough to have her words trailing off as he replies. "I don't *need* anyone."

His arm moves in a blur.

I think it's meant for me, but then the dagger slices clean through Dasha's throat.

Time stops.

A choked gasp escapes her lips, blood spilling down her chest in a crimson arc. Her body falls forward onto the table, her lifeblood soaking into the feast below. It splashes against my skin, hot and metallic.

"No!" I scream, lunging forward.

But it's too late.

Aeson steps past her without a second glance, the blade still gleaming in his hand, his steps soaked in the gore of the only ally I had within these walls.

Behind him, her body slumps from the table to the floor, lifeless.

In the silent seconds that follow, I think this is all but over, that I've lost, failing my mate, my pack, everyone…but then the howls begin.

Distant, at first, but quickly coming closer. Growing louder. Dozens of voices in unison. War cries.

My heart leaps at the sound, but it sinks just as quickly.

Because I know what Aeson is thinking. I see it in the way his grin returns.

They're too far to get to me in time.

"Don't let those sounds fool you." His smile widens. "I'm not done with you yet."

He raises the dagger again, eyes glowing with something inhuman. Something sinister and made from darkness.

He has nothing left to fear.

I brace myself, knowing I have to do something. Quickly. Not only to keep the fight going but to survive.

Because my pack is coming, and they need me just as much as I need them.

I just have to live long enough for them to find me.

CHAPTER THIRTY-SEVEN

JULIAN

Watching Sloane walk away from me, down that shadowed path that led to the unknown, was the hardest thing I've ever done. She didn't look back, and I understood. Because if she had, I might've broken. I might've chased her down and refused to let her go.

But that's not what she needed.

She needed me to believe in her. To trust that she could finish what she started. So I did.

Until the attack.

It came like lightning. A scream, a spray of blood and chaos.

Five of our wolves fell before we even had time to react. They never saw it coming. And that's when I knew— someone among us had warned Aeson. We had a traitor. Our carefully constructed plan shattered in an instant.

There was no time left to stall.

We had to move.

Asher, Theo, and I regroup first. We pull back from the others, give orders, pivot where necessary, and within minutes, we launch into formation. This isn't just a battle anymore. It might be a rescue, and I won't leave Sloane waiting.

My mate is inside that castle, and I can feel her pain.

Not in vague terms, not metaphorically. I *feel* it. A sharp crack in my chest like something had seared right through to my heart. My mate is hurt. And every second we wait, the pain only deepens.

So I run.

I lead the charge with a roar that rattles through the trees. Claws pound earth. Teeth bared. Every wolf at my side follows without hesitation, our intentions set on tearing the castle gates off their hinges, on burning down the walls and everything within.

Most importantly, I won't stop until Sloane is safe in my arms again.

As one pack, we run through the terrain with unstoppable efficiency. I expect another attack before we get to the castle, but it seems Aeson is keeping the rest of his warriors close, meaning this fight won't be spread out. It will be like a bomb detonating once we get there.

Moving through the last section of forest, I sense the dark energy soaking these woods, growing heavier the further we go. My wolf bristles, but the darkness doesn't slow us down. We have a mission to execute and nothing will stop us. Not even the horde of wolves awaiting us when we break through the woods.

Most of Aeson's pack has shifted, their massive forms weaving in and out of the battle like shadows with teeth. But a dozen remain at the rear, still in human form, lined up in formation, bows raised and glinting with deadly metal at the tips.

As we surge forward, the hiss of arrows slices through the

sky. Most miss, embedding into stone and earth, but the ones that strike—gods, they strike hard.

A yelp tears through the air a few wolves down from me. One of ours collapses, an arrow lodged in his flank. It shouldn't be fatal. It shouldn't drop him like that. But he falls instantly, thrashing wildly, foam already bubbling from his lips.

Poison.

The fury in me surges, burning white-hot.

With a snarl, I barrel forward faster. The battlefield becomes a storm. Claws raking flesh, howls cutting through the air, the stench of blood thickening with every heartbeat. I dodge another arrow, my wolf twisting mid-run. The archer that fired it won't get another chance.

But before I can reach him, another wolf blocks my path. Midnight fur, silver eyes wide as we crash together. His teeth snap for my throat, but he's trembling. I feel it in the way his body shudders beneath mine. Even his movements are almost hesitant.

This one doesn't want to be here.

He's not fighting for a cause. He's following a forced command.

I pin him, my claws digging into the soft flesh near his neck. Not enough to kill, just enough to warn. My growl vibrates through him, a low, savage sound that says: don't move again.

He doesn't.

I shift my weight then slam my shoulder into his side, breaking a rib, maybe two. He lets out a pained whine, but remains still, his muzzle pressed to the dirt in surrender.

Good. I don't want to kill wolves like him.

Once I feel certain he's going to stay down, I walk away,

prepared for the next attacker, but it's not a foe who joins me.

Garron's at my side, glancing between me and the fallen wolf. He nods as if he understands. Some of these wolves aren't fighting out of loyalty. They're fighting out of fear, and that doesn't deserve a death sentence.

Up ahead, Estee rips through a shifter twice her size with a precision that borders on brutal elegance. Isla fights at her back, but in her human form for now. There's fire in her eyes, her blades twin streaks of silver slashing through the chaos.

Asher's growl echoes loudly above the cacophony as he takes down a pair of wolves with a single leap. Theo's close behind him, fangs at the ready to finish the kill, dripping crimson.

Still, I can't take the time to see who's fallen, who's still standing, who's bleeding, and who's still breathing. I am not their savior today.

Not yet.

My wolf surges inside me, our bond with Sloane like a beacon through the noise and fire. We can feel her—distant but not gone. Hurt but not broken. We just have to reach her.

Snarling, I charge forward again, no hesitation in my limbs, no fear left in my bones.

My mate is in that castle. And no force, no poison, no army will keep me from her.

I'm nearly there. I can feel her thrumming through our bond, flickering with pain and fury and something I can't quite name. But it draws me like gravity.

Until something slams into me from the side.

The impact is jarring. Bone meeting bone. Claws raking across my flank, hot blood spilling in seconds.

I roll with it, instincts honed to the edge. We crash to the earth, snarling, snapping, a blur of fur and violence.

The wolf on top of me is nearly my size, dark red fur already matted with blood, none of it seeming to be his own. His eyes are wild. Not frightened like some of the others. This one is here to kill.

I twist, trying to throw him, but he's strong, his claws finding purchase along my shoulder once more. Pain blooms, sharp and brutal. He bites down toward my throat.

I rear back and slam my skull into his jaw. The crack echoes in my ears.

He yelps, but only for a second before lunging again. This time, I'm ready. I sink my fangs into the side of his neck, not deep enough to kill, but close.

He bucks, blood flying in droplets between us.

We grapple, a dance of rage and dominance, claws tearing at flesh, fur soaked and slick. My vision narrows, the world reduced to crimson and instinct. He catches my leg, biting down hard. I roar and slam him to the ground, both paws on his chest.

This time, I don't hesitate.

I rip into him with all the ferocity I've held back.

My claws sink deep. My teeth clamp around his shoulder, and I *pull*, tearing tendons and muscle in a spray of blood and raw power. He snarls and fights back, but it's a desperate thing now. I overpower him, every ounce of my strength thrown into this one kill.

Because this one won't stop. Not unless I end him.

With a final lunge, I slam him to the earth again, this time hard enough that bone gives way beneath me. His bellow is cut short as he goes still.

Panting, blood dripping from my jaws, I back away.

He doesn't rise. He won't ever again.

My heart is thundering, my limbs screaming, but I don't stop.

We might be facing hell out here, but Sloane is too, and she's facing it alone.

I lift my head to the sky and release a howl so raw, so furious, it could tear the stars apart. The sound rips from deep within my chest, shaking the earth of the broken kingdom I once called home.

And then I run.

The entry to the castle looms ahead, tall and silent, thick with shadows. I should shift back to open the door like a sane man. But I'm far past that. What I feel now is rage and fear and love so all-consuming it pushes past pain, past exhaustion and logic.

My paws slam against the stone, claws digging in. I don't hesitate.

With a vibrating growl, I hurl myself forward and crash into the wooden doors, shredding them like paper. The hinges scream. The wood groans. And then the entry gives way beneath me, and I explode into the castle like a storm.

Fog clings to the floor, thick and laced with something dark and wrong. The scent of magic slams into me—decay, sulfur, and something sweet like spoiled fruit. But worse than that is the blood.

So much blood.

It paints the floor in uneven streaks. A metallic tang lingers like a veil. I skid on slick stone, scrambling to stay upright.

Gods, what has my brother done?

Sloane's scent hits me next. It's faint and laced with pain.

A snarl tears from my throat. My wolf surges, wrath and

desperation driving every muscle in my body as I leap forward and chase the trail. I scan the staircase ahead, assuming Aeson dragged her back to his private chambers. But my wolf veers hard right, snarling low, a guttural sound of instinct and certainty.

One hallway. Then another, longer corridor that stretches like a vein straight into the castle's poisoned heart.

The trace of my mate sharpens. Not just Sloane's—Aeson's too. And something else…

Death.

My chest tightens, a primal warning echoing in my bones. I push harder, paws tearing against the marble, breath ragged with the burden of fear.

And then I hear it. Sloane's roar of determination. She's still fighting back.

I'm coming for you.

I round the final turn, my wolf taking charge, tearing into the wooden floors as he goes. We enter a formal dining room, but the opulence has been stripped away by the spray of crimson over the table and the dead body at Aeson's feet.

It isn't my Sloane.

Instead, my mate is on her knees, blood streaking down her temple, trying to rise. Aeson towers over her, dagger raised, its blade glinting with something dark.

I don't think. I don't breathe. I leap.

My wolf crashes into him with bone-breaking force. The sound of his body slamming into the stone floor is satisfying, but too quickly, I feel it.

A sting between my ribs. The blade.

Aeson's dagger has found its mark.

Sloane's scream splits the air. "Julian!"

I stumble, legs buckling. Heat flares through my veins,

followed by a cold that feels like it's eating me from the inside out.

I've charged into danger, and instead of saving my mate, I might have just killed us both because whatever poison was on those arrows...

I have no doubt it's on this dagger as well.

CHAPTER THIRTY-EIGHT

JULIAN

Pain explodes through my ribs the second I land, white-hot and blinding. The blade buried deep in my side is more than just steel. It sears like it's been forged in hell, eating into muscle, flooding my system with poison. My body convulses, and for a moment, everything blurs.

Sloane's scream cleaves through the chaos. "Julian! Shift, shift now!"

My wolf's already clawing forward, frantic to protect her, but the agony anchors me, dragging me beneath the pressure of the wound. The air burns in my lungs. My limbs tremble. I can feel the poison racing toward my heart.

"Ah, this is better than I could have planned." Aeson sneers, moving out from beneath me, his movements quick despite the blood dripping from his side. He goes to Sloane before she can get away and grabs her by the back of the neck, wrenching her forward so her uninjured eye has no choice but to look. "You'll get to watch each other die."

No, she fucking won't.

A growl tears from my throat. I force myself upright with

a roar of defiance, eyes rolling back as I call on the power that I know is still within me. I didn't survive two hundred years locked in hell just to die now.

The shift crashes into me like a tidal wave. The pain should be too much, it should shred me apart, but instead it becomes fuel. The world slows, stutters, then flashes gold.

Not just any gold.

Her gold.

Aurora's energy flares through my veins, unfamiliar yet undeniably mine. Not just power. Not just healing. Something wilder, forged only in the realm of gods. It doesn't erase the pain, but it elevates it, turning this agony into something I can wield.

My body starts to slowly mend, and when I stand, I'm not just a man. I'm Alpha King.

Bloodied, burning, alive, and beyond furious.

Across the room, Aeson freezes mid-taunt. His blade is still slick with my blood, his smirk faltering as his eyes widen slightly. "So she gave you a parting gift," he says, his voice a low rasp. "It won't save you…or her."

He lunges for Sloane, dagger flashing.

But she's faster. A shard of glass clutched tightly in her palm slams into his thigh. It sinks in with a sickening crunch. Her own hand bleeds from the force, but she doesn't flinch.

She jerks the fragment free, flinging it across the room, and scrambles to her feet. Her eye is wounded, blood painting the skin beneath it, but her resolve burns hotter than ever.

She reaches me and presses her palm to my chest. "His blood is toxic," she warns breathlessly. "Be careful."

I want to embrace her, but we don't have time.

Aeson snarls at us. "You can't beat me. Not after all I've sacrificed."

He stalks toward us, uncaring that his pants are soaked with his own blood.

The room dims around him, as if the shadows are reacting to his voice.

"We're not afraid of your sacrifices," I growl. "Not even of what they've turned you into."

Sloane pulls the young woman out of the way, dragging her further from the fight. I don't remember her, but she clearly means something to my mate. I hope her death was quick and not painful.

Sloane meets my gaze, our eyes locking for half a heartbeat. There's no goodbye in them. Only war.

I turn away and back to my brother, hopefully for the last time.

"You couldn't just die in that basement," Aeson snarls through gritted teeth, dagger still gripped tightly in his crimson-slicked hand. His voice is venom, each syllable laced with decades of resentment and twisted pride.

I draw both my blades from where they're sheathed at my sides. They aren't coated in poison. They don't need to be. These were forged for war, and tonight, they'll taste the blood of a tyrant.

"I didn't die there," I say, voice low and lethal. "And I'm not dying tonight."

I lunge.

My right blade slices across his wrist, a perfect arc of motion honed by rage and instinct. Steel meets tendon with a sickening snap. Aeson howls as his dagger drops, clattering across the marble floor. I kick it away, the force driving my balance off, and for one critical heartbeat, my side is exposed.

He takes full advantage.

His fist slams into my ribs like a battering ram. Bone

crunches. The breath leaves my lungs in a guttural gasp. I stagger, pain flaring, but I don't fall. Not now.

We lock eyes right before we explode on each other.

We fight like gods damned to earth, ancient and furious. Knuckles slam into jaws. Knees into ribs. Our bodies collide with a violence that shakes the room. We spin, fists flying, blood spraying the walls. I catch his shoulder with one blade, carving deep, but his knee connects with my sternum in response.

We crash into the dining table, plates shattered as the wood beneath us begins to splinter from our combined weight until it finally crumbles. A wave of broken glass gets sent across the stone floor and Sloane jerks back just in time to avoid the flying debris.

She takes a step toward us, fire in her eyes, like she means to finish this at my side. But I raise a bloodied hand to stop her. Not yet. Not this part.

I can't imagine that Aeson was the epitome of a gentleman to her, but he trapped me. He stole my life.

Now, I'm going to steal his.

"You were never meant to rule!" he roars, spitting blood. His next punch slams into my gut like a hammer. I grunt, doubling slightly, my legs buckling from the pressure as he continues. "You're weak and soft. You would've crumbled the second the crown touched your head."

I lift my gaze and snarl, "Maybe. But I'd rather crumble with honor than stand tall with corruption in my soul."

There's so much blood on me that not all of it can be mine, but my skin isn't burning as I would have expected after Sloane's warning. I don't know if that's because of the god energy I sensed earlier or something else; either way, I don't let the realization distract me for long.

I drive my blade into his side.

It sinks in halfway before he jerks back, black blood pouring down his torso like tar. He screams, and it fuels me, even as my arms tremble with exhaustion. I keep going.

"You've tarnished everything you've touched," I growl, swinging my left fist hard into his jaw. "Since the moment you tasted power, you've destroyed everyone who trusted you, including Venaris."

He bellows and surges forward, headbutting me with enough force to snap something in my nose. Warm blood gushes down my face, into my mouth.

Then he moves faster than I expect.

From his boot, he draws a second blade, sleek, short, and jagged. He switches it to his uninjured hand, and the dagger arcs through the air like lightning.

I try to step back, but I'm not quick enough.

The blade plunges deep into my thigh, burying itself to the hilt.

I cry out and collapse to one knee, the force of the hit cutting my breath short. My vision blurs and my muscles seize. Pain consumes every part of me, turning the world red.

Aeson stands over me, panting, bleeding, and grinning. "I didn't destroy this kingdom. *I* made this kingdom. I *am* Venaris." He stares down at me and laughs. The sound is low and breathless but triumphant. "That's more like it. Get down where you belong, *brother*."

I breathe through the pain, my pulse hammering in my ears, the copper sting of blood everywhere. I close my hand around the dagger in my leg, but I can't pull it free quickly enough to use against him.

My gaze lifts and finds Sloane's.

She's still bloodied and bruised, but her eye looks as though it's already starting to heal on its own. She trembles with unleashed fury, every part of her seeming to burn with a fire that refuses to die.

"No." Her attention falls on Aeson, her voice sharp as nails behind him. "You're exactly what we tried to destroy in the Great War. You're what we were supposed to evolve past."

Aeson's head snaps toward her, distracted just for a fraction of a second. That's all she needs.

With a savage cry, Sloane snatches a jagged piece of the splintered dining table and hurls it like a spear. It spins once, twice, before slicing into Aeson's shoulder with enough force to knock him off-balance.

He snarls, stumbling, but doesn't fall.

As he works to get the wood out, I succeed in freeing the knife from my leg.

I expect to see Sloane moving forward, intent on finishing the job herself, knowing that I'm hurt, but she stays back and nods at me as I stand.

She's giving this moment to me and me alone.

Agony nearly blinds me as I walk, but I welcome the pain, determined to use it as a weapon, especially once I notice the newest wound is clean. That last dagger wasn't cursed like the others.

I launch forward, every ounce of my strength focused on the single objective I've carried for two centuries—*kill him.*

I've pictured this moment every day that I was locked away, imagined a million ways to end him. It never mattered how I did it. Just as long as it was done.

Aeson barely raises his arms before I slam into him, blade first. It drives upward into the soft space beneath his ribs, tearing into his gut, deep and final.

He gasps, but I'm not done.

I slam him back, his spine crashing against the stone wall

with a sickening crack. My hand finds his throat, the other still clenched around the dagger's hilt. He thrashes, but I pin him there, keeping him helpless, choking, and cornered.

Black blood seeps from his mouth and pours from the wound, dripping down in rivulets that sizzle against the floor, eating into the stone like acid.

I twist the blade harder.

"This," I snarl, inches from his face, "is for my pack. For every wolf you made kneel and every lie you told. For every future you stole, including mine."

His hands claw at my arms, fingers shaking, lips moving without sound, but none of it penetrates my ire.

"And this…" I lean closer, meeting the madness in his eyes with some of my own. "This is for *my* mate."

I twist again until I feel the crack of something deep inside him. A bone, or maybe his heart. Either way, it's final.

Aeson's eyes widen. He gurgles. Blood spills from his mouth, hot and foul. His legs kick once. Twice. Then nothing. Only then do I release him.

His body slides down the wall, smearing black across the stone before crumpling in a heap. A worthless, ruined shell of a corpse, one who was once a power, unmade by the very truth he tried to bury.

Silence descends like fog, heavy and absolute.

I sway, my body buckling, and crash down beside his fallen form. The blade clatters from my grasp. My breaths come fast and ragged, blood pouring from too many wounds to count.

But I'm alive.

And more importantly, so is she.

Sloane's at my side before I can even think to reach for her. She drops to her knees, arms wrapping around me, cradling my face in her hands. Her skin is warm, her heartbeat a thunderous echo that grounds me in the here and now.

"You did it," she whispers. Her voice shakes with exhaustion, disbelief, and even awe.

I don't know if she means killing him or surviving it.

Maybe both.

Either way, I let my forehead drop to hers, blood and sweat mingling, the fire of war still crackling outside the castle walls.

And I hold on because we're not just survivors.

We're the beginning of something new.

Though, our job here isn't done.

CHAPTER THIRTY-NINE

SLOANE

Standing back and letting Julian face Aeson alone was one of the hardest things I've ever done. Every instinct screamed at me to intervene, to protect him, to fight beside him. But this wasn't just a battle. It was a reckoning. A full-circle moment only my mate could claim.

Aeson had imprisoned him, broken him, and stolen two centuries from him. Ending his brother wasn't just justice. It was survival and reclamation.

All I could do was give Julian the space to take it back. Getting to stab that bastard myself was satisfying enough for me.

Even now that it's all over, I still feel the echo of Julian's final strike in my head. I still hear the crack of bone, the wet choke of that final breath, and the silence that followed. Heavy with everything we've lost and everything we now hope to build.

I get Julian up and away from Aeson's tainted corpse, helping him down the corridor one agonizing step at a time. He's bloody and barely upright, and I'm ready to take him to the first empty chamber I can find to let him rest for a few hours before we face whatever comes next.

But Julian has other plans.

"Do you have anything in this castle that's important to you?" he asks, voice hoarse but laced with purpose as we make it to the landing.

"Nothing that's not replaceable," I answer, realizing I'd yet to bring anything of true value here from Alcaris.

He stops at the end of the corridor, blood dripping from his fingertips, and turns toward me. "Good."

My brows lift. "Julian, what are you going to do?"

"I'm going to burn this place to the fucking ground," he growls, jaw tight. "With Aeson still inside. He doesn't get a funeral, no proper burial ceremony. Not even as Alpha King."

I should feel something, give some sort of pause, but I don't.

He's right. Aeson doesn't deserve firelight and reverence. He deserves to rot in the belly of his broken kingdom.

"As he shouldn't." Though, I do hold some reservations because Julian needs to know. "But we'll have nowhere else to go. My kingdom...it's not sustainable. That's the only reason I was here."

He halts, his hands rising to cup my face gently as if I were made of moonlight.

"Sloane," he says, voice thick with emotion. "We don't need this castle. We don't need a throne made of stone and lies. We'll build a new one. In the forest, in the dirt, in the stars—I don't care where, as long as I have you."

His eyes flick around the hallway, the blackened walls humming with the remnants of twisted magic and everything Aeson corrupted.

"This place is evil," he mutters. "And I won't let it have you or us. You deserve better."

I press my forehead to his, tears stinging the edges of my vision. "*We* deserve better."

He kisses me passionately, a promise in the shape of lips, then he whispers, "So let's burn it all down."

A strange thrill coils low in my stomach, anticipation stirring beneath the bone-deep exhaustion. I loop my arm around his waist and help him toward the front doors. The ruin behind us might have once been called a home, but it never felt like one. Not to either of us.

Clara and Noen meet us in the entryway, both bloodied but still standing. Though, their faces say enough. This war wasn't without its cost.

"What can we do?" Noen asks, his tone clipped, already bracing for orders.

"Find me matches," Julian replies, groaning softly as I force him into one of the foyer chairs. He sinks into it like every muscle in his body has decided to mutiny.

Clara doesn't ask why. Of course she doesn't. The world's best advisor is already halfway down the corridor, her movements purposeful and swift.

I kneel before Julian, inspecting the damage he's trying too hard to hide. The wounds are already starting to knit back together, but what catches my attention is what's not there. No burns or scarring from touching Aeson's blood.

He should have been marked the same way I was.

I open my mouth to ask about it, but Clara's already returned, a small box clutched in her hands.

"What are we burning?" she asks casually, like she's inquiring about dinner.

Julian's voice is rough, low. "The whole fucking castle."

Clara's brows lift, but she doesn't argue. She only glances at me for confirmation.

"Mind if I run to my room first?" she asks.

"Not at all." I nod toward the box in her hands. "Take those with you. When you're done, light a few fires up there."

"Where's Aeson's body?" Noen cuts in, voice like iron.

"Dining hall, back that way," I say with a nod toward the corridor.

He grabs a few of the matches from Clara, giving her a quick kiss before turning for the hallway. "I'll start there."

I glance at Julian. "Are you okay with that?"

"As long as his corpse burns, I don't care who starts the fire."

He's grumpy, beyond tired, and still bleeding a little. The adrenaline has faded, leaving behind weariness and lingering fury. I don't push him. He's earned the right to be whatever he wants.

Once Noen heads toward the dining hall and Clara goes up the stairs, I encourage Julian to stay in the chair. "I know how strong you are, but I'm not. Will you please stay with me?"

He softens instantly. "I'm sorry, Sloane."

I grab his hand as we settle. "You have nothing to apologize for. I'm just worried about you."

"I'm going to be okay. We both are."

His promise rings true, but that doesn't mean I'm okay with seeing him hurt.

We remain silent for several minutes, both of us seeming to reflect on the evening, but our rest is cut short.

The other royals walk through the shattered front doors.

Estee. Theo. Isla. Asher. They're battered but upright, each bearing the look of warriors who've seen the cost of battle. It's all over their faces. The grief, pride, and relief.

"Elyn is here," Estee says first, her voice quieter than usual. "She wants to speak with you two. But she refuses to step foot inside this place."

"Smart choice," Julian says as he pushes himself back up, slow but steady. "It won't exist much longer."

Isla and Estee both look at me with raised brows. I don't explain. Not yet.

"Tell her we'll be out in just a moment," I reply.

Asher steps further in, glancing around. "Do you need help?"

"Fires are already roaring upstairs," Clara calls as she appears at the last landing above the stairs, now with two boxes in her arms, smoke trailing her from the hall she just exited.

"Doesn't seem like it," Julian says, dragging a hand through his hair. He takes a fresh handful of matches from Clara once she rejoins us and strides to the curtains lining the grand windows.

No one speaks as we watch him move, measured and deliberate. The matches flare to life in his hand then vanish into the fabric, igniting the drapes in a wave of flames. The tapestries follow. Then the furniture, one piece at a time.

There's something sacred in the silence. A shared understanding.

This is an ending.

Noen returns not long after, streaked with soot but smiling grimly. "Dining hall and a few other rooms along the way have been handled."

The fire is everywhere now, roaring up the stairwell, devouring every inch of Aeson's legacy. Orange. Gold. Blue. Black smoke curling through the rafters like a curse exorcised. The heat builds and a wall behind us groans as if the castle itself rises in protest. Its bones cry out, mourning the death of a kingdom that never should have come to be.

Julian returns to my side, sweat dripping down his temple, eyes locked on the inferno behind us. "Let's go."

We step into the night just as a stairwell crumbles inside. The flames consume what's left of our past, the smoke rising to the stars above us like a funeral pyre lit for every soul Aeson ever wronged.

The air is thick with ash, heat, and vengeance, but at the same time, it's also fresh, like Venaris being reborn.

Julian's hand finds mine, rough and warm. We don't look back.

Still, our night isn't over.

Elyn waits for us somewhere out here, and I don't presume it's for anything good after the way we departed the god realm.

"We're going to go check on the wounded," Theo announces with Estee tucked into his side.

I nod respectfully. "Thank you. And if anyone asks or seems unhappy, let them know that no decisions need to be made tonight, but the pack members are welcome to leave Venaris of their own free will. We won't keep anyone who doesn't want to be here."

Isla reaches for my shoulder. "We'll welcome anyone we need to. Everyone will have a home and then we can begin working together like we always should have been."

Nothing has ever sounded better to me.

The four of them go off, but Clara and Noen linger.

"You don't have to watch my every move," I say. "The war is over."

She grins widely. "And you have your mate. I know. Old habits are hard to break. I'll go check on our pack."

"Thank you."

She hugs me, almost tight enough to make me wince but then pulls back and winks at Julian. "Don't burn anything else down without me."

"Or me," a welcome and familiar voice says.

We turn to find Garron approaching us. He's limping and there's blood on his clothes, but he's alive and that's most important.

He glances at the burning castle. "Nice touch. I assume you left Aeson in there?"

"He doesn't deserve a proper burial," Julian replies gruffly.

Garron shakes his head. "No, he doesn't. Did you at least let his advisor live?"

The reminder of Dasha has unexpected emotions rising within me. I didn't know her, I didn't even really care for her demeanor, but I understood her. She was doing the best she could given the circumstances, and I can't fault her for that. She also didn't deserve to die for her choices either.

"Aeson killed her when she tried to stop him from attacking me," I say solemnly.

"Well, at least they'll be together," Garron says, confusing me until he adds, "I was here to deliver a message from her brother. He didn't make it either."

I lightly shudder. So many lives lost for such a selfish man.

"I'm sure we'll be delivering plenty of messages throughout the night," Clara says, looking over at me. "We'll go begin on sorting things out. You two wait for Elyn."

She and Noen leave, and I sigh as I watch him take her hand, keeping a protective eye on her. Clara's always been able to handle things on her own, but nothing makes me happier in that moment than seeing her with someone who'll appreciate her just the way I have all these years.

Julian shakes Garron's hand. "Thank you for everything you've done all these years. I hope you'll be able to rest now."

The elder wolf grins. "I don't think that's going to be a problem."

He begins to hobble back the way he came and I start to ask Julian if he wants to rest himself, but he speaks first.

"Where's Elyn?" Julian asks, his tightened gaze skimming over the bloodied courtyard.

"Right here." She steps into view from the shadows as if born from the air itself. Her feet barely seem to touch the ground, and her eyes glow faintly beneath the veil of her midnight blue hood. Her features are sharper, more radiant, and her presence is heavy with divine weight.

She's no longer just Aurora's creation.

Elyn *is* power.

"Nice night for a revolution," she says lightly, her gaze sweeping over the ruin behind us. "Though I could do without the stench of death."

Julian's fingers twitch in mine, but I speak before he can.

"Why are you here?" I ask.

"Well, certainly not to answer your questions," she replies smoothly, folding her hands in front of her. "I'm only here, on Aurora's behalf, to bring a resolution that suits us all."

"But what about the god realm?" Julian presses. "Isn't the goddess fighting her own war right now?"

Elyn's smirk is brief but evident. "The god realm is as it should be. Balanced and stable. But you shouldn't concern yourself with my home when there's much to do here."

This has my brow raising. "*Your* home? You're not going back to Selaris?"

She tilts her head in acknowledgment. "My home is with the gods now. I've been chosen to serve as the bridge between your kind and theirs. So, if the wolves need divine intervention again, they'll speak to me." Her gaze narrows slightly, like she's testing our reactions. "But today, I only come to ask one thing: will the two of you rebuild this kingdom? Or do I need to find someone else?"

Julian and I share a look of confirmation as I answer without hesitation. "We won't abandon our people, and there's no land left for us to return to in Alcaris. These wolves deserve more than what they received under Aeson's rule. We can give them that here still."

Elyn studies me for a long moment then gives the faintest nod. "Then you'll be the Alpha Queen of Venaris now?"

Julian steps in before I can answer. "Actually, we'd like to call it Alcaris. One kingdom, not two."

Elyn's lips curve into a knowing smile. "I thought you might say that." She glances toward the flaming wreckage behind us. "The curse on your land is gone, Sloane. The poisoned water, the dead soil—all of it was bound to Aeson's life. He no longer exists in this world and neither does the curse."

My breath catches. "*He* did that?"

I knew Aeson was vile, but I never once suspected… I want to rage, but there's no one left to rage against. Aeson is gone. All we can do is move forward, and hanging onto that anger won't change the past. It will only affect my future. Our future.

"Yes. You'll see the changes for yourself by morning. The rivers will run clear again. The land will breathe."

Relief stings my eyes. I blink it away and look at Julian. His expression softens—one of pride, and peace, and something so tender it nearly undoes me.

"I'm done here then." Elyn turns to leave without ceremony, as if the fate of a kingdom isn't heavy enough to warrant a dramatic exit. But just as her form begins to shimmer and fade into golden particles, she glances over her shoulder and smirks.

"Oh, one last thing." She winks. "Enjoy your honeymoon."

Then she's gone.

Just like that.

Julian and I stand in the silence she leaves behind, both blinking as if trying to decipher what just happened.

"Was that…a blessing?" I ask slowly.

"Or a threat," Julian mutters.

And then I feel it. Our bond.

But not like before. This isn't the subtle tug I've grown used to. This isn't the quiet ache in my chest or the low hum beneath my skin. This is a wildfire, burning through every broken place inside me and stitching it whole. This is fate crackling to life, loud and undeniable.

Our connection ignites.

It pulses between us, alive and blazing. My knees nearly give out from the force of it. And suddenly, I'm in Julian's arms, and he's in mine, clutching each other like we'll never let go again.

His voice comes through the tether, not just in my mind but in my soul.

"Mine."

It's not a demand. It's a vow.

I finally break. I shatter into light and warmth and everything I've ever wanted.

"All yours," I breathe through the bond, this time not holding back a single part of myself.

The tears come hard and fast for everything we've lost, everything we've survived, and everything we finally get to have. Joy radiates from my core and into the bond. I feel it reflected in Julian, multiplied then sent right back to me.

He cups my face, forehead pressed to mine, both of us trembling. Though, not from fear.

From everything that's real and finally ours.

"I love you," he whispers, voice thick with emotion.

I choke on a sob. "I began falling in love with you in that

cave before I ever knew your name, before I even realized what was happening, and I love you now. I'll love you long after the gods stop watching."

He kisses me like the world has already ended and we're the only two left to rebuild it.

And maybe we are.

Because this moment is what we were meant to have decades ago.

And now?

There's no more war. No more lies. No more shadows creeping between us.

There's only him and me.

Only us.

For the first time in what feels like lifetimes, there's nothing left standing in our way.

And our bond is no longer just a thread of fate.

It's also a kingdom.

Our home.

Together.

Forever.

CHAPTER FORTY

AURORA

Damn those furballs. I kick the chair in front of me —solid marble, ancient, and priceless. It shatters like cheap pottery. A fitting metaphor for my mood.

I stalk across the chamber, throwing open the doors to my back patio and stepping into the open air. The horizon is blanketed in clouds, stretching in endless grays and whites. My sanctuary. My realm. The one place in all the godly spheres that should've remained untouched.

And yet, I let *them* in.

Wolves turned into shifters. God-born mongrels with too much will and not enough sense.

I let out a snarl as I remember the dead bodies on my floor and the way Isla's emotions slammed into me like a wrecking ball. *The guilt!* She wielded that feeling like the world's most precise weapon. One that I'd never experienced until then.

Nobody was supposed to get hurt. At least not *that* hurt. Hell, they weren't even supposed to be here. I'd already decided not to involve them even though I knew the alpha blood would give us the advantage.

But then they had to need me. Had to send word for my help.

Really, they're the ones who should feel guilty. Not me.

I merely took advantage of the opportunity they dropped right into my lap.

Each summer solstice, we indulge in a week of divine sport. A time for us to start friendly-*ish* wars within our factions, flexing our power while bending realms to our whims. This year was the tenth in a row that I intended to win.

And thanks to Theo and Estee's melodramatic, star-crossed-lovers act, I almost lost.

Almost.

The golden trophy now sits smugly on my mantle, glinting in the firelight, mocking me. I should be celebrating. I should be wrapped in silk and wine, surrounded by the gods who helped me claim my victory, getting drunk as well as laid—not necessarily in that order.

But instead, I'm pacing.

Alone.

Thinking about *them*.

What the fuck is wrong with me?

I'm not supposed to care. Those fleabags were a joke gift from my father—living toys made to irk my brother, nothing more. I raised them into something remarkable, yes, but only because it amused me. They were never supposed to matter.

And yet...

They do.

Somewhere along the line, the toy became a cause. Their stubborn hope, their flawed bravery, their endless fucking loyalty wormed its way into me. And now I feel it. This strange, gnawing ache in my chest that doesn't belong to a goddess who's supposed to be untouchable.

Gods, how did I get here?

Laughter rolls toward me from below, carried by the wind from the after-party still raging in the clouds. I should go. I *could* go. I should wrap myself in pleasure and pretense, act as though Lunara never existed, never mattered, never burrowed its way under my skin.

But I stay.

Still waiting for Elyn to return.

She's no longer a wolf. No longer just a healer. She's something more now—something *mine*. A demi-god, crafted by my hands, blessed with my blood, imbued with just enough divine fire to ensure she outlives the world she was born into.

She's perfect, efficient, and most importantly, she gives a damn in ways I *shouldn't*.

That's why she's their liaison now. The wolves' divine connection, their thread to me and my realm, it's all on Elyn. And maybe, just maybe, giving her that title will buy me back the distance I desperately need.

Maybe if I don't look too closely, I can go back to the way things were. Cold. Unbothered. Free.

But I know the truth, even as I lie to myself.

Because somewhere beneath all the chaos, beneath the bloodshed and divine strategy, one of those fleabags looked me in the eye and showed me *kindness*.

And the part of me that didn't laugh in their face?

That's the part that terrifies me most.

The clouds shift, pulling me from my own madness.

It's subtle, barely a ripple in the sky, but I feel it.

She's back.

I turn slowly, already bracing myself for whatever dramatic flourish she's about to appear in.

But there's no burst of light, no swirling vortex, no thunderclap.

Just Elyn—calm, quiet, newly divine in a way that feels *earned* rather than bestowed. She steps onto the balcony, her robes catching the breeze like they're stitched from the light of dawn. Her eyes, once a soft violet, now gleam with an energy that mirrors my own.

"You're late," I say, because I don't know how else to start.

She smiles like she's humoring a child. "And you're pacing."

I scoff and turn my back to her, pretending to find something deeply fascinating about the sky. "Just stretching my legs. Definitely not waiting around like some lovesick mortal."

Elyn steps beside me, her presence quiet but firm. "You were worried."

"No," I lie. "I'm annoyed. That's different."

She says nothing, which is somehow worse.

I sigh. Loudly. "Did they win?"

She nods. "Aeson is dead. The castle is rumble. Sloane and Julian live, as do the other royals."

I hate the rush of relief that floods my chest. It's uninvited and undignified.

"I assume you offered them the choice?" I ask, voice carefully neutral.

"I did. They're staying. But not as rulers of Venaris." Elyn's gaze flicks toward the horizon, thoughtful. "Julian asked to unite the two kingdoms under Alcaris."

I blink at her. "That was his idea?"

She nods again. "You were right about him. He just needed to remember who he was."

"I'm always right," I mutter, crossing my arms.

This time, Elyn laughs deeply, and it echoes off the clouds like music.

"I told them about the curse," she continues after a moment. "That it died with Aeson. Their water will run clean again. Their lands will thrive."

I nod, feeling the tightness in my chest ease just slightly. But there's one more thing I have to do. Just as I did before with Asher's father.

When one of my wolves turns too dark, they don't get a second chance to redeem themselves in the next life. Nothing, not even pesky mutts, will ruin what I've created.

"Elyn," I say, still watching the clouds churn with a low, silvery glow. "Feel like taking a detour with me?"

She inclines her head, curious. "Where to?"

"The afterlife," I answer casually. "Just a quick trip to erase an unwanted soul."

She blinks then slowly walks back toward me. "You're not going to let Aeson reincarnate."

"Of course not," I say, my jaw tight. "That vile creature isn't broken. He's poison. And poison spreads if you don't burn it out at the root. You saw what he did. What he *became*. There's no place for that kind of corruption in my creation. Not anymore. Not ever again."

Elyn hesitates for only a breath before nodding. "Then let's end it properly."

I grin, wicked and sharp. "I knew I chose you for a reason."

With a flick of my hand, the air around us thickens, stars folding in on themselves as a rip forms in the space between one breath and the next. The portal hums with divine energy, its edges gold and black like ink dipped in the night.

We step through.

The shift is immediate.

This part of the afterlife isn't fire and brimstone, not unless I *want* it to be. It's a field. Golden and endless and silent.

And standing in the center of it is Aeson.

Or what's left of him.

He looks like a man stripped down to bone and shadow, eyes vacant, mouth stitched in confusion. He's not snarling or defiant as I half-expected. He's small. Diminished.

"Is he aware?" Elyn asks, her voice soft but guarded.

"Yes," I murmur. "He's tethered here and doesn't know why. He's made his choice to be reborn. Yet nothing has happened. Now he gets to learn the reason."

Elyn stares at him, her posture relaxed. "I look forward to seeing you work."

I nod then walk forward, my skin already itching from the pureness of the afterlife. This isn't a part of our universe I prefer to spend time in.

Aeson lifts his head as I approach, eyes meeting mine, and for a flicker, I see a glimpse of the monster he was. The cruelty. The ambition. The hunger. It makes my job that much easier.

I raise my hand, power crackling at my fingertips.

"I warned you," I whisper unforgivingly. "I don't allow second chances."

Light erupts, engulfing him in a blaze of searing white flames. No screams. No fanfare. Just the snapping finality of a soul coming undone.

When it fades, nothing remains.

Not even ash.

The wind shifts, sweet and clean.

I turn back to Elyn, who watches me with quiet awe. "It's done," I say.

She nods. "As it needed to be."

We step through the fold again, the world sealing behind us with a soft shimmer. We're back on the balcony, the sky beginning to darken as another day comes to an end.

"So," I say, forcing nonchalance. "You're not going back?"

She turns to me, her grin firmly set. "Not until you ask me to. My place is here. With the gods. With *you*."

My throat tightens, and I look away too quickly. "Don't say things like that. I'm emotionally unstable enough as it is."

"I can tell," she says with a chuckle, reaching out to touch my arm.

Her fingers are warm, centering me.

"You've always done the right thing, Aurora," she says softly. "Now is no different."

I shake my head. "Not always for the right reasons, though."

"That doesn't mean what you've done doesn't matter in the grand scheme of things."

We stand there in silence, the clouds parting around us, stars glittering overhead like scattered shards of fate.

"Are you ready to face the other gods?" I say as I turn to head back inside. "I hope you like chaos and deeply repressed feelings, because we have a celebration to make an appearance at."

"I was raised by wolves," she quips. "I think I'll manage."

That earns her a crooked smile.

Elyn begins to walk back inside ahead of me, but she pauses at the threshold. She glances over her shoulder, eyes sparkling with something I don't want to name.

"It's okay that you *do* care about them," she reminds me.

I arch a brow. "Careful. That sounds dangerously like an accusation."

She shrugs. "Caring won't kill you. You're a goddess."

I roll my eyes. "Noted. Now, can we get the hell out of here before I hug you or something equally horrifying."

She holds an arm out for me to lead the way, choosing silence this time.

And for the first time, the quiet doesn't feel empty.

Maybe I do care.

Just a little.

Gods help me.

CHAPTER FORTY-ONE

SLOANE

The sun is up, gilding the sky in soft gold and pale blue—a new day in a new kingdom, no longer blanketed by fire or fear. The smoke that clung to the horizon like a final curse has lifted, revealing the charred stone of what used to be the Venaris castle. Blackened. Broken. Hollow.

No one has gone near it, and no one plans to. There's nothing left to salvage. Nothing worth remembering.

And honestly? None of us want to.

It's been barely twelve hours since the flames reduced centuries of cruelty to ash. Elyn may have told us to "enjoy" our honeymoon, but there's been little time for anything but rebuilding. Even so, the heat of Julian's gaze has nearly ignited my clothes more than once. The man can make a promise with a look, and that promise is coming the moment we have a spare breath.

For now, we breathe in other ways.

We've set up a temporary camp just beyond the tree line, where the forest thins into a wide meadow dotted with wildflowers and thick grass. The earth here is untouched. It's the first time I've seen true beauty in this land. Not the kind painted over lies, but real, thriving beauty. Something that doesn't owe itself to bloodlines or treaties. Something that simply is.

Julian stands a few feet away, speaking with Noen and Clara about how to organize the remaining wolves. His shirt is stained with dried blood as we haven't had time to find new clothes. His ribs are still bound per my demand and he's upright. Alive and growing stronger by the second.

My mate. My Alpha King.

Across the field, Estee kneels beside a small group of injured wolves, her movements fluid, patient, calming. The way she changes bandages and whispers encouragement makes her glow like she was born to heal. She and Theo will be leaving tonight, but they've been nothing short of extraordinary since the moment the battle ended.

Isla and Asher will leave tomorrow. I find myself watching them often—the way Isla's sharp, strategic nature blends with Asher's unwavering presence. They've taken it upon themselves to lead the arrangements for the fallen. Without being asked, they've organized funerals, tended to the bodies, and ensured each wolf will be honored. It's more than I could've asked for. More than I could've handled.

I'll never be able to thank them enough for taking on what might've broken me.

A sigh escapes me, not of sadness but weariness. The ache of too much in too little time. I know I'm not ready to say goodbye to any of them yet. But I won't have to, not truly. This is no longer a fractured realm. Last night, long after the fires died and our wounds were wrapped, we shared a meal under the stars and made a vow.

There will be no more divided kingdoms.

Each of us remains Alpha of our own pack, yes. But our

wolves? They're no longer bound by invisible chains or outdated laws. They can move freely, cross borders, visit the friends they've made through war and loss. There will still be order—we need that. But not control or fear, and certainly not threats of exile just for wanting something different.

We were created to lead. That won't change. But we won't do so with iron hands. Not when we've seen what happens to wolves who are shackled rather than guided.

Not when we've bled to make something better.

Between the remnants of the Venaris pack and my wolves from Alcaris, about sixty chose to leave, seeking new beginnings in the other kingdoms. They'll board the boats tonight and tomorrow with their respective alphas, carrying pieces of our story with them to wherever they now belong.

And then...Julian and I will begin to rebuild.

As if summoned by the very thought, Julian steps up beside me, sliding an arm around my waist. His grin is crooked, knowing, and absolutely lethal. "Noen and Clara have everything handled for the rest of the day, and I've also asked Noen to be my primary advisor. Apparently, he was one of Asher's, and the king had only good things to say about him."

My heart swells at the ease with which Julian slips into this role—the confidence and warmth behind his decisions.

"That's perfect," I breathe.

He kisses the side of my temple. "So it looks like everything's taken care of for the time being. Nothing left for us to do but prepare to head to your castle in a few days."

Gods, the sound of that makes me so damn happy, but he's not exactly right.

"*Our* castle," I correct gently, brushing my fingers over the bandages still wrapped around his ribs. "How are you feeling?"

"Like I'm about to rip this damn wrap off and throw it in the ocean," he grumbles then smirks down at me. "But I'm trying to be a good mate, so I've left it alone. For now."

I laugh, the sound brighter than it's been in days. "How about we go to one of the cabins the others moved out of? I can give you a proper inspection myself."

His eyes darken in a flash. I hear the change in his breathing just before he scoops me up and throws me over his shoulder like I weigh nothing at all. His hands are firm on my thighs, possessive in a way that makes my core pulse.

He doesn't say a word, just moves through the camp like a wolf on a mission.

"Julian!" I object, swatting at his back. "Put me down. You might break something!"

"The only thing I plan to break is the first bed we find," he growls, voice low and full of delicious promise.

Heat races up my spine and spreads across my skin. The way he says it with that unshakable authority and need makes my thoughts dissolve into steam. I cling to him, breath catching, my body already anticipating his.

He starts to run, long strides swallowing the distance with terrifying ease. I bounce with every step, laughing and shouting in protest even though I don't want him to stop.

"Have fun," Clara calls, her voice filled with mirth even through my thoughts.

Of course she's witnessing this. *Everyone* is probably watching Julian haul me across the field like some barbaric Alpha claiming his prize.

But I don't care.

I've waited too long for this moment. So has Julian.

The bond between us might have been blessed by the gods, might pulse with divine strength, but this? This is ours.

This claiming and the heat combined with joy and freedom. It's all ours.

And I'll revel in every second of it.

Julian barrels through the trees with me still draped over his shoulder, his stride purposeful, his breathing steady despite all he went through last night. I half expect him to slow or set me down gently, but he doesn't. He charges forward like nothing will stop him from getting what he wants. What we want.

We reach a small, empty cabin tucked near the edge of the meadow. The door creaks open under his foot as he kicks it inward, the hinges protesting before the space falls into quiet.

The moment we're inside, Julian lowers me, slowly this time, until my feet brush the ground, but even then, he doesn't let me go. He wraps an arm around my waist and cradles my jaw, brushing his thumb gently across my bottom lip.

"You're really okay?" I whisper, searching his face for any sign of lingering pain.

"I am now," he says, voice rough but honest. "You pulled me back from the edge the moment you appeared in that cave."

I lean into him, arms sliding around his neck, fingers threading into his dark hair. "You pulled me back too."

Our powerful stares speak volumes as we consume each other, knowing there's no more need for words.

He kisses me, but it's not urgent like it was before the battle. It's full of need and want like he's pouring all the pieces of his soul into my mouth with every breath and every touch.

I run my hands over his chest, removing his shirt and

unbinding the wrap. "Let me see you," I murmur against his lips.

He lets me strip the cloth away, baring bruised but healing skin. I trace the edge of each scar, each line earned in the name of survival, of us.

Julian leans his forehead against mine. "You don't have to be gentle."

"I want to be," I breathe. "For now."

He lifts me again, slowly this time. I expect him to take me to bed, but instead, we end up in the bathroom. The space is barely big enough for the both of us, but that doesn't seem to matter as he sets me back down.

Without needing to speak, I know this moment is more than just being together. It's about cleansing the both of us from the hell we've been through.

His fingers deftly work at getting my leathers off and his palm slides over the soft skin above my ribs, warming me from the outside in. Our eyes lock as he reaches past me to turn on the water.

We undress each other piece by piece, slowly and filled with wonder. Like we're taking back all the time that was stolen from us. The heat builds—slow and dizzying—learning each other for the first time and remembering everything we already know.

I step under the warm spray of water and Julian follows close behind me, his touch never leaving me for more than a second.

Together, we let the grime and memory of battle wash away, easily losing ourselves within one another until touch is no longer enough. I need to feel all of him, for us to be one, and there to be no barriers.

Julian reaches for a towel and we quickly dry off, our urgency returning only long enough for him to guide me toward the bed, tucked against the far wall of the cabin. The sheets are rough, the small space plain and worn, but it might as well be a palace because we're here. Together.

By the time he's above me, skin against skin, hearts pressed close, our bond is pulsing between us with a golden fire.

"You're mine," he says against my mouth, a promise not a question.

I hold tighter to him, breathless and aching. "And you're mine."

He thrusts forward, making my back arch and my mouth drop open. Gods, nothing has ever felt more right than this moment.

His touch and taste and love. It's all I'll ever need.

He swallows my moans like they're the air he needs to survive and rocks above me with steady movements.

I wrap my ankles around his thighs, somehow needing him closer, until I can no longer tell where he begins and I end.

Our bond thrums with an unleashed intensity, pulsing with power and strength, renewing every cell within our bodies. Our connection glows brighter with every movement, every cry of pleasure and love until we collapse together—sated, tangled, and utterly whole.

"Is it too soon to say I can't wait to do that again?" he murmurs against my neck, sending gooseflesh across my heated skin.

"I was already thinking the same thing."

Julian holds me like he never intends to let go again, and I know he won't.

Because there's nothing left between us but forever.

CHAPTER FORTY-TWO

Dying freaking sucks.

Sure, we're all supposed to die eventually, but I've now died and come back to life twice in this lifetime. Maybe even three times if you count whatever happened to me in the shadow realm.

Either way, the next time I go, it better be centuries from now. Or I'm going to raise hell. Maybe even literally.

But truth be told? I'd do it all over again.

Helping Sloane wasn't a choice. It was instinct. She's the kind of queen this realm desperately needed—fearless, honest, and willing to burn down the world to protect it. And after meeting Julian? I have no doubt he's going to give Theo and Asher a run for their crowns. That male has Alpha King written in the very essence of his soul.

We've only been back in Selaris for a single day, and yet, everything already feels…lighter. Like a fog has lifted. Our people are walking taller and smiling easier. The announcement that wolves from other kingdoms would be welcomed here? That we were finally open, not just politically but personally? Well, you'd think we were throwing the festival of the decade.

Wolves are moving in and out of the castle with armfuls of supplies for our new pack members, laughter echoing through the stone halls. Donations are arriving faster than we can catalog them—clothing, bedding, handmade gifts, even baked goods wrapped in cloth and still warm. And for once, no one's hoarding. They're *sharing*.

I thought my heart was full before. Now I worry it might shatter from the sheer amount of love being poured into this pack. Into *our* home.

As I stand outside on the front steps, taking in the bustle, I spot a pair of our newest wolves walking toward me hand-in-hand. They're both beaming, practically vibrating with excitement, though there's a flicker of nerves in their eyes too.

The male bows deeply. "Queen Estee."

Gods, it still sounds surreal.

But I've grown into this title. I earned it. And now I wear it like armor laced in purpose.

"Welcome to Selaris," I greet them warmly. "I don't believe we've officially met. What are your names?"

"I'm Julie," the woman says with a smile, clutching the male's arm tighter. "And this is James. I'm originally from Alcaris, and he's from Venaris. We found out we were mates right before the battle."

That explains the stars in their eyes and the shakiness in their fingers. A fresh bond, new and sacred.

"Then congratulations," I say, placing a hand gently on both their shoulders. "You've found something precious, especially in a world like ours."

Julie nods quickly, but James clears his throat, cheeks

flushed with color. "Actually, we were hoping to ask you something."

Julie glances at him then back at me. Her lips tremble slightly. "We were wondering if you'd perform our mating ceremony. We know it's sudden, but we just don't want to wait. Not after everything." She swallows hard, her voice faltering. "We've learned all too recently that life can be taken away in an instant," she continues, her gaze misting over. "And we don't want to waste a single moment now that we've found each other."

Her words strike something deep within me. The way her voice catches at the end, the pain behind her smile. I know that look. That ache. Someone she loved didn't survive the fight. Maybe family. Maybe a friend. But whoever it was, the loss is written in the curve of her shoulders and the quiver of her breath.

I step closer and take both their hands in mine. "I would be honored to officiate your mating ceremony," I say, my voice thick with emotion.

Julie lets out a soft sob of relief, while James exhales like he's been holding his breath for days. "Thank you," they whisper together.

"No," I tell them with a smile. "Thank *you*. For reminding me what we were all fighting for. We'll make sure everything is sorted for this evening."

They nod, and I know—deep in my bones—that Selaris is not just healing.

It's blooming.

They walk away, James still whispering softly to Julie as he keeps her steady, his touch both anchoring and tender. I watch them for a breath longer, the way their silhouettes lean into each other like gravity itself is pulling them closer then I turn back toward the castle.

I need a minute. Just one. To breathe. To feel.

But halfway up the steps, a familiar voice cuts through the commotion.

"Where do you think you're going?" Isla's voice rings out.

I turn, and I'm running toward her without a moment's hesitation. I throw my arms around my sister and hold on tight.

Without any warning, I break into silent sobs.

Gods, it's been a hellish week.

She holds me tighter, like only she can. My anchor. My constant. The glue I didn't realize I still needed until this moment. She doesn't speak, and she doesn't need to. Her presence alone is enough.

A voice slices sharply through my bond. *"Where are you?"* Theo demands.

I send back calm reassurance. *"Isla and Asher have surprised us. I'm okay—we're in front of the castle."*

A blur of movement catches the corner of my eye then Theo barrels around the side of the courtyard in full wolf form. He shifts mid-stride, landing in a crouch on two feet, eyes wild until he spots me safe in Isla's arms.

"I thought I was going to have to kill someone," he mutters, rubbing a hand over his face before reaching out to shake Asher's hand with a gruff nod.

"I told Isla we should have warned you first," Asher says, his grin unapologetic. "But she insisted the surprise would be better."

I lean back just enough to glare at my sister. "I would have objected. You were supposed to go home. You've got a kingdom to run."

Isla rolls her eyes. "Cain and Mali have everything under control. Besides, I wanted to tell you the news in person."

My stomach flips. "What news?"

She glances at Asher then back at me, and the expression on her face nearly undoes me. There's something sparkling in her eyes—mischief, joy, love—and before she even says a word, I *know*.

I gasp. "You're pregnant?"

She bursts into laughter. "What? No!"

I freeze mid-hug, blinking. "Wait. You're *not*?"

"No!" She's laughing harder now, reaching into her pocket to pull out a small, ancient-looking phone—chunky and gray with no touchscreen in sight. "Davin's been working on some Earth tech projects for me. I asked him to keep it simple—this one just makes calls. No texts. No distractions. Just a way for me to reach *you*, no matter where you are." She presses the relic into my hand.

I blink down at it. "Oh."

She frowns. "Seriously? That's all I get? 'Oh'?"

"I thought you were giving me a niece or nephew!" I cry, pouting dramatically. "Now I feel betrayed."

"Don't worry, Estee," Asher chimes in, smirking. "We've got plans. That little royal is already on our to-do list."

Theo's chest rumbles with amusement. "Guess we're racing to see who gets there first."

Damn overly competitive men.

"Who says—"

"Please do!" she says, bouncing in place. "I need a little Estee running around in case *this* one up and dies again."

I gasp, scandalized. "Rude."

She just grins and leans her head against my shoulder. "Hey, if anything, it just makes me want to spend even more time with you. Nothing's more important than my sister."

"Also rude," Asher mutters, though the sparkle in his eyes says he wouldn't change a thing.

I wrap an arm around Isla again, holding her close, but

before I can say anything else, a voice knocks the breath out of me.

"You weren't supposed to start without us," my dad mutters.

I turn.

And there they are. Mom and Dad, walking toward us, their steps sure, their faces soft and weather-worn but lit with love.

I burst into tears again, full-blown sobbing this time.

Gah. Maybe *I'm* already pregnant because I can't seem to get a handle on my emotions.

It's a joke, but even still, Theo is watching me closely, a look of wonder in his darkening gaze.

"I'm going to put a baby in you," he says through our bond.

"And I'm going to let you. Right after my family leaves."

"Am I allowed to kick them out?"

My outburst of laughter has everyone else looking at us, but I don't care. We're here, we're together, and the future is brighter than it's ever been.

EPILOGUE: PART ONE
SLOANE

One Year Later...

It's amazing how much a world can change when everyone is finally pulling in the same direction— when the shared goal isn't power or vengeance, but peace, simplicity, and connection.

Even if those goals are as small as wanting a quicker way to visit the people you love.

At least that's what I think as I hurry through the freshly polished halls of our castle, double-checking every detail, smoothing wrinkles in tablecloths that don't need smoothing, and adjusting flowers that are already perfectly placed. I know no one else will notice, but I will. Because today matters.

It's the first time Isla, Asher, Estee, and Theo will be visiting since the final touches were put on the new and improved Alcaris. And I want everything to be perfect.

The castle gleams under the afternoon sun, its whitewashed stone and forest-green shutters freshly painted and proudly trimmed with ivy. The Alcaris flags snap high above the turrets, a symbol not just of sovereignty but of survival and rebirth.

We didn't just repair a home. We resurrected a legacy.

But more than our refurbished castle, the town itself has evolved and grown. The bridge connecting our island to the mainland—the old Venaris—has been widened and reinforced, strong enough now to carry not only foot traffic and single carriages, but multiples of them filled with heavy carts for trade goods and supplies. It's become a lifeline and a symbol of how far we've come.

We moved the marketplace closer to the bridge too, creating a vibrant, central hub where all shifters gather— Polaris, Selaris, and Alcaris alike. The names don't seem to matter anymore. Not the way they used to.

Because now, we no longer act as separate kingdoms.

We're one community.

People come and go between our lands with ease and laughter. There are no borders to fear. No guards giving suspicious glances. Just wolves living their lives freely.

It started with a cell phone. A device that was, unsurprisingly, rejected by many of our people. Then came the ships with bigger motors for quicker travel, but mostly, it was the arrival of more portals.

With the packs united, we've become a realm that welcomes not only all wolves but even friends of the shifters. Which is how we found ourselves uniting with a coven of witches. Ones who were thrilled to help us update a few things with magic in exchange for some royal, god-like blood.

Sure, Theo wasn't pleased at first, but at the time, Estee was beyond pregnant, miserable, and prepared to kill anyone who looked in her direction. When she demanded for her sister and me to be able to come see her and the baby whenever we wanted, she got her way. Quickly.

Now, every island has two portals that only travel within Lunara. One within the royal castles and another for the rest of the packs to use.

But even with the ease of movement, I still didn't allow Isla or Estee to come here until I was absolutely ready to show off the new Alcaris.

A place I'm proud to still call home.

Even better, we've had no uprising. No threats of another war. No issues with the gods.

Everything is just as it should be.

Julian finds me and places a soft touch on my shoulder as I straighten the dining room table for the third time. "They're going to love everything. Hell, they would've loved it before you changed it twice yesterday. Quit stressing, my darling."

I sigh, fingers lingering over the edge of a perfectly aligned napkin. "I can't help myself. I'm so proud of what we've done here—*together*. I just want them to see it. Really see what we've accomplished in such a short time."

He cups my cheeks gently, brushing his lips against mine like a whispered vow. "If they can't, that's their problem. It's no reflection of the incredible queen you've always been and still are."

"Why are you so sweet to me?" I tug on his beard, loving the wild edge he's kept since his time in the cave. "I feel like I don't do enough for you."

He leans in again, voice a soft rumble that slides through me like velvet. "You just being here, breathing, letting me stand beside you as your mate...that's more than reason enough and all I'll ever need. I promise you that."

Gods, every single day I'm reminded how lucky I am to

have been practically forced into that castle, thinking I was going to find a life sentence and instead finding this extraordinary man. My mate. My king.

"Okay," I say, stepping back with a breath of finality. "I'm done. Officially. I won't touch another thing in this house."

"Good," he says, grinning like the smug Alpha he is. "Because they got here two minutes before I walked in."

I give him a shove. "You're…"

"The perfect mate for taking this moment to calm you down?" His deep chuckle sends shivers down my spine, but he's not forgiven. Yet.

"Where are they?"

He takes my hand again, holding tighter this time. "I'll show you, my darling."

I let him lead the way. Mostly because I don't think I have a choice in the matter. He's fallen into his Alpha King role like a seasoned pro, and while I'm powerful in my own right, this man owns me, body, mind, and soul.

There's nothing he can't command out of me.

Thankfully, he doesn't abuse that power.

We reach the foyer to the sound of Estee's squeal. Julian lets go of my hand, and I barely have time to breathe before our bodies collide in a tight, joyful embrace.

"It's been too long," I murmur into her shoulder.

"I *know*," she says, just as breathless.

"Um, hello?" Isla's voice cuts through the moment, dry and dramatic as ever. "Am I invisible over here?"

I glance around Estee to find Isla absolutely glowing as she sits in the nearest chair, hand over her protruding stomach.

"Of course not," I promise as I go to her. "I just wanted to make sure I got my energy under control and didn't hurt my soon-to-be nieces or nephews."

Yes, that's right. It took Isla longer to get pregnant, much to Asher's melodramatic dismay, but the moment she did, the gods gave her two pups. And Asher? He's been unbearable ever since. Beaming and boasting and brooding every time she so much as groans.

I hug her gently around the shoulders. "I've missed you."

"Yeah, yeah. Missed you too." She gives me a look. "So, are you knocked up yet?"

"Not yet." Though it's been discussed, we've decided spending the next decade with only each other when we're not playing alpha sounds rather nice. We're going to have plenty of babies to play with. That will be enough. For now.

"You're lucky," Isla groans as she tries—and fails—to stand. "These two have learned how to kick ribs like it's a sport."

Estee turns toward where Landon sleeps in Theo's arms and sighs. "You won't think that once they're born. It gets better. I promise."

"I was *promised* lunch," Isla interjects, reminding everyone that a pregnant queen requires regular offerings or we risk her declaring war.

"Right this way," I say, and wink at Asher as he mouths a silent apology.

Theo whistles as we make our way down the hall. "I still can't believe how much you two have done with this place. It's gorgeous."

I glance up at Julian, suspicious. He only smirks in return, his expression saying, *I told you so.*

"Thank you," I reply. "It's been a lot of work, but honestly? It's been more fun than I expected. Building something new and lasting, making a home for everyone, not just ourselves, it's nothing we could have prepared for."

"Well, you nailed it," Estee says. "What you two have

accomplished and recovered from in the last year is more than most others could have only dreamed of."

"I second all their compliments." Isla briefly glances around. "It might not have hurt to move the dining room closer to the front, though."

I inch closer to her, wrapping an arm around her waist. "I would be happy to carry you."

"Hey." Asher scoops her up without hesitation. "That's my job."

She snuggles into him, closing her eyes, and the way he trembles from her closeness has me grinning even wider.

We're all the luckiest shifters in Lunara.

LATER THAT NIGHT, AFTER ISLA HAS HAD HER NAP, LANDON has been fed and put to bed, and the men have been appeased, it's finally our girl time.

We take over the sunroom, which Clara insisted we outfit with massive floor cushions, floating candles, and an enchanted ceiling that reflects the night sky even when it's storming. Tonight, the stars twinkle just for us. The wind hums through the open windows, brushing against gossamer curtains as we pass around sweet wine and a tray of spiced pastries Estee brought from Selaris.

"I swear," Isla groans, stretching her legs over Clara's lap, enjoying her orange juice instead. "If these twins don't start respecting my bladder soon, I'm going to shift just to give my organs some space."

"Can you even do that right now?" Estee asks, raising a curious brow as she reaches for another pastry. "You'd probably roll instead of run."

"Oh, bite me." Isla snorts, flipping her off, then grins. "Actually, don't. I'd probably enjoy it too much with these hormones."

Clara chokes on her wine.

"Gods," I say, laughing and fanning myself. "This is exactly what I needed. Do you know how long it's been since I had time to just sit and breathe? Not be queen or mate or anything other than me?"

"You've earned it," Clara says, nudging my foot with hers. "You all have. For once, we're not racing to survive. We're just here living."

The words settle around us like a comfort. We sip and snack and slip into easy conversation. Estee tells us about how Theo cried the first time Landon said 'papa' and how she caught him sobbing in the nursery for a solid ten minutes after putting the baby down last week.

"He tried to say the tears were from a training injury," she says, deadpan. "The man *limped* away from the crib."

Clara rolls her eyes. "Men are such babies when it comes to emotions."

"Says the woman who's already punched two of our guards for *looking* at her man," Isla teases.

She merely shrugs. "Those women looked *too long.*"

Laughter bubbles around the room like magic. For a while, none of us speak. Instead, we soak up one another's company and listen to the soft crackle of the fire mixed with the lull of distant waves.

There's peace here. Real, honest peace.

"I still can't believe we made it," I say after a beat, voice softer now. "That we're all here. Together and safe."

"We didn't just survive," Estee replies. "We built something lasting to be proud of."

"That was our job all along," Isla adds, her hand protectively over her stomach. "To get here so that our kids will never know the world we had to burn in order to give them this one."

That's when we hear it.

Footsteps. Heavy, familiar.

The door swings open, and four imposing men file in like they've been summoned by fate—or, more likely, hunger.

"You ladies done yet?" Julian asks, looking at me like he might just devour me in front of everyone. "Because I've given you three hours, and now I miss my mate."

"I swear you were *just* with her," Asher says to him, exasperated. "You two are ridiculous."

"Really? Because according to your mate, you're just as bad," Clara fires back, smirking as Noen not-so-casually makes his way toward her. "*Whimpering* just because she stayed in the bath too long."

"Yeah. So what," Asher says without shame, wrapping his arms around his mate's shoulders from behind.

Theo lifts a bottle of wine from the corner tray. "I have more wine, and I brought the baby. Can I stay now?"

Landon, somehow wide awake when he shouldn't be and held against Theo's chest in one arm, gurgles as if in agreement.

Estee sighs but can't stop smiling. "He gets away with everything."

"Like his father," I say.

Julian crosses the room and offers me a hand. I take it without hesitation, rising as the night begins to wind down.

As we all move together—mates and friends, kings and queens, family in every way that matters—it strikes me how far we've come.

From fire and ruin to this unity.
To peace and love.
To everything we were always meant to be.
And the best part?
We're only just getting started.

EPILOGUE: PART TWO
JULIAN

The stars are high, the castle is quiet, and laughter still lingers in the halls as if it's always been there.

I carry Sloane in my arms. Not because she needs me to, but because I need it. I need *her*.

Her fingers toy with the collar of my shirt, her head resting against my shoulder. She's warm and soft and buzzing with joy from not only the evening we've just shared with our friends but the entire day.

Even still, underneath that elation, I feel the hum of something deeper that matches my own.

Desire and love and the bond we forged through fire and ash.

We've had a long day. Hell, we've had a long year. But that doesn't mean I'm ready for bed.

By the time I reach our room, her lashes are heavy, but she's still alert, watching me through the haze of candlelight as I set her down gently at the edge of the bed. Her fingers slip down my arm, holding on until the very last second like she can't quite bear to let go.

I know the feeling.

"You didn't have to carry me," she murmurs, breathless. "I could've walked."

"I know," I whisper, leaning down to kiss her temple. "But I like carrying what's mine."

Her lips curl into that wicked smile that makes my pulse thrum. "Possessive much?"

"Only for you."

She laughs softly, and I take my time easing her sweater from her shoulders, letting it fall to the floor. My fingers move with reverence as I unlace the back of her dress, pulling at the ties one by one until the fabric slips free.

She lets it drop around her waist, never breaking eye contact.

Every scar, every curve, every inch of her has been carved into my soul. She's a map I've studied and etched into memory by pain and devotion and a love that nearly never came to be. And yet...

It's *thrived*.

She reaches for the hem of my shirt, pulling it over my head. "You're staring," she says, voice barely above a whisper.

"How could I not?"

Her hands press against my chest, and for a moment, we don't speak. We just *breathe*.

Her eyes shimmer with something I don't quite have a name for. A mixture of awe, hunger, and need. It coils around me like a vow yet to be spoken.

I take her face in my hands, brushing my thumbs over the skin just beneath her eyes.

"You're everything," I tell her. "And I don't just mean to me. I mean to this world. You've changed it, Sloane. For the better."

"So have you," she says softly, fingers curling around my wrists.

The pull between us deepens. Not just desire, but that gravitational force that says this—*us*—was always meant to be. That every detour and battle and loss only sharpened what we'd one day become.

Unstoppable.

"Get in this bed with me," she whispers.

And I do.

Because there's nowhere else I belong than with this incredible woman.

Now and for always.

***

Thank you so much for reading A Reign of Malice, the final book in the Wolves of Lunara series!

I hope you've enjoyed this world as much as I have!

If you've yet to check out my other words, flip a couple more pages and find out more about my back list of books.

Want to chat all things wolf shifters? Come join us in Heather Renee's Book Warriors!

STAY IN TOUCH

Find Heather on Facebook:
Reader Group
Want to talk all things books and get updates before anyone else? Come hang with me in my reader group:
Heather Renee's Book Warriors

Author Page
Teaser and big updates are also posted here:
Heather Renee Author

Newsletter:
I send this out sporadically, so don't worry. You won't ever be spammed by me and you get a couple goodies when you sign up!
http://smarturl.it/HeatherReneeNL

ALSO BY HEATHER RENEE

Paranormal Romance Books:

The Mystics and Mayhem World—These series are connected by characters crossovers, but not the plots. You can read them in any order. Though, this is their timeline order.

Broken Court

A complete New Adult Urban Fantasy series featuring an unconventional and anti-heroine leading lady, a broody love interest, and a fae kingdom with a vile king.

Luna Marked

A complete New Adult wolf shifter series (dual POV) featuring a strong-willed leading lady and a patient, yet fierce alpha male.

Scorned by Blood

A complete New Adult Vampire series featuring a supernatural hunter and the sexy vampire bound to protect her no matter the cost.

Fated to the Wolf

A complete New Adult Witch and Wolf series (dual POV) featuring an abandoned witch, a rogue wolf, and their broken bond.

The Hidden Realm

A complete New Adult wolf and dragon shifter series (dual POV) featuring a feisty wolf shifter just looking for her freedom and a broody dragon trying to save his world.

Mystics and Mayhem Novels

This includes *Christmas Mates*, *Fractured Mates*, and *Shattered Mates*. Each book is a standalone and between the three stories, you'll find a holiday gathering with all the shenanigans, vengeance to be had, and risks to be taken.

Individual Series

Wolves of Lunara

A New Adult Romantasy trilogy with a murder mystery, fated mates, reincarnations, royalty, and swoon-worthy wolf shifters.

Raven Point Pack Series

A complete Upper Young Adult Paranormal Romance series featuring wolves, witches, vengeance, and fated mates.

Shadow Veil Academy

A complete Upper Young Adult Urban Fantasy Academy series featuring shifters, elves, witches, and more.

Elite Supernatural Trackers

A complete New Adult Urban Fantasy series featuring witches, demons, a smart-mouthed female lead, alpha males, and a snarky fairy sidekick.

Royal Fae Guardians

A complete Young Adult Urban Fantasy series featuring fae, magic users, a sweet romance, along with snark and humor.

Standalone Fantasy Books

Ignite Me - A spicy wolf shifter story featuring a lost heir, the mate who doesn't want her, and the enemies who wish them dead.

Cage Me - A spicy wolf shifter story featuring a shadow cursed wolf and a mate who's on the run.

Marked Paradox - A Young Adult fae story about a realm divided and one fae to bring them back together.

Contemporary Romance Books with Harper Reed:

The Wicked Duet

A mafia romance with enemies-to-lovers, forced proximity, and more than a bit of unaliving before there's a happily-ever-after.

Ruthless Truths

Tangled Deceit

The Unexpected Series

A Spicy RomCom trilogy featuring three best friends and their happily-ever-afters!

A Mutually Beneficial Proposal

A Mutually Beneficial Mistake

A Mutually Beneficial Secret

Standalone

A Royal Oops

A Spicy RomCom with royal antics, an epic second chance romance, and a kingdom that needs their new queen.

ABOUT THE AUTHOR

Heather Renee is a USA Today Bestselling author who lives in Oregon. She writes Paranormal Romance and Fantasy novels with a mixture of romance, humor, and sass. Her love of reading eventually led to her passion of writing and giving the gift of escapism.

When Heather's not writing, she's spending time with her loving husband and beautiful daughter, going on their own adventures. She loves to hear from her fans, so visit her website: www.HeatherReneeAuthor.com and check out the Contact Me page for ways to connect.